WOUNDED BLUE

DARBY KERN

WOUNDED BLUE

BY

DARBY KERN

PUBLISHED BY

ATHANATOS
PUBLISHING GROUP

Wounded Blue
By Darby Kern

Published by Athanatos Publishing Group.

ISBN: 978-1-64594-042-5

Chapter 1

Dana Hujet ran for the first time in almost seven years and while her body protested, her survival instincts propelled her forward over the hard, dirty ground.

It wasn't that she hadn't wanted to run; she simply had nowhere to run to. Her entire universe had been a ten by twelve room in the basement of a house where she had been held. There were no windows and the only light came from two ceiling fixtures fitted with dim bulbs that her captor replaced at irregular intervals. The walls were cinder blocks painted dark gray. In fact, the only color in her life had been a blaze orange blanket that stood out against the white sheets that had turned dingy and threadbare over the years since she'd been coaxed into that van on a rainy spring afternoon. She had been twelve at the time.

Now nighttime continued to rob her world of color. Even the blood that flowed from the deep gashes on her arms and legs looked black instead of the rich, crimson hue it would have in the light. She had paid a steep price for escaping her dungeon.

Keep running. Keep going. If you stop now, you're dead.

There was a road ahead of her but whether it was fifty feet or a quarter of a mile away she couldn't tell. She was getting more light-headed with every step and the uneven ground of the field kept her from running in a straight line but she believed she could make it, she had to believe it. There were lights on the street and cars passing—somebody would stop for her. Somebody would save her.

She imagined how happy her family would be to see her again. Her bear of a father who could wrap her up in his arms and eclipse the sun; her mother with a gleaming white smile and bright green eyes; the sister that loved unicorns. She couldn't remember their names right now but she was sure that once she was rescued, they would be reunited quickly. She was looking forward to opening the birthday present from Grammy that arrived in the mail the morning she went on that fateful bike ride.

She hoped it was an iPod.

Her bare foot landed on an uneven piece of earth, turning her ankle and sending her crashing to the ground. She stretched her hand out to stop but still managed to land on her face. She gasped for breath, but only managed to inhale the dust. Against her will she coughed, hacking from deep in her throat.

She rolled onto her back without a thought and groaned in pain. A coughing sob escaped from her dirt covered mouth. What she saw next robbed her of whatever hope she had left.

A brief flash of headlights illuminated a figure walking towards her. Unfortunately, it was the one person she wanted to never see again—the only person she had seen for years. Even though the light obscured his features she recognized the faded green work pants and the Milwaukee Brewers windbreaker that he wore even though the temperature was in the high seventies.

Dana rolled back onto her stomach. She buried her face in the earth as it burst from her mouth, sending dirt into her nose and eyes. Her emaciated body shook with each staccato moan that escaped her lips as the last bit of energy evaporated. The dream of seeing her family again faded and the pain from her wounds that had been delayed by her defiance descended on her. It had taken all of her courage, all of her fear, and all of her love of family to make this attempt at escape. She had tried and failed. At least she had tried, she told herself. Her eyes closed. In an act of providential mercy, she quickly lost sensation in her appendages.

Dana knew in that moment that she was going to die and, considering the alternative was returning to her darkened chamber, she was fine with that.

She watched with blurred vision as her pursuer approached and squatted to get a closer look. She noticed for the first time that his work boots were stained with something dark and wondered if it was blood—her own or one of the other girls being kept in the concrete dungeon.

For a moment Dana thought that he was shining a flashlight in her eyes. Her fading synaptic functions caused fireworks to explode behind her half-closed eyelids and something instinctively told her that she was about to die.

She felt her body moving and focused her vision just enough to see her warden had picked her up and was turning her around.

He was sitting on the ground now and he had moved her body so she was leaning back against him. He placed one hand on her head and one on her shrunken abdomen, rocking her the way you would rock a child.

His mouth was close to her ear and she could hear him whisper, "There, there. There, there."

The fireworks overwhelmed her. Then everything faded and she was gone.

Chapter 2

I knew that there were people having a worse morning than me but at that moment I just couldn't help feeling selfish.

Physically, I was at the wheel of my Chevy Impala heading west on Bradley Road towards a crime scene at the northwest edge of suburban Milwaukee, but mentally I was still in Dr. O'Connor's exam room where only half an hour ago I'd learned that my lifestyle would need to change.

"Your cholesterol level is elevated but still within the 'normal' range," O'Connor said reading the results from a recent blood draw. He tapped the edge of his clipboard on the desk. "Your blood sugar is definitely in the 'too high' range though."

I rubbed my hands together as if we were beginning a game and said, "Okay, I'll bite. What's too high?"

"Yours was at 278."

"What should it be?"

"Between ninety and one hundred."

The news didn't come as a shock. I'd been eating badly, sleeping irregular hours and not exercising much lately, lately being the last ten or twelve years. I was six feet tall and running about two-thirty, not morbidly obese or anything, but not exactly Hugh Jackman.

And as much as I was loath to admit it I wasn't a spring chicken anymore either. On my last birthday I was officially closer to fifty than forty and my body was beginning to catch up with me. I couldn't eat three donuts for breakfast, chase it down with a twenty-ounce coffee (two sugars) and not expect my gut to end up hanging over my belt anymore. The body that I saw in the mirror when I stepped out of the shower wasn't exactly a babe magnet anymore... if it ever was.

I guess things needed to change. How come changes can't be fun? Why do changes always have to be a drag?

"So… what are you telling me?" I knew what he meant; I just wanted him to give it to me straight and actually use the word. It was an interrogation technique.

"It's diabetes, Ken. My guess is you'll probably be able to manage a good chunk of it with diet and exercise but at some point, you're going to need to go on medication."

I sat up a little straighter on the exam table. The paper cover ripped a little.

"But I'm not going to have to give myself the shots? The insulin shots?" I realized that I said *the insulin shots* as if the doctor didn't know what I was talking about.

O'Connor just shrugged.

"We'll see. Right now, you need to get set up with one of our dieticians that specialize with diabetes. You'll need to start monitoring your glucose levels right away." He leaned forward in his chair. The look on his face was pretty serious. "I'm not kidding though, Ken. You need to pay more attention to your diet, and you need to exercise every day—regardless of where your levels end up. You need to run, ride a bike, do something active. High carb meals—pizza, pasta, subs? That kind of stuff has gotta stop, buddy."

The problem was O'Connor had just described all eight of my last meals, except the drive through I'd had for breakfast, but I was sure that if he knew he would have mentioned that too. On the rare occasions that I brought a lunch with me to work it was always leftovers and included a large mound of potatoes or something starchy. And don't get me started on the soda…

I could just see busting out a Tupperware container of vegetables in the break room in front of the other guys. My stock was low in the squad at the moment; this sure wasn't going to help any.

The call from Lieutenant Gold had been a welcome interruption to our conversation and I politely, but quickly, took my leave.

I crossed 107th Street without fully stopping and pushed down on the accelerator. The car leapt forward covering the mile to 124th in 45 seconds. On my right Dretzka Golf Course was a blur. I hadn't played a round there in forever anyway so I didn't feel like I was missing anything.

The crime scene was in a field that used to be Starlight Drive-In, a two-screen movie theater that lasted well into the 1980s. The screens were long gone and the grass had overrun the parking lot twenty years ago. The building that housed the snack bar and projection booth was still more-or-less standing but these days it only housed a collection of rodents. Even the heroin addicts that previously used it as a shooting gallery didn't bother with it anymore.

I'd seen a couple movies there when I was a kid and a few more when I started dating in high school. I know I saw one of the Porky's movies on the north screen with Barbara Klaser. That night turned out to be more embarrassing than anything else.

The memories of teenage fumbling got my mind off my health issues for a few blissful moments, but when I pulled to a stop on the gravel shoulder an empty Coca Cola can rolled from beneath the passenger seat and came to a rest next to this morning's fast food bag. It was a pretty rude reminder of my current health situation.

Diabetes… Well, Doctor O'Connor said I might be able to control it with diet and exercise. Yeah, I got this. I can fix it.

I'm better at fixing stuff than changing.

I grabbed the trash and tossed it into the back seat. Out of sight and out of mind, right? I unplugged my phone from the charger and stepped out of the car.

Chapter 3

There were already two S.U.V. black and whites parked on the shoulder, along with a Buick sedan that I didn't recognize but assumed belonged to the detective that caught the case. I looked inside for any kind of clue as to whom it belonged to but there was nothing giving it away.

The crime scene was in the 4th District and even though I'd grown up not that far from here I still only knew a couple of the cops that worked out of the precinct house on Silver Springs Drive. Most of the cases I catch are in the 1st or 2nd, the section of Milwaukee that the locals usually referred to as "Downtown." But as a Detective with the Sensitive Case Unit I am expected to investigate anywhere inside, and on occasion outside the city.

The Sensitive Case Unit, or SCU as the acronym-obsessed police department referred to it, is tasked with investigating cases that require a delicate touch; elder and child abuse, racial crimes and, on occasion, homicide—provided there was an unusual pathological element to the crime. The members of the squad pronounced it "skew" and for us it's an honor to serve on the elite team.

I walked through the overgrown field making my way towards the spot at the far side where two uniformed officers and a detective stood talking and comparing notes. The detective was holding a cup of coffee. He looked up when he saw me approaching.

"That was quick," he said. "Dave Collins, out of the fourth. Are you the guy from SCU?"

I introduced myself without slowing, moving past Collins and his offered hand to where the uniforms were protecting the scene. When I stepped over a patch of weeds I could see the body clearly for the first time.

I read the entire scene in an instant collecting any number

of details and filing them away mentally. I'd transfer them to my notebook when I got back to the car; right now I just wanted to get a feel for the space and what may have happened here.

The girl was dark skinned, probably Middle Eastern or Indian. She was barely over five feet tall and so bony that I figured she weighed about sixty pounds. C.S.I. would figure out the details later. The only clothing she wore was a dirty, blood-soaked t-shirt that was probably white several years ago and a pair of panties that looked too big on her emaciated body. Probably a cute kid once upon a time.

It was obvious that she had bled to death, the result of a number of wounds all over her body. One cut on her left arm was so deep I could see the bone. There were similar cuts on her legs and the blood and tears in her shirt suggested there were more underneath. She was laid out supine with her arms close to the torso.

I hate the ones with dead kids...

I looked at the other cops and said, "What do we got?"

"Dump job," the shorter of the two uniforms said. His tag told me his name was Kussmall. "Teenage girl. Looks like someone cut her up good."

I kept from saying that he was stating the obvious. A blind man could look towards 124th Street and could see the path where the grass was still matted down from her being dragged through.

This dump hadn't happened all that long ago.

"Who called it in?"

"Couple of kids found her about an hour ago," Kussmall said. "They're at home with their parents right now. Their mom was so ticked off that they were playing here she's probably tanned their backsides by now."

"I got the number," Collins said holding up his own pad.

"How come SCU got called in?" The girl looked like she was over eighteen; this looked like a run-of-the-mill homicide and dump job, if such a thing existed.

8

The taller uniform spoke for the first time.

"I spotted something when I came around this side."

I took a step around the body, taking care with where I placed my feet but I had to squat down to get a better look at what the cop was pointing out with his pen.

On the inside of her right forearm the number 326827 was tattooed in faded blue ink. Underneath them the words, "nur Offiziere" showed in slightly darker ink.

I looked up at Collins who shrugged and looked away. He didn't know what it meant but he wouldn't admit it out loud—at least not to me. Most of the time when a detective turns a case over to SCU he's happy to wash his hands of it. This guy, probably in his first year on the squad, seemed like he was gonna be a jerk about it.

"I've seen this stuff before Detective," Kussmall said. "But it was in high school history. And in movies."

"Yeah, we all know the Nazis tattooed numbers on the Jews in the concentration camps," Collins said. "But what's it say underneath?"

I looked at Kussmall and said, "You speak any German?"

"Not much. Just the menu at Maders."

"Not all the girls made it to concentration camps," I told the uniform cops, pretending Collins wasn't even there. "Some of them ended up in brothels around Germany and other occupied countries. If they were special they would get tagged."

I pointed at the words.

"It says, 'Officers only.'"

Chapter 4

"That doesn't make any sense," the taller uniform cop said. "This girl is barely twenty—if that. She wasn't in any Nazi camp seventy or eighty years ago."

"That's why they call SCU," I said. "If it wasn't a weird one, I wouldn't be here."

"But what's it mean?" Collins said.

"Well, there's a dead girl with cuts all over, lots of scarring and signs of previous abuse, sexual and otherwise, she's barely dressed and it looks like she hasn't been clean in months."

"Runaway?"

"Could be, Officer Kussmall. But what is she running from?"

I heard the sound of a buffalo approaching through the tall grass and turned to see my partner, detective Lloyd Washington tromping through the weeds towards us.

"Glad you could make it, Wash," I said. "Any sign of C.S.I.?"

"I passed them on the highway. They'll be here in about five."

Wash stepped up to the body, completely ignoring the others and practically pushed Collins out of the way. He squatted low and looked her over.

"Don't mind us," I said as if I hadn't done the same thing to Collins when I'd arrived. But I was used to Wash bulldozing his way into and through an investigation. He was a good detective but he never stopped climbing; never stopped striving. I know that he considered being African American a disadvantage, even in a racially diverse city like Milwaukee. He figured he would have to work twice as hard to make his bones with his fellow cops and probably the public as well.

So, he usually came on pretty strong.

"What does this mean?" Wash said, pointing at the tattoo.

I explained the tat and everything else we knew. It didn't take long.

"I'm assuming she bled out, but lack of blood here suggests she did it somewhere else."

"Genius observation. You should make First Grade by the end of the week."

When the others looked at me like I had just spit on my partner I just smirked and my dismissive head shake told them that this sarcastic banter was just a game that we played, and they didn't need to worry about him throwing gunshots my way.

"C.S.I. will be here soon," I said. "While they're doin' their thing we can check Missing Persons. My guess is we'll need to go back a ways."

Wash pointed to old wounds on the girl's legs and nodded.

"Some of these look like they're several years old."

"If it weren't for the crazy tats, I would assume it's just domestic abuse," I said. "Like I said, let's wait and see what the autopsy shows."

Wash held out his hand and I pulled him up to his feet.

"You still looking for Brewers tickets for Sunday?" he said.

Chapter 5

The Man With A Goatee unscrewed the cap from the bottle of bleach and splashed it all around the small room. He used old rags to scrub the walls and a new mop he'd bought at Walmart to clean the floor. After seven years the room was, no doubt, covered with physical evidence that Dana Hujet had been there. There was probably hair and skin all over—maybe even blood. In the corner was a bucket that she used for a toilet. That would have to go as well.

The Man With A Goatee was not a forensic expert but he'd seen enough television shows to know that the slightest trace of evidence could get him a lethal injection. Well, not in Wisconsin—there was no capital punishment—but it could prove that the girl had been there, probably over a long period of time, and that was enough to convict him.

He'd been fond of Dana; she was probably his favorite of the girls he kept hidden away. She was quiet and submissive, qualities he liked in his girls. There had been some who were always carrying on and that got on his nerves. He'd gotten rid of them quickly.

But Dana had been special; she reminded him of Marta, the first girl he'd felt anything for. She was also the first girl he'd been physical with. He loved the way her dark hair and brown eyes complimented her olive complexion. Her skin was so smooth and her voice was soft and gentle. She was perfect. She was the template for his ideal woman; who he looked for in every girl he met but never found. But there was only one Marta, and she was not coming back.

The Man With A Goatee wondered how much he needed to scrub the room. How much of the bleach was enough to wash away the remains of a young woman who'd lived in this space for so long? And would the bleach leave any kind of telltale markers? He had to believe it would. But these were things no one had ever taken the time to teach him. Maybe if he'd taken home economics in high school instead of industrial arts classes… But then something told him that they didn't cover DNA disposal in Home Ec. either.

The fumes were giving him a headache. He'd planned on throwing a coat of paint on the walls and floor as well but it wasn't going to happen anytime soon; not until the room had vented some of the smell of sweat and excrement to the outside.

He gave the entire floor a quick once-over with the mop before covering the bottle and heading for the door. A shower sounded good right now. Sweat ran down the side of his cheek and he wiped it off with the back of a hand too quickly to realize he probably rubbed bleach onto his whiskers.

He cursed loudly and was surprised to hear a whimper from one of the other rooms.

He could feel the anger burning at the bridge of his nose as he shouted, "You shut up in there!"

The whimpering ceased.

The Man With A Goatee held the mop in his armpit as he carried the bleach in one hand and the mop bucket half-full of dirty water in the other.

Yeah, a long shower, he thought. Then maybe some Pepper Steak at The Black Kettle followed by an early evening with one of the girls.

All through his shower and lunch he thought of Marta.

Chapter 6

The squad room for the Sensitive Case Unit is on the fourth floor of a building on Wells Street, not far from the Milwaukee Public Museum and the Public Library in what the tourists, they called West Town. The S.C.U. moved in shortly after it was created in the early 1990s, taking over space previously used for jobs that had been taken over by computers located at an unknown and, presumably, secure site.

The room smelled of mildew and burnt coffee and every time I walk in from the hallway I have to stifle the urge to cough. Our last lieutenant said he'd bring in an air purifier someday but he never did. Some days I wondered what the percentage of cops dying in the line of duty versus cops dying from something they caught from working in a moldy office was. Considering ninety percent of our job was spent in the squad or other rooms on the floor my guess was that I had less to fear from a skel with a gun.

When Wash and I arrived the squad room was empty. Only our civilian Police Administrative Aide, Claire Mullen, was at her desk.

"Did we miss a memo?"

"I stepped out to the ladies room and when I came back the squad room was empty," Claire said.

She was a nice looking girl, red hair and green eyes but without that charming Irish lilt that would drive the guys over-the-top crazy for her. She always dressed professionally but when I turned my desk around so it wasn't facing her I found myself becoming more productive.

It didn't help that somewhere in the world I had a daughter about the same age.

Wash just walked to his desk.

I stepped back into the hallway got a drink from the bubbler. One thing I liked about this building was the cold water. At that moment I needed a cold drink. I was even willing to put ice in a glass of scotch, but that would have to wait until after five—probably later if we didn't make any headway in this case.

It's one of the truisms of being a cop that the first forty-eight hours are critical to any investigation, but forensic evidence from a crime scene often takes days, even weeks to process. So far, we had little to go on.

I returned to the squad and turned on my computer. I logged into the department database and started looking for similar crimes or anything that had a Nazi-like hate component. I'd gotten as far as typing in "Nazi" and "tattoo" before Lieutenant Gold stuck his head in the door.

"Brady, can I see you out here?"

I saved the witty reply and stepped out into the hallway, tucking in my shirttail as I walked.

Gold waved me to follow him and we walked down to the Viewing Room next to Interview Two. Two was a room we used a lot; it had the most comfortable chairs and a long table that immediately intimidated the punks we questioned there. It was also the room we used if someone was having a birthday and there was cake. We liked Two.

The Viewing Room was not as special. It was probably a broom closet or storage room before someone cut a hole in the wall and installed a one-way mirror. It was cramped and usually smelled like sweaty detectives, not an odor that you'd put into a bottle and try selling. Still, it's better than when they let us smoke in the building.

Gold and I stepped into the cramped space where Detective Ray Schmidt was standing with his hands on his bulging waist. I'm sure he thought he looked like Superman but he was really projecting the frustration I knew he was feeling. There was a problem in Schmidt-ville and I was being called in to fix it. I was already interested to hear how he was going to ask for help without actually asking for help.

I nodded my head in greeting.

"Brady," he said. I could hear his contempt in that one word, my name.

"What's going on?"

Lieutenant Gold stepped between us and said, "I want you to take over this interview."

Schmidt started to protest but the Lieu stopped him with a hand. I was impressed with the way our diminutive boss, only two weeks in our squad, already had control of the wild bull of SCU. Schmidt wasn't a bad detective but he wasn't what you'd call a light touch. He was a heavyset, blustery clod who would look right at home working on the docks until somebody asked him to actually do something physical. Not that he was lazy, it's just that he ran a twelve-minute mile and threw his weight around an interrogation like Michael Chicklis in Meatloaf's body. Before he lost weight, that is.

"You have the jacket?" I asked. Gold handed me the manila file. It was about half an inch thick and I paged through the pages while Schmidt gave me his own rundown between sputters and throat clearings.

I knew a lot of the details already; the case had come to SCU a few days ago and even though Schmidt caught the case I still managed to go through the paperwork he left on his desk when he left the squad room. I probably knew the details better than he did because details are what I pay attention to. Schmidt always looked for the easy answer because, funnily enough, it was usually the correct answer. But on those occasions when the answer wasn't right in front of his face he tended to miss the minutiae.

When Schmidt finished his brief I shut the folder and turned to the Lieu.

"So, what do you want me to do?"

"Can you get him to give it up?"

"Probably." I turned to Schmidt. "How'd the tough guy

routine play with him?"

"You wouldn't be here if I'd gotten anywhere," Schmidt said. "If it were up to me, I'd go back in there with a phonebook and find out what I want to know."

"Anybody ever tell you you're not supposed to say that in front of the boss?" Gold said looking Schmidt in the face until the dope actually turned sheepishly towards the window. He turned to me and said, "Can you do this?"

"Yeah, I can do this." And I turned and walked into Interview Two.

Chapter 7

Interviews and interrogations are funny things. Some cops love doing them, some hate it. I don't waste time thinking about whether or not I enjoy it. It's a fact of my job and I'm going to do it whether I want to or not.

It just happens that I have a pretty good track record with getting confessions from suspects. Six months earlier I'd done a marathon interview that turned into an interrogation with a guy who murdered six elderly people and collected their Social Security money. As clear cut as the case seemed to be, I still needed a confession and after seventeen hours I got it. It was a pretty big deal and for a while I was the flavor of the month in the squad.

Since then I haven't closed a case. I've helped the other guys but for some reason none of the cases I've caught have been satisfactorily resolved. Not by me anyway. I was in a worse slump than the Brewers, who occasionally won, and my fellow detectives were beginning to see me as a screwup. It's not funny how fast you can become the red-headed-step-child in a squad like this.

Helping Schmidt was advantageous for both of us. He was never going to get this guy to talk and I needed the karma points.

There's an unwritten rule that you would never lay hands on a suspect if you don't know for certain that he's guilty. There's a lot less of that kind of questioning than most people would think but I'm not going to say it never happens. I wouldn't even say that I've never done it. Some of these guys that end up sitting in this room; it's the only way you'll get them to tell you their name.

I could tell by looking that Billy Trava wasn't one of those kids. He looked like he'd been taking beatings all his life and if I punched him he'd shut up like a clam. Schmidt knew he had the right guy, and I thought he was right, but I wanted to hear him say it himself.

Billy was slouching in the chair with one arm draped over the table where he was drumming his fingers. He wore a heavy Chicago Bears jacket despite the fact that winter had been over for a while and under these lights his dark skin glistened from the sweat. The jacket was his security blanket. He was tall and skinny like a basketball player but he looked small sitting behind the table. He was scared and tired, not the best combination for me to work with but I was going to get this done.

Billy Trava had killed his infant son and disappeared the mother. We had enough evidence to put him away for the killing but I needed to find out exactly what happened before some shyster came in and told him to shut up. I needed to do this right, for his kid's sake if not for my own.

This is where I needed to put on an Academy Award performance.

I walked into the room with the file, looked at Billy Trava sitting at the table, looked at the number outside the door as if I'd maybe entered the wrong room and finally stepped inside.

"Billy Trava?"

Billy looked up at me and I swear he almost looked amused for a second.

"You gonna beat up on me?" he said.

"I don't have the energy," I said, dropping the file on the table and sitting not opposite from him, but around the corner where I could see his entire body.

"Where'd the other guy go?"

"I don't know. Which other guy?"

"The other cop who's been screaming at me for the last three hours. Thinks I killed my kid."

"Other cop? Big guy?" I held my hands up over my head as I asked, giving the impression that Schmidt was six inches taller than me when he was really an inch shorter. "Smells like he was just rolling sausages at Usingers?"

"Yeah, I guess," Billy said. "But I don't know nothin' about no Usingers."

"It's a German sausage place over by the river," I said. "Bad joke. Sorry."

I opened the file and looked at the top pages silently. We sat that way for a couple minutes while we silently sized each other up. "Okay," I said looking up at him. "You're Billy Trava? Right?"

"Yeah, I'm Billy Trava. Who do you think that other guy's been talking to for all this time?"

"I'm sorry, I'll probably be asking you some of the same questions that Detective Schmidt asked you. I didn't get to hear what you told him. Just bear with me, okay?" I didn't talk down to him or raise my voice. I wasn't trying to establish a hierarchy that put him at the bottom; I was trying to get him to like and trust me enough to start talking. Schmidt probably made that easier for me; I was the good cop following up on his bad cop and he was bound to like me better. We hadn't planned it that way but it was working out nicely.

I asked him a few other basic questions: his address, his birth date, where he worked—stuff he wouldn't feel like he needed to lie about. I needed him to be in a habit of telling the truth. That way lying would feel awkward and I might be able to spot his false statements easier.

He answered my questions with a bit of frustration in his voice but he wasn't trying to be antagonistic. That was going to work for me too.

In my head I knew I was talking to a monster; a guy who would murder his infant son and probably kill his girlfriend too. But I wasn't going to learn anything from the monster. I needed to talk to the human being sitting next to me; the part of him that was scared silly. The part of him that actually felt remorse about what he'd done.

I was about to make a new friend.

Chapter 8

"So, tell me what happened last Friday." I leaned forward on the table and looked him in the eyes giving him my full attention.

"I told that other guy—"

"I know. I didn't get his notes though. And besides, I'd rather hear it from you. I know you'll tell me the truth. That other guy will give me his opinion, and that's not good for you."

He looked at me like he was considering what I was saying, which I'm sure he was.

"Last Friday?" He finally said. "Well, I came home from work and—"

"What time was that?"

"I don't know exactly. Nine-thirty or so. That's when I usually get home."

"Okay," I said making a note on the back of his rap sheet. "Sorry for interrupting you. Keep going."

"I got home from work and Erin—my girl Erin—she was watching some movie on the DVD." He started scratching the tabletop as if he was writing with his finger. "She was mad 'cuz James wouldn't go to sleep. He was all cryin' and stuff."

"James is your son, right?"

"Yeah."

"Did James cry a lot?"

"Seems like he's always cryin'. Erin ain't much of a mother. She don't have those material instincts, you know?"

I did know and said so, ignoring the malapropism.

"She started getting loud, cussing me out for not helping, as if me going to work at the restaurant didn't pay the rent and get us food."

"So, what did you do?"

"I bolted, man! I didn't want to listen to that all night!"

"What time was that?"

"Maybe, like ten."

"Okay," I said. "You were gone by ten o'clock?"

"Yeah. Maybe earlier even."

"Where'd you go?"

"I went over to my man Russell's place."

"And Russell can verify that?"

"He wasn't home, but I knew where the key was. I let myself in."

"Nice," I said. "It's good to have friends, right?"

"Russell and me been friends since grade school."

"Old friends are the best friends."

He confirmed the sentiment with language I wouldn't use in front of my mother. I could tell he was loosening up a bit. I kept up eye contact with him and listened closely to every word he said. He'd already lied to me a couple times but he thought I didn't know. I wasn't going to bust him out on anything yet—I wanted to keep him talking.

"And when you left at ten o'clock—that was the last you saw Erin or James?"

"That was it. I slept at Russell's place. When I went back to my place on Saturday afternoon the cops were already there."

"Huh," I said chewing on my pen. "Who do you think called the police?"

He shrugged and grunted, "I don't know. Ain't you got that in your papers there?"

I paged through the stack and found the right page.

"Yeah. Yeah, here it is. One of the neighbors called about eleven-thirty. Said there was a heck of an argument going on."

"I was gone by then."

"Right, you were at Russell's." I leaned back in my chair. "Did you go right to sleep when you got there?"

"What do you mean?"

22

"Did you go right to sleep? Or did you watch television, or eat something or... whatever?"

"I might've had a beer. I watched some TV and fell asleep on the couch."

"At Russell's?"

"Yeah."

"You didn't watch TV at your place?"

He hesitated for a moment before saying no. "Erin had the TV on but I didn't watch nothin'. I wasn't there long enough."

"Yeah, you said that..." I sat forward and started playing with my lower lip, trying to look like I was deep in thought about something.

"What?" he said.

"Well..." Now I hesitated for a moment. "It's just that your neighbor—the one that called this in—said that they didn't hear anybody leave the apartment until later."

"They're wrong? Who was it?"

"They said that there was lots of commotion and then someone went up and down the stair a couple times, but it was after eleven o'clock."

"I told you, I was at Russell's by then."

"I know. I know. Is it possible you got the time wrong? Something like that?"

"I didn't."

"Okay, it's just that..."

"What?"

It was a key moment and I had to sell a certain amount of confusion. If I blew this he was going to clam up. I could almost hear Gold and Schmidt holding their breath behind the mirror.

"It's just we know you were in the apartment after eleven."

I was hoping for a certain look, a certain attitude in response to my statement. He could have been defiant. He could have gotten angry. I was hoping to see some fear in his eyes. And I got what I wanted.

"W-What do you mean?" he stammered.

I reached over and placed my hand on his arm.

"Hold on, don't worry. I'm not accusing you of anything. I'm just saying that you were in the apartment. Don't get all…" I waved my hands around my head.

"But I wasn't…"

"You used the toilet, Billy," I said. "And then you didn't flush it."

His head started shaking as he dug deep for an answer. In his nervousness he looked like he had palsy.

"That was… from when I was there before."

"Billy, they run tests on that kind of thing. I don't know how an adult can do that kind of thing and it sure ain't the job I'd ever want, but… there it is. They proved it was you and that you dropped it after eleven."

"No. No. No. No," he said, shaking his head from side to side. "I didn't do this."

"Slow down, buddy. All I'm saying is you used a toilet. That's it. Just relax."

He settled down and I waited until his breathing was back to normal.

"You okay, Billy?"

"Yeah. Yeah, I'm okay."

"Can I get you something? Can of soda? Coffee? I'm sure we got some donuts around here somewhere."

"Soda's good."

I asked him what kind and he asked for anything with caffeine. I stood up and gave his shoulder a gentle squeeze as if I were reassuring him.

"I just wanna go home," he said in a tired voice.

"I know. I'm sorry this is taking so long. Just a little longer." I grabbed the paperwork and took a step toward the door. "I'll be right back."

Chapter 9

Schmidt and Gold met me in the hallway.

"This is you getting this guy to confess, huh?" Schmidt said. "You gonna get him a Happy Meal next?"

"You're just mad 'cuz I have rapport."

"I stick around long enough you'll probably file adoption papers for this dirt bag."

"You don't like the way I do it? Fine. You go back in there with a rubber hose and see how far you get. You worked that plan for three hours and didn't get bupkus. I'm gonna walk back in that room and I guarantee the first thing he tells me is he was in the apartment."

"Ten bucks says you're wrong," Schmidt said.

I turned to Gold and said, "You're our witness."

Gold handed me a can of soda.

"Just get this guy's story."

I returned to Interview Two resisting the urge to pop the top on the soda and drink it myself. I almost asked Gold for another can but I figured after Dr. O'Connor's diagnosis this morning it probably would do more harm than good. I needed to keep my head in the game.

Billy Trava was sitting up at the table drumming both hands now. I popped the can and set it in front of him.

"You sure you don't want a donut?"

He shook his head, then opened his mouth like he was going to say something but didn't.

"What is it?"

"I..." He was having a hard time telling me what I already knew. "I was in the apartment."

I gave him my mildly surprised look and said, "Okay." He didn't offer anything else; he just sat back and looked at the tabletop. "Did you see what happened?"

He shook his head.

"Listen Billy," I said leaning towards him and stretching a hand across the table. "If you saw what happened you need to tell me. If Erin did something to James…" I left it hanging. I knew Erin didn't do anything to the kid. She was a victim too and I needed to know where she was.

"I don't know what happened."

"Well, I'll tell you. Someone squeezed their hands over his mouth and behind his neck and gave him a shake." I demonstrated the grip on an invisible baby.

It was worse than "a shake" but I didn't want to show all my cards. I needed him to think he had some room to maneuver.

"Then they swung him by the leg and hit him against the wall."

Billy's face fell. He shifted in his seat, trying to cover up how nervous he was but his body language gave everything away.

"Did you witness any of that?"

He did a full-body flop to one side of his chair.

"Billy, listen to me. If you witnessed something you gotta tell me." I slid my chair around the table closer to him and leaned down to make eye contact. "You don't seem like a bad guy. You don't seem like the kind of guy that would do something like this. If you saw what happened…"

He snorted up a nose-full of snot before it ran onto his upper lip, then wiped his face on his sleeve.

"I know you were there, Billy," I said in a gentle voice. "Tell me what happened." I waited almost a minute before I spoke again. "There were drugs in the apartment. Were those yours?"

He seemed surprised that I'd brought the drugs up.

"I don't care about the blow, Billy. You hear me? You're not here because of a stupid drug charge. I just want to know about James and Erin. You don't seem like the kind of guy that would do something to his own kid, but if you were hopped up… that's a different story. You wouldn't have been in control of yourself. You know what I'm saying?"

The way he looked at me I couldn't tell if he spotted my trap or if he wanted to give me a hug. There was genuine fear in his eyes and I could see tears forming in the corners. He slid his chair back and buried his face in his hands.

"Listen to me Billy, if you didn't mean it—if you came home from a hard day at work, needed to do some blow to unwind and then did something to James 'cuz he just wouldn't stop crying…"

He sobbed, a loud, air-sucking sob and I knew I had him.

"You wouldn't do something like that on purpose—I know you wouldn't. I know how tough it can be. I got a couple kids myself. Sometimes it's too much."

"I wouldn't do nothing to hurt that boy…"

"James?"

"Yeah."

"I know that. And I don't believe you'd do anything to hurt his mother either. Not unless you weren't in control."

"I loved 'em both."

"I know you did, Billy. I know that. But the cocaine—it made you do something you didn't mean to do, didn't it? Because I know you wouldn't hurt them on purpose."

"I wouldn't."

"It was the coke, wasn't it? It made you hurt them. You're not a monster, Billy. You're a good guy. But the coke…"

His body shook as he sobbed, then he finally broke into a full-throated wail.

"The dope made you do it, right? You wouldn't hurt either of them on your own, but the dope took control and you hurt them?"

He managed to get just enough control to say, "It was the coke made me do it."

I slid my chair until I was right next to him and wrapped my arms around him. His body collapsed against mine and he cried like a baby.

An hour later I walked out of Interview Two and handed

Gold the signed statement.

"That was a day's work," Gold said.

"You can take it out of Schmidt's check."

Schmidt stopped me from walking away by putting his hand on my chest.

"This is still my case you know," he said.

"Yeah, it's still your case," I said. "Good job closing it."

I pushed past him and returned to the squad room.

"And you owe me ten bucks."

Chapter 10

I spent the next couple hours going through files, hard copy and computer, looking for similar M.O.s to what we'd seen earlier. There were lots of hate crimes, lots of racially motivated hate crimes, but none that included tattooing a number on a young girl's body like the Nazis did. Wash and I were working on the idea that whoever did this was someone we hadn't come across before. The girls condition showed that whatever happened had been going on for a long time—years for sure. This guy had been at it for a while, so what happened that this girl was found today? She was dumped somewhere where she would be found fairly quickly. This time of year, a traffic helicopter would have spotted her body if those kids hadn't stumbled onto her.

Somebody made a mistake and we needed to capitalize on it.

I have no idea how the memory popped into my head, but there it was like it had been hanging out off to the side of my mind and now it was waving a hand at me.

But it wasn't a full memory, just a thought.

"Wash," I said spinning around in my chair to face him. His desk was a dozen steps across the squad. "Do you remember me telling you about a missing girl case when I was working in The Second?"

Wash didn't look up from the file he was reading.

"Nope."

"It was a girl with dark hair. A teenager."

"You think this is her? The girl we found today?"

I scratched my chin and thought about it for a second.

"Nah," I said. "The ages aren't right. That was, like, eight years ago. That girl would be in her early twenties today."

"Our vic could've been early twenties. She's pretty messed up."

"You guys wanna keep it down," Schmidt said from where he was typing up the report in his corner of the squad room. "I'd like to get this done by quittin' time."

"Hey, if you want, I can do that for you too," I said. "Everyone knows you can't spell anyway."

"If you'd ever close a case you could do your own report, maybe get on the news again."

"Maybe you oughta roll that report in a cone," I said. I didn't need to finish the thought—he knew what I meant. He also knew enough to shut up and leave us to what we were doing.

"I'll give Voight a call later and see what he remembers." Jason Voight was my partner in The Second. He was retired now, living in the burbs on disability after being injured in the line of duty. I don't want to make any judgments about him because that sidewalk was pretty uneven and the sprain looked bad but I sure wish I could retire at fifty-one and collect three-quarters of my pension. All that nonsense aside, Voight was a pretty solid detective and a stand-up partner.

"Brady," I heard Gold call from just outside his office. He waved me over and told me to close the door.

Now what did I do?

I still wasn't convinced that this was the guy to run our squad; I didn't know a whole lot about him when he arrived and the past couple weeks hadn't given me any real clues to his personality either. He was dark skinned, like a Middle-eastern and his name, Joshua Gold, gave me a strong indication that he was at least partly Jewish. I'd worked with Irish bosses, German bosses, even a black boss—excuse me, African-American—but Gold was the first Jewish boss I'd ever even heard of. So far, he hadn't come on too hard but I assumed he was just being passive aggressive.

He sat behind his desk and looked over at me.

"Are you gonna be able to get this thing with Schmidt cleared up?"

"What's to clear up? The guy's a jerk."

"I appreciate it that you got his guy to talk but I can tell you didn't do it for him."

"That's my job," I said probably sounding too forceful. "Schmidt can hardly write his name in the snow but I don't squeeze his shoes when he goes a couple months without a collar."

Gold didn't back down at all.

"It's been more than a couple months for you," he said.

"No Lieutenant, it's been about an hour but that mouth breather in there is going to get the credit even though you saw me do it."

"You think I won't give you credit for closing this one?"

"I think once Schmidt files his paperwork on this case it won't matter what you say. He'll erase another name from the board and I'll still have my list that hasn't changed in almost six months."

"I have an idea," Gold said. "Quit feeling sorry for yourself. You're a good cop in a slump. Pull up the big boy pants and do what you do."

I don't know how other people in his command responded to him but trying to sound like my dad wasn't going to win him any points.

"Super," I said only barely managing to keep the sarcasm from my voice. "Anything else?"

"What's going on with this case you caught today?"

I ran the case for him, telling him what we knew. It didn't take long. I told him there were some uniforms canvassing and we were running cold cases while we waited on the examiner's report. I didn't tell him anything he couldn't already see or didn't know. It was pretty much what police do: collect and analyze data.

It only occurred to me while I was telling Gold about the case how much the whole thing annoyed me. It wasn't just that a young girl was dead, or that some wicked things had been done to her physically and, no doubt, mentally. What hacked me was that this kind of thing had happened in my city. Milwaukee had a large German population and a tradition going back several generations but it had never birthed the Neo-Nazi groups that had popped up in other cities like Skokie. There had been a fair share of racial intolerance but we were a far cry from Berlin, Munich or Nuremburg in the 1930s. I didn't know if that concentration camp tatt was someone's sick joke or what but it definitely sent me to an angry place.

I wanted to catch this scumbag, and the canvasses and the M.E. report couldn't come fast enough for me.

I'd hardly finished getting Gold up to speed when there was a rap on the window that separated his office from the squad. Claire pointed at me, then held up two fingers.

"You need anything else," I said, "or can I get this?"

Gold told me to go and waved me out of his office.

As I walked to my desk Claire turned to me and said, "It's about your friend, Amanda."

Amanda wasn't really my friend. She was someone I tossed a twenty to every now and then in exchange for some information. She wasn't completely reliable but she'd helped me a couple of times. She was twenty-two going on fifty and between her chemical dependencies and the boyfriends who regularly used her for punching bags she had a pretty rough existence. It wouldn't surprise me to find out she was dead. Or that she'd done it herself.

I grabbed the phone and hit the button for line two.

Chapter 11

Lakeview Hospital is on Bluemound Avenue, across the street from the Milwaukee County Zoo. It's pretty small compared to some of the other medical campuses in town that seem to grow a new wing every couple of years. A kid I went to elementary school with was born there and he reminded us every time we went on a field trip to see the animals. You can imagine some of the jokes we considerate grade schoolers made, but the dope just couldn't stop sharing this portion of his life story with us. I guess some kids never learn.

I entered the hospital through a sliding glass door and flashed my shield at the woman sitting at the information desk. I told her who I was looking for and she quickly told me where I could find her, including detailed instructions about how to get there. Hospitals never seem to have direct ways to get from one place to another.

Amanda was curled up in a chair, asleep in a waiting room near the E.R. when I found her. Her left arm was in a cast from her fingertips to just below the elbow and her brow had four butterfly bandages where she'd just received stitches. There was a bruise lower down on her cheek that was going to be purple tomorrow, even against her cocoa skin that so many of the boys seemed to find alluring. She'd probably been pretty cute before she discovered crack and turned into a pincushion for every guy with a rock. By the time I'd found her she was trying to turn her life around. She'd done a decent job too; getting off the drugs and risking her life to give me some information that helped me close an important case. There's no question that she had more guts than brains, qualities which probably helped earn her this trip to the Emergency Room.

I squatted next to her chair and put a gentle hand on her

knee.

"Amanda," I said quietly.

She woke with a start. I'd probably awakened her from the first decent sleep she'd had in months. She recognized me and smiled.

"Hi Ken."

Such a simple greeting, there was nothing weird in her choice of words but the way she said it made me feel uncomfortable, like she had a crush on me or something. I think she could tell I was a little embarrassed and held up her cast.

"It's not as bad as it looks," she said. "My arm bone is only fractured but my wrist is broken. I guess the Catholic churches won't be interested in me anymore."

"What do you mean?"

"Wasn't it you that was telling me how the Catholic churches in Europe have collar and wrist bones of all the Apostles?"

I didn't remember telling her that but it wasn't impossible. When I was a teenager my mom took us to Germany for my grandparents wedding anniversary. We'd visited a half dozen of these cathedrals and they all had that kind of thing. I'm not sure how they actually identified St. Peter's shinbone but there you go. Who was I to say it wasn't legit?

"What happened?"

She looked away at a television that was playing a muted news broadcast.

"Oh… Johnny didn't like that I didn't have dinner ready when he got home from work. Didn't matter that it wasn't even two in the afternoon."

Johnny D was her dirt bag boyfriend, another piece of human waste who'd only escaped a deuce on a domestic abuse rap because she'd dropped the charges. He'd beaten her pretty good that time, his coup de gras being a closed-fist punch that knocked three teeth down her throat—literally. I knew I was wasting my time but I said it anyway.

"You gotta get away from that guy, Amanda. He's not

gonna change and one of these times he's gonna kill you."

"You don't know him—"

"Yes I do," I said interrupting her. "I know him better than you do. I see punks like him every day. They think they're tough but they only beat on little girls. They wouldn't last three seconds in a fight with a real man."

"Maybe you should give him a beating."

"Maybe I will," I said.

When she turned back to face me her eyes were pleading.

"Please don't," she said.

"I'm not kidding, Amanda. Guy like that doesn't change. He'll keep beating you as long as he can get away with it and he'll get away with it until he's in jail or dead."

She turned back at the floor, looking at it like she was counting the tiles.

"Do you have someplace else you can go?"

She thought about it for a moment and said, "I got a girl-friend lives in West Allis. I can probably stay there."

"You gotta stay away from Johnny."

"I will."

"You have to," I said more forcefully.

"I will."

She didn't convince me completely but I knew it was the best I'd get from her.

I'd seen girls like her all my life. Hooking up with the wrong guy and getting hurt but never doing anything about it, as if being alone is worse than being in a hospital. Or worse.

I guess it's true what they say: the heart wants what the heart wants, even if it's no good for you.

I handed her my phone and said, "Call your friend. I'll drive you over."

Chapter 12

Johnny D was a grease monkey with patchy facial hair and dirt under his fingernails. Previous experience told me he was twenty-four years old, five foot eight and about a buck and a half—soaking wet. That same experience told me exactly where I could find him.

He was at the far end of the bar at Smokestack, on Fond du Lac Avenue, a smelly neighborhood tavern that didn't seem to get the message about the smoking ban in public places. The place had been there for eighty or ninety years so the smell was probably permanent at this point anyway. Stale cigarettes and beer...

I breathed through my mouth as I walked past the other derelicts and crank-heads, most of whom were as wrong as snow in August. I wasn't there for them; I couldn't have cared less what they did or what they were holding. I was gonna state my case to the greasy bag of crap and be on my way.

Unless he resisted. Then I was gonna have some fun.

He was hunched over a basket of deep fried cheese curds, a glass of beer warming itself on the counter. It was almost full but I didn't figure it was his first. He'd probably been at the bottle since this morning. He needed the courage to slap around a girl almost half his size.

I slid onto the stool next to him and grabbed a curd from the basket. Before he could say anything, I'd dunked it into the soufflé cup of overly sweet barbecue sauce and shoved it in my mouth.

"Hey! What do you think—" he managed to say before he recognized me. Then his face fell. "Oh… hey."

"Let's talk," I said.

Johnny D sat up and made a show of brushing the crumbs from his hands.

"Yeah, okay," he said. "What do you want to talk about?"

"What do you think, you puss bucket?" I couldn't believe he wanted to play games with me.

He turned towards me, placing a hand on the bar and said, "This is probably about Amanda, huh?"

I grabbed his hand and squeezed. It was boney and I could feel a finger coming out of joint as I applied pressure.

His howl attracted attention from the other hop heads. Two surly dudes down the bar stood up to get a better view of what was happening.

"Just sit down," I said, turning to them, "unless you wanna see how hard I punch."

The dudes went back to their drinks while Johnny D moaned. I let go of his hand and pulled him by the collar until his face was a couple inches from mine.

"Now you listen to me you little waste of DNA. If I ever hear again that you laid hands or anything else on Amanda, I am gonna rip your arm off and beat you to death with the bloody end. You hear me?"

He nodded his head with some vigor.

"I can't keep her from going back to you," I said. "Believe me, I tried. But you know how women are. They do all kinds of dumb stuff that doesn't make any sense so's I don't hold it against her. But if you hurt her again you can take it to the bank that I am gonna bury you deep—someplace they won't ever find you."

He was trying to not cry and his whole body was shaking with the effort. He managed to say, "You're a cop."

"I am a cop, and I have a pretty good reputation in the department. They think I'm a swell guy. If this turns into a matter of 'who do you believe?' you can bet the house that you're gonna lose. You're a dirty scumbag with a record of beating on girls. Nobody is gonna go to bat for you. You will end up in a hole so dark that closing your eyes will only make it brighter."

"Oh my god…" he choked out.

"Do you hear what I'm telling you?"

"Yes."

"Do you?"

"Yes!"

"If you hurt her again, I will do damage to you," I said.

"Okay," he said. "Okay."

I sat staring at him, not moving. I wanted to see how long he could last without flinching. It wasn't long.

"What?" he said.

I didn't say anything, just continued to glare.

"I'm not going to hurt her again," he said. "I swear! I'll leave her alone."

I was beginning to get a headache and I didn't know if it was from the smell, my blood sugar or from not throwing this chump a beating. Either way, I needed to get moving.

"I'm serious," I said.

"I know. I know."

"Do not hurt her again."

"Okay, I won't."

He tried, but couldn't look me in the eye when he said it. If I'd cared enough to check I probably would have found his pants soaking wet. He was plenty scared, which was how I wanted it.

I slid off the seat and said, "Get some ice for that hand." I walked out without looking back.

Chapter 13

I wasn't ready to go home yet. I had a head of steam from talking to Johnny D and I really didn't want to go home to Carrie and the kids with that kind of mad-on. It was bad enough I was going to be preoccupied with this girl we found earlier, I didn't need to be carrying Johnny D's bags as well. My first thought was to grab a drink someplace—it was after six and I was off duty technically. I'd called the squad and left a message for Gold that I was done for the day but the truth was I was too fired up to just head home.

Somewhere in this city was a guy who kidnapped, raped, starved, cut up and dumped a girl. Somewhere else was a family wondering what happened to their daughter and/or sister. The whole day had gone by and I still had no clues leading me anywhere. As distinctive as this dump job was, with the cutting and the tattoo, I still had nothing leading me to the skel that did this.

That's just the nature of police work sometimes. Sure, there are times when the pieces fall into place easy and you track down the chuckle-head in a day. That's the kind of stuff you see on television all the time. The reality is that finger prints don't come back instantly with a match since most people never get printed in their entire life; Crime Scene Units take days to give definitive answers, or any answer at all for that matter. The wind and rain are corrosive elements to a crime scene, washing away evidence as carelessly as we flush the toilet.

Even in this day and age of computer technology making an identification can take days, if not weeks. And that's assuming a family member isn't responsible for a D.O.A. being in that position and making an I.D. is in their best interest. There's no more shock left in me for what families will do to each other.

We cops are good at what we do but there's still a wide margin for error. There are cases on the board in the squad that never get cleared. Some names that have been written for years, their cases open but no evidence coming in.

That's why the early canvass is so important; the uniforms talking to the kids right away, asking people in the nearby homes if they saw or heard anything, checking the immediate area for clues before they're gone, all this stuff is crucial to making a collar.

I told myself that was the reason I came back out to the drive-in—to see if I could see anything we'd missed before but that wasn't true. I needed to blow off some steam.

I'm prone to tension headaches at the back of my skull when I know I should have given someone a beating but restrained myself. And that's how I was feeling now. Johnny D needed a tune up, and I was the guy to do it, but as a favor to Amanda I held back. Now I was hoping the fresh air would keep me from a migraine.

I slowed down as I drove past where the Forensic Evidence team's truck was still parked. They were still gathering evidence even though the body was taken away hours ago. I don't envy those guys their hours and the work they have to do; I love being a detective but I guess I'm too gregarious to spend my days crawling through long grass or hunkered over a microscope in a lab. I couldn't do what they do and they couldn't do what I do.

I decided not to stop. I wouldn't have made any difference anyway and they'd only want me to stay out of the way. The last thing I wanted was to slow them down.

I turned on Bradley Road and headed down the hill, back towards the city.

There was really no good reason why I turned on Granville Road; it's not a major artery of traffic or anything. The only reason I knew about it at all was that I dated a girl who lived in some apartments between Bradley and Brown Deer Road. That was a long time ago and she was happily married, the mother of two adopted kids and living a half hour north in Grafton. She'd been quite a good-looking girl back then, but when I looked at her Facebook page a while back I found that she'd settled into married life and let herself go. She seemed happy.

Granville is a two-lane road that probably hadn't been re-surfaced in twenty-five years. Traffic and weather, not to mention shifting earth caused by the runoff, had left the surface with a series of dips and uneven patches. The centerline was probably six inches higher than the shoulder and grooves from semi tires left it treacherous to walk across.

Especially if you were a raccoon like the one that ran out in front of my Impala.

I have no love for rodents but hitting something that size could mess up my car but good so I jerked the wheel and jumped on my brakes. The Impala skidded to a stop on the shoulder, spraying up gravel that flew like birdshot at the re-treating animal.

There was no other traffic on the road so I just sat there while I waited for my blood pressure to return to normal. I resisted the urge to take a shot at the raccoon with my Smith and Wesson, knowing that my headache would be coming back—full force.

I needed something to eat, and soon.

The raccoon ran to a chain link fence a few feet off the road on the other side of a ditch that the DNR probably would term a "Navigable Water Way" these days even though you couldn't float a kid's sail boat in it. It stopped, turned around and ran in the other direction, probably look-ing for a place to crawl under. The other side was a junkyard and I couldn't begin to imagine how many rodents were liv-ing in that dump.

It was pretty big as junkyards go, though you wouldn't have noticed just driving by. It covered about a hundred yards of Granville Road but it looked like it went back three times that far. It was weird that I'd driven by it a couple dozen times in my life but never taken any real notice of it. It's like those strip malls that are so ubiquitous that you don't see them unless they have the pizza joint you're looking for.

It was the fence that caught my attention. Chain link, seven or eight feet high, but at the top there was a roll of razor wire, not just the barbed wire that has surrounded farms for the last hundred and sixty years; this stuff was designed to accomplish extreme damage to whoever went through it. The blades on that wire cut long and deep; wicked stuff.

I imagined what the damage from razor wire could do to a person and, at least in my mind, it looked just like the cuts I'd seen on that dead girl's body earlier that day.

It didn't take much for that to thought to take root in my head.

There were plenty of places that used barbed wire at the top of their fences but not a lot that had this type of razor wire. The Army Reserve unit on Silver Spring Drive used it but off the top of my head I couldn't think of another business or property that would go to the effort. Even the airports still used regular barbed wire.

Could it be possible that this girl climbed through a razor wire fence? I couldn't imagine what could have been going on in her mind to do something like that. I knew her life had to have been hell just by looking at her but that was just nuts.

My god, what had they done to her?

I pulled further to the shoulder and got out of the car to get a better look at the fence. Without crossing the ditch, I could tell it was about eight feet tall but the razor wire added another foot and a half. Climbing through it would take a supreme act of the will or monumental desperation.

The C.S.U. report couldn't come quick enough for me. I wanted to see not only what killed that girl but what exactly had been happening to her in the years before she died. There were signs of malnutrition and abuse, probably sexual abuse as well. I had to believe that would be enough to make a person willing to subject themselves to the kind of destruction and pain that those blades would do. I've heard stories about people cutting their own arms or legs off to escape from various perilous situations. Desperate people can do all kinds of things that seem crazy.

I grabbed the links of the fence and gave it a shake. It was pretty firm; a person could easily climb it.

Was I really beginning to think that this junkyard was where the girl had been imprisoned? Could I have found the place so easily?

Like I said, that C.S.U. report couldn't come quickly enough.

It wasn't impossible, but was it likely? What did I know for sure? A girl bled to death and was dumped a few miles from here. She was covered with deep lacerations that *could* have been done by razor wire like this.

I needed something to eat. I was beginning to chase shadows.

Chapter 14

"Is there something I can help you with?"

The voice came from my left, but on the other side of the fence. He was a mousy little guy, wearing navy blue Dickey work pants and shirt.

"Is this your place?" I said.

"This is my salvage yard, yes." The way he said it he sounded like my dad in one of his quieter moments. It was something in his cadence—something... European maybe.

Milwaukee was a city with plenty of European immigrants, especially from Germany and Poland. When I was growing up there were whole neighborhoods where nobody over fifty spoke English. This guy was probably one of the kids or grandkids. My guess is he grew up in one of these homes and heard that sing-song quality from one or both of his parents. I wasn't good at this kind of thing but he sounded German.

I made my tone as conversational as I could and said, "Have you been here for long? I dated a girl that lived in the apartments over there a few years back but I don't remember your yard here."

He made a half-hearted look over his shoulder.

"I've been here for seventeen years," he said. "My father owned it before then. Is something wrong with your car?"

His question confused me for a second. Then I remembered nearly hitting the raccoon.

"No," I said. "I almost hit an animal. I guess it surprised me. I'm just getting some air to clear my head before I start off again."

"You're a police officer?" he said. "Is something the matter?"

"How'd you know I was a cop?"

He pointed to my waist where my shield was clipped to

my belt. My windbreaker must have ridden up a bit when I grabbed the fence; it was snagged over the grip of my Sig Sauer leaving my belt-line visible.

Wow, I really needed something to eat.

"Yeah," I said. "No, there's nothing going on. I'm just… waiting for my blood pressure to go down."

He stood there with his hands in his pockets, just staring like he was sizing me up. Suddenly I wanted to punch him.

I looked down the road and saw a small, hand painted sign that said Witt Auto Salvage.

"Are you Witt?"

"I'm Stephen Witt," he said pronouncing it Vitt.

"You tell me Mister Witt. Is something wrong?"

He rubbed his chin and shook his head.

"No, officer. There is nothing wrong. I'm just wondering why a police officer is lurking around my property."

Okay, this guy was wrong. I don't know what he was up to but he was definitely up to something.

After a couple decades on The Job I had a pretty decent sense of these things. Maybe I couldn't guess ethnic backgrounds from a few spoken words but tell when I was talking to a dirt bag. He may have been running a chop shop or selling dope—I couldn't guess, but he was dirty. If I'd had time or inclination, or even probable cause I would have taken a stronger look at this guy. Legally there was nothing I could do about him.

"Take it easy, Mister Witt," I said. "I told you I almost hit an animal. I'm not lurking. In fact I'm just taking off."

Stephen Witt, huh…? Well, right now I needed to get something to eat and a sweaty, little German junk dealer wasn't going to slow me down.

"Have a nice evening officer."

"It's *detective*," I said as I humped up the small hill to my car.

He was still watching me when I drove away.

Chapter 15

I made a call to the station house on my way home and asked the Sergeant to run Stephen Witt. He didn't love the idea of doing me a solid but he said he would. I knew I could count on the info being on my desk when I arrived tomorrow.

For the rest of the drive home I put in my Dire Straits, Love Over Gold CD and tried to forget the picture of the sliced-up girl that had been stuck in my head all day. Before Telegraph Road ended, I was pulling into the alley behind my house in Wauwatosa.

I parked in the space beside the garage that was too small for my Impala but just right for Carrie's Passat. Fortunately, it was a pretty good neighborhood and I didn't need to worry about anybody breaking in. Still, I never left anything important in the car overnight.

One of the things I liked about this area was that the lots weren't too big. I didn't like mowing grass and our back yard mainly consisted of a concrete slab patio where we kept our grill and some lawn chairs. I could even watch the sun set over the trees from there.

"Hi Ken!"

My neighbor, Bruce Havercorn, was carrying a couple bags of trash to his garbage bin.

I liked Bruce. He was about my age but quite a bit shorter. He started shaving his head a couple years back when his hairline receded too far for his liking. The guy even did my income taxes each year for a box of cigars.

"Is it that day?" I said pointing at the bags in his hands.

"No," he said. "You got a couple days. We're taking the kidders to Wisconsin Dells tomorrow morning."

Bruce and his wife Danielle were the perfect parents as far as I could tell. Trips to the Dells or Chicago were fairly common for them. As far as I could tell they were perfectly normal and to be honest, I was jealous. Bruce worked nine to five, Monday through Friday, never missed a birthday party or his kids' field trip. Danielle ran a home business, one of those women's things that gave her a decent income and still gave her time to raise her children.

I told him to have fun and walked up the steps to the back door.

Carrie and I bought the house a couple months after we got married, when we realized we were going to need more room for all my and her two kids' stuff. Eight years later it was still cozy, and there still was room for more stuff if we wanted. We'd made a couple of bedrooms in the basement for Toby and Diane and turned one of the upstairs bedrooms into my office. Carrie turned Diane's old bedroom into a scrap-booking studio and stocked it with the tools of her trade/hobby.

It was nice having the kids' rooms downstairs.

Carrie celebrated her thirty-seventh birthday in spring but I thought she could pass for thirty. Even after giving birth to two children she still had a smoking figure and a face that could, and did, stop traffic. What she saw in a mug like me I couldn't say.

Toby and Diane liked me too; at least as much as any fifteen and fourteen-year-old could like a stepfather who happened to be an overly protective cop. We got along great and they seemed to trust me.

And I wasn't going to apologize for being over protective. Somewhere out there I had two kids from a previous marriage that I hadn't seen in twelve years. My own flesh and blood and they had no interest in seeing me; a testament to how big a jerk I'd been to them and their mother. Toby and Diane were a second chance for me and I didn't want to mess up again.

Carrie was the last shot I had at happiness. And she made me want to be a better person. She was kind and merciful, and it sure didn't hurt that she was as sexy as anything God had put on this planet.

As I pushed open the back door of our house, I was reminded that she wasn't perfect.

I couldn't tell what the smell was, but I knew where it was coming from. She'd pushed some food into the garbage disposal and then forgot to run the darn thing. It was an old habit for her and a pet peeve of mine, one of many. I'd long since given up on telling the kids they needed to rinse their dishes before putting them in the dishwasher.

I walked to the sink, turned the water on and flipped the switch for the disposal. The blades bit on whatever was in there, grinding it to a manageable size before washing it away.

I shut it off just as Carrie walked into the kitchen from the living room with a bowl in her hand. She was wearing a pair of cutoff shorts and a Milwaukee Bucks t-shirt and whatever passive aggressive comment I'd planned on making faded from my mind when she smiled and kissed me.

"Did you eat yet?" she said.

"Uh... no. And I need to talk to you about that."

"You want me to make you something?"

"No," I said. "Just listen. I saw O'Connor this morning."

"Oh yeah. How'd that go?"

"He says I have diabetes."

She curled her lip and tilted her head, giving me a look of surprise.

"Apparently, I haven't been eating so good," I said.

"Okay," she said slowly. "What do we do now? I mean, what do we do about this?"

I leaned against the counter and shrugged.

"I don't know," I said. "He gave me a packet of papers— med guides, whatever. He doesn't think I need to get on any medication or anything right now."

"Then it's not that bad?"

"It's diabetes."

"But you don't need to give yourself insulin shots or anything?"

"O'Connor says he wants to see what I can do with diet and exercise first," I said. "My guess is I need to put the kibosh on carbs and sugar."

Carrie didn't bother saying anything. She knew the way cops ate—she knew how I ate. Carbohydrates and sugar were probably seventy-five percent of what I ate and drank. Now I needed to start eating like a rabbit if I wanted to live any kind of normal life.

I needed to find out if I could still drink scotch. I'm sure beer was off the table.

Carrie reached over and took my hand.

"Well… let me know what I can do to help."

I pulled her closer and kissed her forehead.

"I will," I said moving my hand to the small of her back. She pressed her body against me and kissed me on the mouth. I could taste mint chocolate chip ice cream.

Chapter 16

Before the Impala had driven away down Granville Road the man with the goatee knew that things were about to change. Just the fact that a strange car appeared and a man that could only be a police officer was taking an interest in the razor wire atop the fence less than twenty-four hours after one of the girls had forced herself through it unnerved him. Fortunately he seemed interested in an area far away from where the girl, number 326827, had received the wounds that killed her. At some point he'd need to get over there and clean up that mess as well. He'd seen the way she was bleeding and there was no way that she hadn't left a blood trail.

He wondered if it could be seen from the air. Could a police or news helicopter spot it by accident and somehow trace the girl back to the salvage yard? What if a dog, or a little kid stumbled upon it? What kind of story could he spin to make someone believe it was anything but a desperate girl trying to escape a life of imprisonment?

He'd have to work on that.

He thought about it the entire way to "The Cooler," the building where he kept the girls. Two of his dogs followed him while he considered a scenario where they had caught and shredded some poor animal.

Only the blood was on the wrong side of the fence. And how could some critter have had their blood splattered so high up on the barbed wire?

No, he'd have to get out there and clean it up first chance he got. Maybe even burn the long grass she'd run through.

It still barely registered with the goateed man that she was dead, even though he'd held her for her final moments. 326827 was gone for good.

In a way he didn't mind. She was the one that caused him

the largest amount of grief; she didn't eat and had become dangerously thin. Not like that supermodel skinny that was en vogue and nauseating. She was flesh and bone and not much else. The encounters they'd shared had not been enjoyable lately since she'd given up struggling. The last few times he hadn't even bothered to tie her hands to the iron rings in the wall.

He knew now that she had begun to formulate her escape plan and was just biding her time, waiting for the right moment to take flight. That was why she didn't put up a fuss. That was why she laid there in silent acceptance of all he did to her.

And now she was gone. 326827...

She was the last six-digit number he'd tattooed on anyone. Shortly after applying her ink he'd noticed that all the pictures of concentration camp prisoners only had five digits so he'd started cutting down on the extra number. There may have been six-digit numbers in Aushwitz or Dachau or any of the camps but he didn't have pictures of them. Besides, it had become a game with him, choosing the numbers for his little beauties. Five digits gave him the chance to use postal zip codes. 90028 and 90210 were the first he used, the first based on the addresses he heard all the time as a kid on game shows, the second from the television show based in Beverly Hills.

Both girls were still with him, though he would never allow himself to think of them as girls. They were cattle. They were playthings. They were objects existing solely for his pleasure.

They were his tribute to Marta.

As he reached into his pocket for his keys the man with the goatee kicked some gravel at the dogs, forbidding them to follow him into "The Cooler." He unlocked and opened the door, sliding inside and closing it before his loyal mongrels could follow.

Inside was a corridor that ran the entire length of the

building. There were eight doors, two of which were open. One of them was the room that he had scrubbed out; the other was an unoccupied cell where nobody had stayed for over a year. The other six had residents. A single wooden chair sat against the wall.

The Man scratched the hair of his goatee and smiled. He liked choices. And he liked not having to settle himself to just one choice.

He stepped to the third door and opened a small sliding port. Inside the girl was sitting on the mattress, wearing clothes that hadn't fit properly in years.

Her hollow eyes turned and met his.

"Good evening," he said.

She didn't reply. She'd been trained not to say anything. She just sat there, resigned to the fact that her night was going to be filled with horrors.

The Man smiled and slowly undressed to his briefs, folding his clothes neatly and placing them on the chair. He unlocked the door and went inside, ignoring sobs of relief that came from the other rooms.

Chapter 17

"I need you to talk to Toby," Carrie said. "He's been in his room since this morning. I couldn't even get him out for dinner."

Toby was like any fourteen-year-old boy. If he didn't want to eat there was a problem.

"Did he say anything?" I said.

"Just mumbled and grumbled a bit. Nothing that made any sense."

Carrie had grilled a chicken breast for me while I threw a salad together with whatever looked like it was worth eating. It wasn't easy holding back on the croutons and smothering it with French Dressing. I mixed some olive oil and balsamic vinegar with Italian spices and drizzled it on the lettuce instead.

I used the last piece of chicken to sop up the last of the homemade dressing from the plate.

Maybe I could get used to eating like this.

"I'll go talk with him," I said after I'd finished the last bite.

My relationship with my step kids had always been good. I don't know if it was because I was so good to them or because their real father had been such a bastard to them and their mother. I know he'd smacked all three of them around but I'd never even given the kids so much as a spanking. Carrie? Yes. The kids? Never. Not that I was a pushover; they'd been grounded and put on restrictions frequently, but I'd never resorted to corporal punishment. I suspect they'd appreciated that.

Toby's room was the largest in the house and looked like the typical kid's room. Beatles posters on the wall, my old twenty-seven-inch television on a dresser and clothes scattered on the floor. The turntable and LP collection set him apart from most kids his age but they were mine anyway. I let him have the setup when Carrie said she didn't want the California Audio Lab cabinet speakers in the living room. They looked obnoxious but they sounded great.

I pushed open Toby's door and leaned into the opening.

"You okay?" I said.

Toby was lying on his bed, his arm covering his face. A tuft of red hair was all I could see north of his nose. He didn't move when I spoke.

"Come on Tobes. What's up?"

"Nothin'," he said quietly and in a tone that made it clear something was wrong.

"Wrong answer, Tobes. And just to be clear, I'm not letting you off the hook until you talk to me. Your mom wants to know what's going on too."

"Then tell her nothing is going on," he said. "'Cuz nothing is going on."

Not for nothing I'd been a cop for almost twenty years. He was trying to send me a message without saying anything and I didn't think it had anything to do with Carrie.

A walked in slowly and sat on the end of his bed.

"All right, it's you and me talking. What's going on?"

He was quiet for long moment, but I knew not to bother him. He'd talk when he wanted to and I wasn't going anywhere. I'd sat silent in some interviews for hours waiting for the other person to speak—not that I wanted to treat this like an interrogation.

Toby was silent for almost a minute before he whispered, "You said we would go to a Brewers game this summer."

A Brewers game? That's what he was upset about? That's why he'd been moping around?

Well... okay. I didn't remember telling him we'd go to a Brewer's game and that made it even worse. I could have given him a dozen reasons why it happened yet but none of them would matter. I'd let Toby down and now he was ticked off.

"Yeah. I did, didn't I?"

"Summer's more than half over and we haven't done jack yet," he said. "We hardly even see you."

He was right, I had been working a lot of hours. On top of that I had been moonlighting, doing security at a club on Fond du Lac Avenue called Kryptonite. The late hours had me sleeping most of the following days—more time I wasn't spending with the kids.

It wasn't that I didn't want to do things with the kids, in fact I'd been justifying the extra work by saying it was so we could take a family vacation. A week at Disney World or Yellowstone sounded great but I couldn't expect the kids to be thinking long term. They wanted to do something now.

"I owe you, don't I?"

"You said we'd go to a game last month," Toby said. "Back when the Brewers were playing good. Now they're playing lousy and..."

He was going to say he didn't want to go anymore but caught himself.

"Well," I said. "I was talking to Wash this morning about some tickets he wanted to sell. I'll tell you what, let's talk to mom and about it and hopefully we can go to the game this weekend."

"Just you and me or all of us?"

"If you want we can make it just the two of us," I said. "Diane might want to go too."

"Nah, she's got some date this weekend."

Diane had a date? This was the first I'd heard of that. She was only fourteen years, what kind of date was a fourteen-year-old going to go on?

I suppose things had changed in the last thirty years or so, but I sure didn't like the idea of my daughter going on dates yet. I decided to talk to Carrie about it later.

"Well, we'll have to see. I don't know how many tickets he has anyway." I grabbed his arm and pulled him up towards me. He came off the bed in a stiff, comical way. I was amused that his stiffness was a sign that he was loosening up. I put an arm around him and gave him a hug. "I'm sorry, Tobe. I wanna make it up to you."

I held out a fist and he pounded it with his own.

"Do your mom a favor and eat some dinner, okay. You need to keep your strength up if you're gonna be a cop,"

"Yeah," he said. "I may not want to be a cop anymore."

"What's wrong with being a cop?"

"Your hours suck," he said.

I couldn't disagree. But it was an honorable job and there were lots of worse things I could be doing.

"Yeah, well... You don't gotta decide today," I said. "Go talk to your mother, okay."

Toby was already up the stairs by the time I stepped out of his room. I was headed for the stairs when I heard another door open and Diane stepped out.

"Hey Dad," she said. "How do you like my dress?"

I flipped on the light in the hallway to get a better look.

It was like getting hit in the gut with a baseball bat. Diane wasn't the flat chested tween she'd been... not that long ago. The outfit she was wearing accentuated her budding maturity, something I didn't want to see from my teenage daughter. The dress was cut across the middle of her thighs, several inches above her knees and the top was a thin tank top that embraced her body like a sock. If it had been flesh colored she would have looked nude. For the first time in my life I appreciated the color turquoise.

"Has your mother seen this?" I said.

"She helped me pick it out," Diane said with one of those head quivers that kept her from having to vocalize the word, "duh."

"You don't like it," she said before I could find anything to say.

"You look great Diane," I said. "I'm just not ready for you to grow up. Toby said you have a date this weekend..."

"It's not a date," she said holding her hands up to stop me. "A bunch of girls from church are going roller skating, that's all."

I was surprised to find out that kids still went roller skating.

"You're going dressed in that?" I said pointing at her new outfit. "You wipe out in that and you'll be hurtin' for certain."

"I'm not going skating in this," she said. "Besides, I can tell you don't like it so I'll probably never wear it anywhere."

She turned back to her room. I could tell she was hurt by my reaction.

"Diane, just come here."

She stopped her retreat but it took her a moment to turn.

"Come on," I said.

She turned and sheepishly walked back towards me.

"I told you, I think you look nice."

"But?"

"You're fourteen years old, Diane. You don't need to look and dress like you're eighteen yet. You need to enjoy being a kid. Milk it for as long as you can."

I didn't feel like telling her about the girl we'd found that morning, the one that didn't look any older than her except for the multiple lacerations and signs of sexual abuse. That and the fact she was dead.

I'd worked too many cases where young girls dressed like Diane was dressed kissed their mom goodbye on a Friday night and ended up on a slab at the morgue. Or in an alley behind a gentlemen's club.

Or in a field where they bled to death.

"I like the dress," I said. "You look nice. I don't want you to wear it outside the house."

She gave me the arms folded, bent-knee, rocked-back-on-one-foot defiant pose.

"That doesn't even make any sense. I look good but you don't want anyone to see me?"

"No, that's not it. I want to have some control over who sees you. Believe me, Diane. I know boys. I know what they look for and I know what they think. It doesn't matter that you're a good girl—good girls get hurt all the time."

"Not every boy is like that, Dad."

"I know," I said. "But enough of them are."

She actually stomped her feet in a petulant manner.

"Do you have any idea how much it sucks having a cop for a dad?"

"Nope," I said. "But I can tell you what it's like having a dad that didn't give a crap what his kids do." I didn't tell her that her stepsister could tell her what it was like too. "Someday you'll appreciate it. I won't be that lucky."

She turned and walked back to her room. I could tell she was hurt.

"Yeah, I really feel lucky…" she said.

I spent a couple hours on the computer, searching the internet for ideas about what could have happened to the girl we found that morning. There were a couple S&M websites that made me think she could have been involved with something along those lines but I eventually gave that up. This girl had been starved and tortured over a long period of time. She looked like she'd been raped multiple times. I didn't understand the whole sadomasochistic thing, but this was clearly something different. Something even worse.

When I stepped out of my office the whole house was quiet. I didn't even hear Toby or Diane moving around downstairs. Carrie had been watching television but now the living room was dark and the TV turned off.

I hoped she was waiting for me in bed.

I checked to make sure all the doors were locked, brushed my teeth and shuffled quietly to the bedroom.

Carrie was lying on the bed, still wearing the t-shirt but her cutoffs were on the floor. She was only partly covered by the bed sheet.

I sat on the bed and leaned down to kiss her neck.

And found her fast asleep. She didn't even stir when I kissed her.

I guess I waited too long.

I tip-toed out of the room, back to my office and turned the computer back on.

Chapter18

"Preliminary exams confirm that she bled out," Wash said, reading from the coroner's report. "A couple of the cuts nicked arteries, blah, blah… We figured that."

Lieutenant Gold dismissed Wash's discourteous comment with a roll of the eyes.

"Are you two any closer to knowing who she was?"

"We're still looking through the books," I said referring to the piles of missing person files that covered both of our desks. "So far, we got bupkuss."

Gold knocked on my desktop in an absent-minded way, but I could see that wheels were turning in his head. I didn't know this guy at all but I could tell he was engaged in this case. Maybe he wasn't as big a tool as I thought.

I decided to test the waters with him.

"Lieu," I said, stopping him from returning to his office. "Mind if I run something by you?"

Gold was as surprised hearing it as I was by saying it. He looked at me and shrugged.

"Go ahead," he said.

"Last night, after I left I went driving around by where we found the body."

He nodded and gestured for me to continue.

I told him about Witt's junkyard and the razor wire on the fence.

"This Witt guy… He's wrong," I said. "I don't know what it is but something about this guy is wrong. I can't say for sure that it's got anything to do with this case but something in my gut tells me that it does."

"Your gut close many cases for you?"

"A few," I said. "I got a pretty good intuition about these things."

"And you think that razor wire fence could account for her lacerations?"

I thought for a second and said, "Absolutely."

"Okay," Gold said. "What do we know about the guy who owns the place?"

I reached over and grabbed another file on my desk.

"He's in the system," I said. "I haven't looked at his jacket yet but I got it here."

"Let me know when you've given this guy a shake," Gold said. "For now keep trying to find out who this gal is."

"Who she was," Wash said, his face buried in another file.

"Nice, Washington," Gold said. "You got somebody at home that loves you?" He said the last part as he was heading back to his office.

"Touchy little heeb," Wash said after the Lieutenant had closed his door.

"He probably hasn't seen as many dead bodies as we have," I said setting Witt's file off to the side and digging into the missing person stack.

I don't care how long you're on The Job, dead bodies never get any easier to see. It doesn't matter if it's a ninety-year-old guy that had a heart attack in his favorite chair or a five-year-old girl caught in gang crossfire; they all suck. We all find ways to cope but whether it's denial or gallows humor we never get used to the junk we investigate.

When I first started on The Job the north side of Milwaukee was going through a series of gun shootings that made the years of Mafia wars seem tame. At least five a week for almost two years, and they were all over stupid stuff like jackets or t-shirts.

I'd been partnered up with an old-timer who was on a downward slope. Fischer was a good cop but he'd been hanging on for his twenty-five years and the fact was, he started too late in his life. He'd been in the Army, spent time in Viet Nam and then gone backpacking across the United States for two years before going to the academy. He was sixty-two years old by the time he could retire. He was the

61

classic cop in denial.

Me and Fischer were the first to arrive at a half dozen of these shootings, almost all of which were black kids—teenagers or early twenties. Yet Fischer was always there with a quip or little joke, like that guy on Law & Order. I was ready to puke in my hat and this guy was playing like Jerry Seinfeld. After a couple of shootings, he told me his secret: he didn't personalize the dead kid at all. He didn't give him a name or any more humanity than he needed to do his job.

"Then I go home and drink myself to sleep," he told me.

Wash made jokes like Fischer, but I never got the feeling my latest partner was an oiler. I certainly never smelled booze on his breath. His wife was Asian, maybe she had him doing some whacky meditation or something…

Everybody has their own method. Mine usually involved sarcasm of some kind. It never made it easier but at least it kept me from doing something I couldn't undo.

"Brady, check it out."

I looked up from the sheet I was reading to see Wash pointing to the hallway.

Lance Padget, a Captain from Internal Affairs was drinking from our bubbler—what people from outside the state would call a water fountain or drinking fountain. He finished his drink, wiped his chin on his suit jacket and walked into our squad room.

"Are you lost Captain?" I said as he passed my desk on the way to Gold's office.

If he heard me he didn't show it.

I don't know what they did to recruit for Internal Affairs, but they must have a heck of a benefits package to rope these guys in. Either that or they have some kind of dirt that they're using to blackmail them. The truth is it's not much different from what you see on TV cop shows; the rank and file cop hates I.A.B. and call them "Cheese-Eaters" or "Rat Squad" among other things. Cops have to put up with enough crap, from the public that hates them, to the media trying to make them look bad and politicians using us for their own purposes that the idea of cops investigating cops is infuriating. And who are these guys? How are they above suspicion? Do they have some genetic test that proves they're somehow above taking a bribe? Or that they refuse gifts from dubious sources? Or that they wouldn't whack somebody who tried to get over on them? Yeah, they were the Rat Squad all right. Best not to kick the garbage can.

"What do you suppose he's here for?" Wash said when the door to Gold's office was closed.

"They ain't here for me," I said. "That's all I care about."

It was mostly true. I hadn't done anything that would concern I.A.B., but I also wasn't going to let the cheese-eaters screw over someone in my squad. I'd even stand up for Schmidt if I thought he was in a bogus jackpot; because that's what cops do.

I looked back at the sheet I was reading, the missing persons file of a girl named Mary Lynn Wersching. She'd gone missing four years ago while she was on her way home from school. One minute she was walking on a sidewalk with her backpack, the next she was gone, backpack and all. She'd be twenty years old now; it could be her that we found yesterday.

"What do you think?" I said showing Wash the picture.

He took the sheet and squinted at the picture.

"I don't think so," he said handing it back. "This girl's face is more heart shaped."

"It's been four years, bro."

"I'm just sayin' I don't think so."

I dropped the file on a pile of maybe—a pile that was getting frustratingly tall.

"Brady!"

Gold was standing in the door of his office. He waved for me to join them.

"You sure you didn't do nothing?" Wash said.

I made a fist around the pen I had in my hand and tapped it on the desktop. I couldn't imagine why they'd wanted and it was bugging the crap out of me. Something was happening and I knew I wasn't going to like it.

I stood up and walked to Gold's office.

"Close the door." It was Padgett, not Gold giving the order. He sat at the Lieu's desk, writing on a page, not even bothering to look up.

I pushed the door in a careless manner that made it swing most of the way shut. I didn't bother pushing it closed—I don't know why. Okay, I did know why. It was a private act of rebellion.

Padgett pointed to a chair and said, "Sit down."

I'd been shining a chair all morning and wasn't interested in sitting down, not for this guy.

"I'm good."

Gold stepped behind me and pushed the door shut.

"It's okay," he said. "Grab a seat."

When I didn't move he cocked his head towards the chair, a tight grimace on his face. I got the impression that Gold didn't like this chump any more than I did. I sat in the chair and sat back, folding my hands on my stomach. It was as indifferent as I could make myself look.

Padgett stopped writing and set his pen down.

"You worked with Paul Murphy, didn't you Detective Brady?"

It wasn't really a question.

I looked over at Gold, then back at Padgett and laughed.

"Are you telling me you don't have access to all our case files?" I said. "You know I've worked with him."

"What's your opinion of him?"

"What is this all about?" I said only moderately relieved it wasn't about me.

"Just answer the question."

Gold took a step forward.

"Hang on," he said. "You don't need to talk to my detective that way. He's not under investigation."

"He's not exactly making what I need to do easier."

"Good," I said. "I'm not interested in making your job

64

easy. I'm not here to help you bust good cops."

"Is Murphy a good cop?"

"Good enough to get assigned to SCU."

"That means he's capable," Padgett said. "It doesn't mean he's good."

"What are you doin'?" I said rising from the chair. "You want me to say something you first tell me what this is all about. Because this is just dumb."

Gold grabbed my arm and urged me back to the chair.

"Take it easy, Brady," he said. "We gotta let him do his job."

"I wanna know what this is about, Lieu! This is baloney and you know it."

"No I don't know it," Gold said. "Apparently, Padgett has evidence and I haven't been in this unit long enough to know anything about Murphy."

"Evidence of what?"

"He's a drug abuser," Padgett said matter-of-factly, like there was no chance in his mind that he was wrong. Whatever information he had was enough to satisfy him that Murphy was a doper.

Or he could be fishing, hoping I would give him something by accident.

"I'm not buying it," I said.

"Shows what a great detective you must be," Padgett said not even bothering to hide the sarcastic tone. "Work in the same office and you can't see the signs?"

"He's not my partner," I said. "And he's been on loan to stakeout for most of this year. I can't remember the last time I seen him in the office."

"What about out of the office?"

"I don't remember!" I wasn't just covering for Murph. I really had no idea when I'd seem him last. I guessed there was still snow on the ground and it was the middle of summer now.

"Listen Padgett," Gold said. "You wanted Brady's opinion of the guy, you got it. If you got something else…?"

"He hasn't got jack, Lieu," I said. "He's fishing. I don't know if things are slow in the rat cage or his wife just left him but he's got nothing on Murphy."

"I got enough evidence to end his career," the florid-faced rat said.

"Then what are you doing here?"

"I need to know how big this thing is."

"What thing? You said he was on dope."

"He's addicted to amphetamines," Padgett said. "Makes me wonder if anyone else at SCU has any similar issues."

"You wanna test me for drugs?" I said. "Gimme your coffee cup. I'll give you a sample."

"It might come to that, Brady."

Gold put his hand on my chest, stopping my advance on the cheese-eating piece of trash. I hadn't had so much as an electric brownie since I joined the academy and I wasn't about to let this guy get away with insinuating otherwise. He had evidence on Murphy—so what? That didn't give him the right to cast dispersions on SCU or me.

"I got your sample right here," I said balling up my fist.

"Take it easy, Brady," Gold said. He straightened his arm, firmly but effortlessly pushing me back towards the chair.

As hard as he tried Padgett couldn't look completely calm. He knew he'd be wearing his own blood if Gold hadn't stopped me.

It was good for both of us that Gold stopped him. Getting ticked off wasn't something he could act on; me beating the dog crap out of him would have cost me my job, for a few months at least but more likely forever.

"You need him for anything else?" Gold asked Padgett raising his voice slightly.

"I'm good."

I shook my head and said, "That'll be the day," as I left Gold's office.

Chapter 19

Stephen Witt had spent two years in the De Pere Correctional facility for assault. Apparently, the mousy guy I'd talked to on the side of the road had taken a swing at another guy in a bar. Not only that—he'd laid the guy out. Apparently, he did have some stones.

But if I'd suspected him of being my killer the timeline was probably wrong. Wash and I figured the girl had been held prisoner for several years—Witt had been in the hoosegow until fourteen months ago.

I told Wash to call me if anything came in on the girl or we received any leads, then I left and headed over to see Jason Voight.

Voight was living in Brookfield, a few miles outside Milwaukee. It was a nice neighborhood with mid-century homes, manicured lawns and well-maintained shrubbery. A cop's salary wouldn't get him a house like this, and he was making three-quarters on disability. Good thing his wife came from money.

I parked my car in his driveway hoping it wouldn't drip oil onto the concrete.

Voight answered the door in shorts and a t-shirt that said, "Here Today, Gone To Maui." He smiled out of one side of his mouth and held out a hand. I noticed the skin on the back of it had become shiny and thin, more evidence of the soft life he'd been enjoying.

"Howdy Kenny," he said. "It's been a long time."

There was a hint of rebuke in his tone. I just shrugged and shook his hand.

"What finally brings you to my homestead?"

"What? Come on Jason, no small talk?" I said.

"Are you kidding?" Voight said. "You know me. I've

never been big on small talk."

"You've never been big on talking at all, you crusty old dog. I just figured we'd spend a few minutes catching up."

That got me another crooked smile. He pushed the door open further.

"Come on in," he said. "Can I get you a Rumchatta?"

"I'm on the job, Jason." Not that I wouldn't have loved a Rumchatta.

"That's right. And you've got yourself a new boss from what I hear."

"You hear pretty good," I said stepping into the house. It was tastefully decorated with a strong woman's touch that seemed to make Voight uncomfortable. He hurried me through the living room into the kitchen where he already had a drink waiting on the counter next to an auto magazine. He was still a gear head.

"I still have some friends on The Job. They still drink my liquor if I offer it to them."

"I'll take a soda if you got any," I said, then realized I didn't need the sugar. "Or better yet, a glass of water."

This diabetes thing was gonna stink...

Voight opened the refrigerator, pulled out a bottle of water and tossed it to me.

"Did Carrie put you on a diet or something?"

"Something like that," I said. I didn't feel like giving him a health update or anything.

"You ever see Randi anymore?"

I shook my head. I hadn't seen my second ex-wife in years, and that was okay with me but I didn't appreciate him mentioning her, as if he and I had some personal history beyond being partners for a while.

"She was something, that Randi," he said.

I don't know if he noticed a look on my face or realized he was being a jerk but he quickly changed the subject.

"So, how's The Job been treating you? I saw you on the news."

"That was a while ago, Jason."

Voight shrugged and said, "Yeah, I guess it was."

He swirled the ice around in his drink while he tried to figure out what to say next. I thought about letting him off the hook but decided against it.

After a moment he sat at the kitchen table and took a drink.

"I don't understand why anyone would want to be a cop anymore," he said. "Nobody respects the shield these days. All these mobs chanting that they want dead cops—and why? Because cops defend themselves when someone attacks 'em? What a bunch of garbage."

I couldn't disagree. In the last few years there had been a couple high profile cases where cops had killed suspects they were arresting. Race agitators had made it looked like there was a racial component and turned the public against law enforcement. Protestors took to the streets, most of them peaceful, but not all of them. In New York crowds chanted, "What do we want? Dead Cops! When do we want them? Now!" Police killings followed in several cities around the country. The majority of people still trusted us but in some neighborhoods our job was darn near impossible.

"Yeah, Jason. It's getting to be a drag. Lucky you got out when you did."

I saw his eyebrow shoot up as he wondered if I was insulting him. He had to know that the rest of us thought it was pretty lame using a twisted ankle to retire and collect three-quarters of your pension but I had never said anything to him about it. There were a few times I felt like I would take that deal if given half a chance, but I'd feel like a jerk. Most cops would.

He watched me for a moment and then decided I wasn't trying to bust his chops.

"So, what brings you to my abode?" he said, taking another drink. "It's been a while. I assume this is a job-related visit."

"You have a better memory than me Jason," I said, the flattery intentional. "I'm working a case now that reminds me of something we were mixed up with a few years back."

"We were mixed up with quite a few things."

"It was eight or nine years ago, down in the 2nd. A fourteen or fifteen-year-old girl disappeared coming home from Wilson Park."

Voight sat back in his chair and scratched his chin.

"I remember we never found her," he said. "Something come to earth on it?"

I pulled a chair out from the table and sat down.

"I thought so for a little while but the ages aren't working."

"What do you mean?"

"Do you remember the girls name, or what she looked like?" I said.

He waved a hand at me and said, "You got the files."

"I know," I said. "We're digging through them but I haven't found it yet. I was wondering what you remembered about her."

"What you said; fourteen years old, rode her bike to the park and never came home. Her friends at the park said she left around dinnertime. We never found her or the bike."

"Her name?"

"Berman or Beeman or something like that."

"Do you remember what she looked like?"

"Five foot nothing. Dark hair. Dark skin. She may have been middle eastern."

"Was there was a racial component we ever considered? Anything at school or anywhere?"

"No, not that I recall," Voight said. "I don't remember getting much of anything on that one. It was like she just disappeared into thin air." He leaned forward and said, "What's going on, Ken? Is there another one?"

"We found a girl the other day. She was in bad shape— bad enough I thought it could be her."

"But the ages don't work?"

"I don't think so," I said. "The girl we found was younger. Maybe eighteen or so."

"What's going on in this world?"

"It's worse than that, Jason. You don't wanna know even if I could tell you."

"But she looked like her?"

"Dark hair, dark skin. Like I said, she was in bad shape. Starved for sure. But she could have been middle-eastern or Jewish."

Voight sat back and folded his arms.

"Speaking of Jews," he said, "What do you think of Gold?"

"I could always use a little more," I said. I knew what he was talking about, I just didn't feel like making it easy. I took a slow drink of water.

"I'm talking about your new boss. How do you like him?"

"Am I supposed to like him?"

"It never hurts," he said taking a drink of Rumchata. "Come on, Kenny. What do you think of the new guy?"

"He's a boss," I said. "It's not like we hang out or anything. He's only been in the squad a couple weeks so I don't hardly know him. Why? You got some dirt on him?"

"You remember Shaw? Our boss over in the 2nd?" I told him I did. "Apparently, he knew Gold when he was coming up. Did it pretty quick too."

"So, he's good?"

"Or he knows someone."

"You don't think he could get there on his own merits?"

"If you can tell me what those merits might be..."

I stood up and said, "I gotta go. You mind if I take this with me?"

I held up the bottle of water.

"I don't want it anymore," Voight said.

A few seconds later he was leaning against the jam of his open front door watching me walk to my car.

"I'm not kidding, Kenny. You need to look into this Gold. Word is he's got some deep, dark secret he's protecting."

I laughed.

"Don't we all."

Chapter 20

When Amanda opened the door and saw me her face fell, as if she had been expecting someone else. It took me about half a second to realize who that could have been.

"You said you weren't gonna talk to Johnny D, Amanda," I said by way of greeting.

"What? Are you tapping my phone now?"

"That would be illegal," I said. "And there's no way I could have gotten it set up by now."

"Then how did you know?"

"I'm not a detective for nothing. You told me yourself."

People are always a bit surprised when you can tell them exactly what's going on based on the look on their face. They think that you're Sherlock Holmes or something and don't get what an easy trick it can be for someone trained to notice things.

Amanda pushed the door open and gestured for me to come inside. It was one of the older houses, built around the nineteen-twenties when it looked like happy days were here to stay. There wasn't a whole lot for yards and the homes were built about ten feet apart, but that was okay. Milwaukee County has a great park system.

She was wearing the same clothes she'd had on when I dropped her off last night. Her hair was wet, as though she'd washed it in the sink. The cast was still dry so she clearly hadn't taken a shower.

"Where's your friend?"

"She's at work," Amanda said. "I've been watching her DVD collection."

The movie "collection" was a copy of "Grease," Season two of "Girls" and a handful of Disney animated features.

"And when is Johnny D getting here?"

"He said he'd be here after he showered."

"So…" I said. "He'll be here sometime next week?"

She ignored my joke and said, "He told me you saw him last night."

"And I'm gonna see him when he hurts you again," I said. I didn't give him the benefit of the doubt. I knew if these two got back together he was going to hurt her, and I wasn't going to let her think otherwise.

"He said he's going to change."

"I'm sure he did. He might change for a while too, but he's never going to change who he is or what's in that heart of his. If you think…"

I stopped talking. She'd heard me say this to her before. I was wasting my time. The heart wants what the heart wants…

Okay. I was gonna lay off and let her make her own choices. She wasn't my daughter no matter how much I pretended she was.

I held up my hands in a gesture of surrender.

"Forget it," I said. "You do what you want."

"Ken…"

I pulled a business card from my pocket and handed it to her. When she didn't take it I dropped it on a nearby coffee table.

"If you need me, give me a call."

I could see her looking out the front window as I put the Impala into drive and pulled away from the house. She looked like the lost child that she was and I could tell that she was hurt that I left.

I guess there was some satisfaction in that.

I was a couple blocks away when I saw Johnny D cutting through a yard and turning onto the sidewalk. He was wearing a jean jacket despite the summer heat. His injured hand was pressed deep into the pocket.

When he was parallel to my car I jumped on the brakes and came screeching to a stop.

Johnny D turned towards me quickly, looking afraid. When he saw it was me he froze.

Our eyes locked for a long moment and I could instantly tell what he was feeling; he thought I was there to kill him. In the daylight of a sunny afternoon this jack-wagon thought he was about to die.

And that was okay with me.

Without breaking our eye contact I slowly brought my hand up and made a gun with my hand, the kind of gesture that gets a kid expelled from school these days. Then, with a quick laugh I hit the gas pedal and took off.

It was a very different smell that greeted me when I arrived home later that afternoon; this one I didn't mind. Garlic sautéed in olive oil always meant I was gonna have a good dinner. It was one of my favorite smells in the world and since dead and decaying things often assaulted my senses it was also very welcome.

Carrie had spent hours preparing her meat sauce probably because she knew how much I loved it. Toby and Diane liked it okay, but as far as I was concerned it was her best recipe, one she said she learned from a roommate a few years back. I never pressed her to find out who that might have been because I never cared, I just appreciated that they knew how to cook and didn't mind sharing recipes.

When I stepped into the kitchen Carrie was on her tiptoes, reaching into an upper cabinet for a colander. I never knew why she kept it in so high a cabinet but I certainly enjoyed watching her stretch her body to grab it. She was wearing an apron I'd brought back from a rib joint I'd eaten at in Memphis a couple years back and, even though she was fully clothed, in my imagination it was all she had on.

She hadn't heard me come in and was surprised when I put my hands on her.

"Hey!" she squealed and moved my hand down to her waist. She turned her head and kissed me over her shoulder.

"At least let me finish making dinner."

I pulled her closer and kissed her harder. When my hands traveled this time she didn't object.

After a moment she turned around to face me and we continued kissing hungrily.

A noise from the other room brought us back to reality. It was followed by Toby saying in a completely insincere voice, "Sorry."

It was enough of a buzz-kill.

Carrie gave me a quick peck of a kiss and said, "Tonight."

"I gotta work at Kryptonite tonight," I said. "I'll probably be late."

Kryptonite was a part time gig I did for cash, working the door at a club on Fond du Lac Avenue. I wasn't supposed to be moonlighting but if I ever wanted to take the family to Disney again, I needed to do something to supplement my income. And it wasn't a bad job besides; the owner was a friend of mine from grade school so he paid me decent to sit on a chair and watch the crowd. Every once in a while, I got to break up a fight or pull some jerk off one of the girls that worked there. There were plenty of interesting people there and the dancers were easy on the eyes.

Carrie didn't love me going to Kryptonite in my spare time but she understood that it helped us out financially so she let me do it. She also knew it was a favor to my buddy.

"I'm not gonna promise to be awake," she said.

"I know," I said moving away from her so she could continue making supper.

"Diane asked if she could go to Mayfair with her friends tonight."

"What'd you tell her?"

"I told her to ask you."

I opened the refrigerator to get something to drink. As the cool air hit my face, I was surprised to see how many sugary drinks we kept, not just soda but sweet tea, fruit juice and a pitcher of Kool-Aid. I closed it up and grabbed a glass from a cupboard.

"Is something wrong?" Carrie asked.

"I been meaning to tell you." I got some ice from the dispenser on the front of the fridge and filled the glass with water.

"Tell me what?"

"I had to see Doctor O'Connor the other day. My blood work came back."

Carrie turned to me and wiped her hands on the apron. There was something about this completely innocent move that turned me on and made me wish the kids weren't home.

"Is everything okay?"

I stared at her for a moment and thought about how lucky I was. I was married to this beautiful woman who had hardly lost a step as she approached middle age. Even better, she loved me. She wanted to be with me and take care of me. I know when I told her about the diabetes she would be concerned and do everything in her power to make it easier for me. I could see her clearing out the pantry of anything with sugar and tossing everything with excessive carbs. She'd take care of me alright.

But everything would change, and I didn't want it to. Even though I knew it had to happen I didn't look forward to changing.

So, with that in mind I did something I hated.

"Everything looks good," I said taking a drink of water and leaving before she asked me any questions.

"So," I said raising a forkful of lasagna to my mouth. "Mom says you want to go to Mayfair tonight."

Diane had hardly raised her eyes from her food the whole meal but now she allowed me to see the green of her pupils. It reminded me of some of the skels I'd interviewed, and that bothered me. I knew instinctively that there was something she wasn't saying.

"Mom said I need to ask you."

"Are you gonna ask me?"

"Will it do any good?"

I shrugged.

"Can't hurt," I said.

"Can I go to the mall tonight?"

"What do you think I'm gonna say?"

She looked at her brother for help. He just smiled and took a bite of bread he'd sopped tomato sauce on.

"I don't know," she said. "Yes?"

"That's it? Just yes?"

"Yes, and have a good time." She paused a second and said, "Don't get into trouble."

I sat back and pretended to think about it.

"Yeah, that's all pretty good," I said.

Carrie gave me a grin, the kind that silently asked me to stop torturing Diane.

"Okay, you can go," I said. "But on one condition."

You'd think I'd kicked her feet out from under her. She fell back in her chair and huffed.

"Don't worry, it's not something that's gonna kill you," I said.

"What?" she said irritably.

"I want you to change your clothes. I don't want you going out like that."

She probably thought I hadn't noticed her short shorts as she entered the room, or that her shirt was so loose that if she leaned over to tie her shoes anybody could see all the way down to South America. My own daughter—stepdaughter didn't seem to think much of my detective skills and I didn't think much of her fashion sense.

"Come on Dad," she said. "All the kids dress like this nowadays. It's not that big a deal."

"Okay, first of all: not all the kids dress like that. Secondly, I don't care. Even if they did you wouldn't. I'm responsible for you and I don't want you going outside like that."

"Do I embarrass you or something?"

"He didn't say that—" Carrie started before I interrupted her.

"No, you don't embarrass me. I'm not doing this for me."

"How is dressing like I'm Amish going to benefit me?"

"The less you can do to give other boys the impression you're a sex object the less likely I'll be finding your body in a field someplace."

I said it without thinking. What was really strange about it was, I wasn't angry. It just came out, the way it would come out if I were talking to some kid on the street that I didn't really care about. Somehow the idea had taken root in my head and it wasn't gonna budge.

That girl in the field could have been my daughter.

Carrie and Toby stopped eating and were staring at me.

The silence was pretty long and very uncomfortable.

"I—" Diane forced out. "I'm not going to end up in some field."

"I know," I said in an even tone, making it clear I wasn't angry but the point was not negotiable. "Because you're going to go change your clothes before you leave the house."

Diane was till staring at me and I imagined she was trying to decide if she wanted to go out at all.

"You aren't going to win this one, Diane," Toby said.

It was the last thing anybody said for the rest of the meal.

Chapter 21

I stood at the end of the bar nearest the door and sipped my Diet Coke, keeping an eye on the crowd, really only four randy, middle-aged men, and the door. Kryptonite was a better than average joint but it was still what would be called, euphemistically, a gentlemen's club. It was dark, except for the stage, which held two stripper's poles. The music was almost strictly eighties and nineties and way too loud. Carla, the lone waitress moved from table to table refilling drinks.

It wasn't a very busy evening—weeknights usually weren't, so the "B-Team" was onstage. They weren't ugly or anything, just less experienced. To the guys sitting at the table buying shots or cocktails they were just fine. It's not like they'd come in for good conversation or anything; they were there to see naked girls dance or do some kind of gymnastics on the pole, brought in by a compulsion or the sign outside that said, "Women's Clothing 95% Off."

Milos, the owner of the fine establishment, and I had been friends since grade school, long before I'd ever considered being a cop. He gave me my first cigarette and I'd shown him his first girly magazine. He'd managed to make his end pay off with the club while my old man whipped me with a tree branch the first time he caught me smoking, nipping that in the bud before I ever got addicted. If somebody had told me in third grade that I'd get paid to hang out in a place with naked girls I'd have thought they were crazy, yet here I was, living some kind of dream… only drinking diet soda.

I looked it my watch. It was 12:30. I'd been sitting for two and a half hours and hadn't had to so much as raise my voice. Everybody was on their best behavior. Another hour and we'd be calling it quits for the night.

I turned away from the stage and waved to Milos for another drink. He came over and grabbed my glass, refilling it with the gun.

"I never thought I'd see the day you'd be drinking diet soda," he said. "Don't you know that stuff will kill you?"

"So will women but I'm not ready to quit them yet."

"That's because your wife is a hottie. I still think you should get her onstage here."

If I thought he was serious I would have punched him. This was just the way we talked to each other, never saying quite what we meant but making our point anyway. Milos wasn't the kind of guy that would go on about what a beautiful wife I had any more than I would tell him how stupid it was that he dated his employees. It was easier to make jokes about herpes sores on his lip.

"Let me know when your daughter turns eighteen."

"Okay," I said, slapping the bar. "That's the last I ever want to hear you say that!"

"Take it easy, Kenny. I was just kidding." He held up his hands in surrender, knowing from my reaction that I was serious. "Settle down."

"I'm sorry," I said. "I'm just a little sensitive about her right now. She's full on into the teenager thing and I don't like the way she's been dressing."

Milos spread his arms in a gesture that took in the whole club.

"Are you kidding me? Look where you are, Hoss. Don't tell me you're getting religion or something."

"Because I don't want my daughter looking like a whore you think I'm getting religion? If that's the case maybe I should."

"Touchy today," Milos said. "Bad day at work?"

I wasn't going to run the whole case for him; that would just make me angrier. Knowing that we would pass the crucial first forty-eight-hour time period without gaining any ground on the investigation hacked me off pretty good but there was nothing I could do. We had a guess at the cause of death but we still had no idea where the actual murder took place. We still didn't even have an I.D. on the victim.

She was too young. That's all I knew for sure. Too young to be dead in an overgrown drive in theater parking lot. Too young to have suffered what she'd suffered through. Too young to be cut to pieces the way she was.

Too young...

When did I become such an old man? I was starting to think like one of those old dudes who sit on the porch and yell at kids to stay off their lawn. Dumb kids. Stupid generation. Crazy kids, like Diane.

Or like Lana, the dancer onstage whose stage name was Wild Orchid. She told me once that she was twenty-one and trying to earn some cash to get back into college where she was studying psychology but never seemed to realize she was a troubled, needy child who would never be able to help anyone else because she'd never get her own act together. Over nothing stronger than ginger ale she'd told me her life story, including the way her dad had run out on the family when she was four and how her stepfather molested her when she was twelve. I don't know if I have a sympathetic face or because they know I'm a cop, but these lost girls seem to like dumping their dirty laundry on me even though I can't clean it. Would I like to throw Lana's stepfather a beating? Of course I would. Was I gonna do it? Nah, that wasn't gonna happen.

I'd taken on a project with Amanda, and that was enough for me right now.

And Diane...

I could already see her blossoming into a young lady and I just wasn't ready for it. I'd dropped the ball with the kids from my first marriage and I swore that wasn't going to happen again. I'd worked hard to keep it from happening again. I would protect Carrie, Diane and Toby and I wasn't about to apologize for it.

I looked back at Milos, who was staring at me. Suddenly I felt light headed.

"I gotta get some air," I said.

"You okay, Ken?"

"I got this sugar thing," I muttered heading for the door.

It was still warm outside, even at that time of night. The cars were speeding by on Fond du Lac Avenue and the highway behind Kryptonite. A truck or a bus must have passed by recently. I could smell diesel. Fresh air—I wasn't gonna get it.

I moved around the perimeter of the parking lot, trying to walk off whatever was happening to me. I needed to get a blood/glucose monitoring kit—or maybe O'Connor would set me up with that, I didn't know. I ended up by my car where I knew I had a bottle of water. I grabbed it and slammed the tepid liquid, drinking it in a few gulps. In a couple minutes I was feeling almost human again, except for the water that sloshed uncomfortably in my stomach.

"Ken?"

The gentle voice came from behind me, near the back door of the club. When I turned around another one of the girls, whose name might have been Nikki was standing next to the dumpster. She was wearing skinny jeans and a windbreaker. Despite the heat I could see her trembling.

"Are you leaving?" she said.

"I was thinking about it," I said. "There isn't much happening tonight that Milos and Carla can't handle."

"Think you could give me a ride home?"

Brother... This was all I needed. I knew Milos had been bringing her home and asked her about it.

"I don't... I don't want him to bring me home tonight."

"Is something wrong?"

"No. I just want to go home."

She told me where she lived and I was happy to find it wasn't out of my way. I went inside and told Milos I was heading out but I didn't tell him about the girl I was providing taxi service for.

It was only half an hour later when I slid into bed next to Carrie and pressed myself against her, giving her soft kisses on her neck.

A soft moan came from the back of her throat as she stirred and slowly awakened. I was kissing her neck beneath her ear when I felt her body shudder. She was awake.

"You smell like a bar," she said turning towards me to kiss me on the mouth. I didn't respond and we kissed hungrily for a couple minutes while our hands traveled each other's bodies. I was pushing her t-shirt over her head when I heard her say, "Looks like I won't be getting much sleep tonight."

She wasn't wrong.

Chapter 22

When I got to the squad the next morning Gold was sitting on the corner of Schmidt's desk addressing the guys. He stopped what he was saying as I approached and gestured at the cup of overpriced coffee I had in my hand.

"You bring one for everyone?" he said.

"I sure didn't."

He made a show of looking at his watch to let me know he was aware that I was fifteen minutes late.

"Next time use the pot in the coffee room," he said. "We got a lot of work to do today."

Before I could stop them the words were out of my mouth, not loud or anything but loud enough that Lieutenant Gold heard me.

"Sure thing, Golda."

Nobody had been talking but the room suddenly became even more silent, as if the air conditioning system had just stopped and the traffic outside had come to a complete stop. For some reason I thought of that movie, "Backdraft," and the way the smoke drifted from under the door, then got sucked back in before the whole place exploded.

Gold didn't explode but I knew he meant business the way he told me in a slow, even voice to meet him in his office when the squad meeting was over. The other detectives were conspicuous the way they didn't look at me.

The conference ended with Gold giving everybody but me and Wash their assignments for the day. There was nothing new on the boards for SCU so Schmidt was getting loaned out to the 2nd for the day. I felt bad for the chumps that got stuck with him but at least he had something to dig his teeth into. I was looking forward to another day of paging through old case files and photographs looking for my victim's identity.

I followed Gold into his office ready to take my lumps.

"Close the door," he said as he sat behind his desk.

When I turned back to him, he had his glasses on and was writing on a packet of forms.

"Am I gonna have a problem with you?"

"No," I said. "I don't even know why I said that, Lieu. I'm just tired."

"You look like a bag of crap, Brady. Did you get any sleep last night?"

I didn't feel like telling him that I was moonlighting against the department's regulations or that Carrie and I were getting' busy until the birds were chirping their merry, morning music.

"It's this case. It ain't helping my sleep any."

"You want me to give it to someone else?"

"No," I said, probably too forcefully. "I just need one break and I'll nail this jerk."

"One break and we'll solve the Lindberg killing too," he said, reminding me how tenuous our job could be at times. "I need you to keep your head in the game and find this guy. The Captain is tracking this too and wants to know what we got."

"Wash and me are still tracking old cases for a pattern. We found a couple abductions that have similarities—same age, comparable looks, that kind of thing. If it's the same guy he's been at it for a while."

"And you didn't get anything from the scene?"

"Still waiting on the lab," I said.

"All right," Gold said. "Let me know if anything turns up."

I muttered something affirmative and turned towards the door.

"And Brady," he said.

I looked back. He didn't look up at me when he said, "I don't care what's in your heart, just don't let it come out of your mouth. Not in my squad"

A couple hours later a courier arrived and Claire signed for a package. It was the report from CSI and the results of the autopsy. There wasn't a whole lot that we hadn't already figured out but a few facts were suggestive.

The girl had died from bleeding out as a result of her many cuts and lacerations but the report said she would likely have died from malnutrition soon enough. The dirt under her fingernails was common enough for the area and included trace amounts of oxidized metal, which wasn't strange either except that there was more than the man on the street would be carrying. A two-page section of the report detailed the abuse, sexual and otherwise that her body had taken over a period of years.

There was one nugget that we wasted no time bringing to Lieutenant Gold.

"They're fairly certain that her name is Dana Hujet," Wash said when we brought it to the boss. "She disappeared about seven years ago, riding her bike home from McGovern Park."

"How old would she be now?"

"Nineteen or twenty."

"Did they get a positive I.D. from the family?"

"Not yet, Lieu," I said. "I wanted to run this for you before I called them. I still need to find them."

"And you guys didn't find her jacket in your search?" He wasn't accusing us of negligence, he made that clear with his tone. He was just wondering if we'd chipped away enough of the mountain to find her file.

"I never saw it," I said.

Wash shook his head and shrugged.

"Okay," Gold said. "Let's get someone in for an identification and we'll go from there."

"I got it," I said.

"I'll pull the original paperwork and see what we can find," Wash said.

As I was leaving his office Gold said, "Let's hope that's the break you needed."

Chapter 23

It took a few phone calls to track down someone from the Hujet family. In the years since their daughter had been taken, they'd changed their phone numbers and like most people in America these days used their cell phones exclusively. Once we realized the old numbers were no good someone had the bright idea of checking with the Bureau to see if they'd left a good number. It was the father's mobile.

I told him we might have some information and asked him to come to the squad. I hated putting him through this, maybe giving him an ounce of hope and then telling him that we think we may have found his little girl and, oh by the way, she's dead.

Some days you just feel like a bag of crap.

Giving someone bad news is the worst part of the job, but if you can control the environment, control the temperature of the room you can do it without creating a huge scene. Some people are always going to be more demonstrative than others; they're the ones you can't do anything with. You just give them the news delicately and offer any comfort you can. I do it as privately as possible and hope for the best. If we're in our house there will always be a room available. If we do it at their house you never know what sister, brother, cousin, neighbor will be hanging around and go into hysterics.

Wally Hujet didn't seem like the kind of guy that was going to go to wailing and gnashing his teeth but you could never tell. The last job we had on file for him was a janitorial gig at Marshall High School and the lead detective's notes said he seemed like a solid, blue collar joe. They'd run him through the whole interview process—that's standard procedure when a kid goes missing. We take a close look at the immediate family so we can eliminate them if nothing else. Clearly the guy who caught this case was satisfied that he was innocent. The mother looked good too.

I'd never seen Mister Hujet before, but when he entered the squad room, I could tell at a glance that the last seven years had taken their toll on him. He looked tired and his shoulders slumped with grim resignation. I saw in his posture that he had been called before, maybe many times, and it had never amounted to anything beyond more grief.

Now, if we'd done our job right, I was probably going to be confirming his worst fear and I didn't know if that was better than giving him an ounce of hope that she was still alive and prolong his agony.

No matter what I learned in the next few minutes I just wanted to catch the guy who was responsible for Wally Hujet's torment and make him hurt.

Hujet checked in at the catching area and Claire waved me over with an apprehensive look on her face.

Wash got up with me and we went to meet him.

"You said that you wanted to see me," Mister Hujet said by way of introduction. There was a hint of irritation but he wasn't being jerky or anything. He just wanted to get it done.

I introduced myself and Detective Washington.

"Would you like a coffee or something to drink?"

"A bottle of water would be great." He didn't bother pointing out that it was almost ninety degrees outside.

We lead him to the break room across the hall and Wash gave him a bottle from the stock in the refrigerator. We all sat down at the table.

"You said you might have some new information about Dana?"

"Yeah, well we think so," Wash said.

"What does that mean?"

"Mister Hujet—"

"Just call me Wally, all right. I spend enough time in all these different precincts you'd think I was a crook. Just call me by my first name."

"Okay, Wally," I said. "You sound like a straight shooter so I'm gonna level with you. We found the body of a girl that we think might be Dana."

He sucked a bit of air before he said, "So… this girl is dead?"

"She is, yeah."

"And you think it's Dana? But you're not sure?"

"The description sounds like her, but it's been a few years and…" How was I supposed to finish that sentence? She'd been serially abused? She'd been cut to ribbons? She'd been violated in almost every way imaginable?

"Are you saying she died… recently?"

Wash sat forward and looked Wally Hujet in the eyes.

"Yes sir. This girl died within the last week."

Hujet looked like he was about to get sick. He held his head in his hands.

I reached across the table and set a gentle hand on his arm. It was a useless gesture but I felt like I had to do something. If I could give him a scrap of strength it might get him through this.

"So, this girl…" he said. "If it's Dana… she's been alive all this time?"

"If it's her, yeah."

"Where's she been?"

He looked up at me when neither of us answered right away.

"We don't know yet, Wally. We think we may have some good leads but I'll be honest with you, we just don't know exactly yet." It was probably more than I should have said but I didn't feel like I could lie to this guy.

"You're going to need me to identify her, aren't you?"

I drove Wally to the morgue and asked him to wait in the hallway while I had a quick word with the Medical Examiner, a spotty kid who looked like they'd pulled him off the

89

playground of a high school.

Was I really that old?

Dr. Judson was actually in his thirties but new to the position of M.E. I explained to him in no uncertain terms that I didn't want Wally Hujet seeing any more of this girl than he needed to. It would be best if he could make the ID off her face alone. If it didn't work that way, I wanted to find a way without him seeing what some sick bastard had done to this girl.

Judson had the corpse laid out on a table and covered with a sheet, just like they showed on every cop show or movie. What those shows could give you was the smell of the lab; the chemicals, the cleaning agents and the decaying remains of a human being. Sometimes it was too much for a hammerhead like me. I couldn't imagine what Wally was feeling at the moment.

"Doctor Judson is lifting part of the sheet," I said. "I just want you to tell me if you recognize her as your daughter. Can you do that for me?"

Wally took a breath and nodded his head. I saw him tense up like he was about to take a punch in the gut.

"Are you ready Mister Hujet?" Judson asked.

Wally nodded again.

I wished the doctor would quit stalling and move the sheet.

As if he knew what I was thinking Judson lifted the sheet and revealed her face.

Wally took another breath and looked down at the girl's face. I could tell immediately that he recognized her from the way his face seemed to collapse in on itself. He started sobbing.

"Wally," I said.

"I think it's her," he said. "I'm pretty sure."

I was surprised to hear him suggest doubt. Every bit of his body language said he knew it was Dana.

"She's got a... birthmark on her foot," he said. "On the

90

bottom."

"Which foot?" I said.

"I don't remember. The right one... maybe..."

Judson covered her face and moved around the table to her feet. When he looked up at me I nodded, giving him permission to lift the sheet.

What Hujet saw first put a look of confusion on his face, then his lip started trembling and I could see exquisite pain take over his body. He stretched a trembling hand towards the table, holding it a few inches away from the girl's foot.

He looked at me and nodded.

I reached out to him, getting a grip on his arm to keep him from collapsing. I could feel his body trembling as he sobbed. When he did lose his steam he leaned against me.

Judson grabbed a chair and slid it over behind Wally. I lowered him into it and gave him an awkward pat on his shoulder.

"Is there anything I can get you?" I said.

He sobbed, just staring ahead at the body of his little girl and I could see everything he was imagining at that moment: the day she was born, him holding her in his arm and showing her off to his friends that visited the hospital. A toddler playing with her dolly or stuffed animals. Taking pictures of her on her first day of school; the girl wearing a brand new backpack and excited for the occasion. Teaching her to ride a bike. That life was over. Wally Hujet was never going to walk his baby down the aisle. He was never going to hold his grandchild by Dana.

"What...?" he said and then ran out of steam. I squeezed his shoulder and he found the strength to continue. "What happened to her? Where...?"

"We're assuming she was held someplace," I said. "I know how dumb this sounds but this part of the investigation is in its early stages. We don't have a lot of answers for you yet."

"How'd she...?"

Judson stepped up and said, "She lost a lot of blood, the result of multiple lacerations."

My look shut him up.

"She looks so tiny."

"Like I said, we're still looking into the details. There's an active investigation and we're doing everything we can to find who's responsible for your daughter's death."

"Her name is Dana."

"You're right," I said. "I'm sorry. We're looking into Dana's death."

"Can I see her?"

"You don't want to do that, Mister Hujet. Just think of her like she was; your little girl."

"My little girl…" he said. "My baby."

"Maybe we should go see about your wife, Wally. How's that sound?"

For the first time his gaze left the sheet that covered the corpse of his child.

"Yeah," he said. "Let's go see about her mother. She's gotta know about this."

I drove Wally back to his car and told him I'd come along and talk to his wife. I wasn't surprised that he was quiet on the ride, I just wanted to know that he was okay.

"Are you all right, Wally?"

"I don't know," he said after a moment. "I'm, uh… I'm not surprised I guess. I been living in fear of this day for a while. Still… we been holding onto hope. For seven years there was a chance that Dana coming back. That our girl was still somewhere waiting to be found."

He didn't mean it in any accusatory way but I felt a rebuke, more from myself than the grieving father.

"Now I found out she was out there the whole time," he said. "I can't imagine how scared she was—or what she was going through."

"You weren't wrong to hope."

"Yeah, what good did it do? It just makes today harder—and it didn't help save my girl."

"I don't know about these things, Wally. And I don't know if I believe in other worlds and such, but your hope wasn't a waste. Maybe your hope, and your wife's hope… maybe Dana was able to get some strength off that. Maybe that's what kept her going the whole time."

Huget thought about it for a moment before turning to me.

"Yeah? What do I got now?"

Chapter 24

Wash and I spent the rest of the day reviewing everything we could on Dana Hujet's initial disappearance. Her mom and dad couldn't give us anything new; it had been so long and they were just too overwhelmed at the moment.

There was lots of information on the case, but lots of it was contradictory and much of it just didn't help at all. Even the basic facts were far from clear.

Dana had been at McGovern Park with a couple friends. Around dinner time they all hopped on their bikes and headed home in different directions. Dana and her bike were never seen again. These were the only solid facts we had.

A couple kids that were interviewed seven years ago said there had been a white truck trolling the neighborhood. Others said it was a white van, a couple people said something about a rumpus in the park, but the police had never been called. One lady said the cops had been called and they had been the ones to take away the girl. It had been looked into but there was not a single report filed by any cop in the city regarding anything in McGovern Park that day and no record of a call to that area.

It was a whole lot of nothing.

It was from looking at the ME's pictures of Dana and that tattoo on her arm that reminded me of the guy at the junkyard, Stephen Witt.

There was something about the guy I just didn't like. I don't know if it was the mousy way he acted or the way he spoke with a German accent when his family had been in the United States for decades. He told me the junkyard had been his for seventeen years and it was his father's before that. So, what was with the Colonel Klink dialect?

It wasn't that the guy was German either. If I held that against him I'd have to hold it against me too. I was proud of my heritage even though I like living in America. Still, I had to admit there was a German component to this crime.

"nur Offiziere" the tatt said. "Officers only." What on earth was that even supposed to mean? Was it possible there was some kind of brothel in Milwaukee, a city with a very strong German population, where young girls were the main menu? And why put the ink on them? And why in German? And why number them the way Nazis did?

Dana Hujet's body turning up didn't solve anything; it just made for more questions, questions I had no answer for.

Stephen Witt… This guy didn't look like he could hurt a spider—so what was that two-year bit he did in De Pere all about? He laid out some guy in a bar? I knew he was wrong when we'd had our little chat a few nights back but I figured he might be running a chop shop or moving some drugs maybe. I didn't see this guy as violent and I usually have a good nose for that kind of thing.

"Why does your face look like it's gonna pop?" Wash said breaking the silence in our corner of the squad room. He was sitting at his desk, across from mine, rubbing his eyes with the heel of his hand, the same as I had done about five minutes earlier.

"Because I'm still not putting the pieces together. So much of this doesn't make any sense."

"What would your boy Sherlock do?"

"He'd send Watson out to the country to do the heavy lifting."

"Not that you're any kind of Sherlock Holmes, and I definitely ain't no dope like Watson, but I wouldn't mind taking a ride out to the country for a while. Get some fresh air."

I didn't bother telling him that Watson wasn't a dope, that they made him that way in some movies because the writers thought it would make Sherlock look smarter. I'd been telling him for years he ought to read the original Sherlock Holmes stuff by Arthur Conan Doyle but he wasn't interested. He'd make some half-whacky comment about print being dead and go back to writing his reports.

"Did you get a chance to look at the jacket on that Witt guy I told you about?"

He leaned forward, grabbed the file from one of several piles on his desk and opened it up.

"I looked at it," he said. "I'm not seeing any connection to the Hujet girl though."

"I don't know," I said. "It's just a feeling that I have."

"That this guy is wrong or that he killed our girl?"

"I'm not ready to say he killed the girl. There's something definitely wrong with him though."

Wash laughed.

"There's crazy people in every house on every street," he said. "That don't make a case."

"I know. I'm not saying he did it."

"You're saying something. You've had his file sitting around for a few days now. You must want to look closer at him."

"You know Wash, I got as much reason to go after this guy as anyone else. We got nothing here. We'd be doing just as well with a Ouija Board or a Magic Eight Ball."

"Shut up, man. You know these things don't close up so easily. Stuff takes time."

"I know," I said standing up. "But try to tell that to the grieving father and mother."

"Try telling a grand jury that you like a guy because of a 'gut feeling.' It's probably got more to do with your diet than anything else."

I was about to go grab a candy bar from the break room until he said that. I hadn't mentioned anything to him about my diabetes so his comment caught me short for a moment.

"Yeah…" I said. "This from a guy with irritable bowels?"

He laughed and I'm pretty sure I heard him foul the air as I walked to the bubbler to get a drink.

Chapter 25

By the time our tour ended I was pretty wiped out. Lack of sleep and staring at files and computer screens all day didn't do much to keep me energized. That's what the black coffee was for. But now I was winding down and I still hadn't made any headway in the case. I decided to get some drive thru and catch some air.

I knew the food was bad for me, especially the soda I ordered, but what the hey—Dr. O'Connor wasn't around and at least I ordered a twenty-ounce instead of the thirty-two. I told myself I needed the sugar to get me moving.

I took highway 43 north and got off on Good Hope St. In no time I was on Granville Road, turning into Witt's Salvage Yard.

I probably knew I was going to go there when I left the office but I never made a conscious choice. Even as I turned in it occurred to me the only reason I did was because the gate was open. I needed to think of a reason to be there, like, immediately.

Or maybe I could just count on my innate ability to fib.

The salvage yard didn't look as big from the inside, mainly because there were automobiles stacked up, forming fifteen-foot-high canyons and blocking any view of the whole property. I knew from the outside that it stretched out nearly half a mile and there was no way I was going to get a look at all that tonight.

Near the gate was a dingy, gray house, two stories and stained from things that had been leaned up against it at various times. The front door and porch faced the salvage yard rather than the road.

Next to the house was a chain-link fence enclosure that served as a paddock for three of the gnarliest looking dogs

I'd ever seen. Before I'd turned the key of the Impala these mutts were barking up a storm, showing me the business end of their teeth and letting me know that I wasn't going to get any rhythm from them if they got loose.

If there was a store someplace that sold junkyard dogs these three were the ugliest by a mile and when I stepped from the car I thought I could smell mange. I sure didn't need any of them taking a chomp out of me.

"Hello officer," Witt said from behind me. Somehow this guy had a knack for sneaking up on me and I didn't like it. It sure didn't do anything to get me to trust him. "Don't get too close to the fence. The one in the middle—his name is Jurgen—I've seen him actually climb the fence when he gets angry."

"Climbs the fence?"

"He takes a running start and leaps most of the way."

I pointed to the barbed wire at the top.

"How does he get through that?"

"I haven't seen him do it since we put the sharp wire there," he said.

"How long has that been?"

"Oh," he said, rubbing the hair on his chin and pretending to think about it. "It's been several years. I doubt he could actually complete the climb today."

"I don't wanna find out.

We both smiled awkwardly, staring at each other.

"Is there something I can help you with?" he said. "Perhaps you damaged your car the other night?"

"No," I said. "No, my car is fine. I just thought I'd stop by. My brother-in-law lives north of Chicago—he's kind of a gear-head. The guy just bought a Sixty-Six Mustang... Stingray, I think. He said it's like the one in that Steve MacQueen movie."

He smiled and shrugged.

"Anyway," I said. "He's looking for an oil pan that's not all rusted out. He swears he's looked or called every salvage place between Chicago and Racine. Can't find one. I just thought I'd help him out."

"I'm surprised he couldn't find what he was looking for."

"Really? You think you have one?"

"No," he said flatly. "I am certain I do not. But there are many salvage yards. I suspect one of them had what he needed."

"You think they lied to him?"

He shrugged again and said, "It could be they didn't want to look. He called them on the wrong day."

"It must be nice to make the rules like that," I said. "I can't imagine what that would be like in my line of work."

"I don't suppose a police officer can turn a blind eye to things."

"Not if he wants to keep his job."

"It's the same for us. You have to do business to stay in business."

"But you can't help me?"

"No, I'm sure I don't have anything from a 1966 Mustang."

I was about to ask him if I could look around when a phone in the house rang. For a moment he ignored it and continued staring at me.

"If you need to get that…" I said.

"Please excuse me," he said backing away. He turned and loped to the house.

I couldn't complain about that. I wanted to take a look around on the QT and now I could.

There just seemed to be so much wrong about Stephen Witt that it was hard to blow him off. He was hiding something and he was doing it intentionally. I don't know if I tipped my hand somehow asking about the car parts. I don't know a ton about how cars work beyond the basics so I didn't try to pretend I was a gear-head myself. If I played that character too strong he was going to catch me. And all I really wanted was a quick look around.

I walked away from the dog pen towards the automotive bone yard. As I looked down the avenue there didn't seem to be anything too weird, just the remains of once proud vehicles that had either outlived their usefulness or met an untimely demise. It occurred to me that every car there had a story, or even a few stories. At one time every one of them sat new on some dealer's lot with a shiny engine and a shiny coat of paint. Each of them represented some type of freedom for whoever bought it, whether it was freedom from public transportation, freedom from being stuck at home or freedom from just standing still. I thought about couple getting busy in the back seats. I thought about kids driving across the country with a ring to propose to their sweethearts. Maybe there were even a few people who ended up in the trunk of some of these cars back in the days when the Mafia had a strong presence in this city. I remembered the times I'd hidden in the trunk as we snuck into the drive-in theater.

The drive-in theater.

Dana Hujet.

She had never wandered far from my mind but now she jumped directly into my headlights. It was the razor wire fence that first lead me to Stephen Witt's salvage yard. Why was I so attracted to this guy for a crime that he had absolutely no connection to? My gut instincts were not bad but this was a whole new way to investigate a case—by not investigating. There was not a piece of evidence that pointed me in Witt's direction but my that little man in my stomach told me I needed to keep an eye on him. I was missing something, just one crucial link in the chain.

I just didn't know what the chain was attached to.

I had wandered twenty or thirty yards into the bone yard when I saw the white, Econoline van parked in an area behind the dog pen. There were hundreds of cars around me, even a few vans, but there was something different about this one. It didn't look like it belonged here.

Unlike all the other vehicles, somebody had washed this

one recently.

I pulled my phone from my pocket and was moving to get a better angle on the van when somebody cold-cocked me from behind and I hit the dirt.

I could hear the dogs going crazy as somebody with white Chuck Taylor sneakers walked around and booted me in the face.

Chapter 26

I knew I was going out, but I could still hear what was going on around me; the crunch of the gravel under the rubber sole of the sneakers, the dogs barking and Witt running from the house shouting.

I pushed myself up a few inches, but my strength disappeared and I face-planted on the hard stones.

I dreamed of Terri, my first wife. We were young when we got married, but not as young as lots of couples. And we'd had quite a few good years, along with two kids; Jake and Nicole. I was on The Job at that time already, working in the detective squad, the job I'd wanted since I was a kid. Then I'd started seeing things that nobody should have to see because they should never happen. If I was going to stick with this gig I'd need to develop some thick skin and find ways to deal with it. Terri saw through me pretty quick and decided she didn't want to be, or have the kids anywhere near me.

That part was pretty bad, but the marriage was great at first. I dreamed about the great time. The week we spent at The White Gull Inn in Door County when we'd left the room for breakfast and an afternoon bike ride through the state park. What I wouldn't give for half of that energy now...

The first thing I felt was something cold behind my neck. It wasn't uncomfortable but it sure was a change from the molten ice pick that seemed to be sticking out of the back of my head.

When I opened my eyes, I saw I was lying on a couch in what I presumed was Stephen Witt's living room.

The whole place was painted in the same dingy color as the outside but was considerably cleaner. It wasn't spotless but it had clearly been dusted in the last week. I wondered what kind of woman he was married to; the decorations were feminine but there were very few of them. The walls had pictures in frames, but they were faded and out of style. My guess was that they were pictures of the old country. The most recent piece of "art" was a nude African American woman with a piece of scarlet cloth draped over her arms. Her breasts were a male fantasy of defied gravity. All of this painted on a piece of black velvet.

The couch was a turn-of-the-century sectional with criss-crossing line patterns whose geometry made the ache in my head worse.

I sat up, noticing for the first time the piece of tissue stuck in my nose. I pulled it out and found the end colored red with my blood. It hadn't dried so I must not have been here too long. If the pain was any indication I was still in the early stages of recovery.

I heard footsteps in another room and turned to have a look. Through a wide, arched doorway I saw the kitchen… well, the refrigerator anyway. I assumed it was the kitchen. The fridge had an automotive calendar with a scantily clad model reclined over the hood of a muscle car. I recognized it right away; we had the same calendar in the break room back at the squad. Ours wasn't hanging up, regulations prohibited that kind of display, but it was sitting on a shelf over the coffee table. We used it to mark off days we planned to take vacations.

Witt walked into the living room with a frozen piece of meat still wrapped in white butcher paper.

"I was wrong," he said. "It's a piece of flank steak, not rib eye."

Apparently, we'd had a conversation I didn't remember. He handed me the wrapped meat.

"What was this for?" I said.

"To keep your nose from swelling. You asked if I had a steak to use as a compress."

"Frozen doesn't work. The idea is to use something that will move with the contours of your face." I held up the ice pack from my neck, which turned out to be a bag of corn.

"This is perfect."

"Ah," he said, setting the taking the meat back and sitting on the other end of the couch. "So, why do people use steak for an ice pack?"

"I don't think most people do anymore," I said. That's probably one of those things from fifty or sixty years ago that pops up in movies or TV shows every now and then."

I leaned back and put the corn on my nose. I probably looked like an idiot but it certainly felt good.

"Thanks for your help, Mister Witt. Did you happen to see the punk that tagged me?"

"I saw him as he was running away. He looked black or Asian but I really couldn't tell. He ran when I came out of the house."

"Does this kind of thing happen very often?"

"This is the first time anyone has been assaulted in my salvage yard, if that's what you mean. I'm sure items are stolen from me from time to time."

"Even with the dogs and the barbed wire?"

"If someone wants something, they will always find a way to get it."

"How does your wife like living in a salvage yard?"

He hesitated and for a brief moment I wondered if I'd stepped too far. It was an innocent question, but it was a private question. I didn't want to reveal that I was looking at him that closely.

"I'm not married," he said. "I have a nephew that stops by sometimes or stays when his girlfriend kicks him out of their house. Otherwise, I'm alone here."

"That's not information you want to be passing along to strangers, Mister Witt."

"But you're a police officer. I thought it would be safe to tell you."

"You're safe from me," I said as I shifted and sent a new wave of pain through my head.

"I have some aspirin if you want," he said seeing my pain.

"That'd be nice. And some water too." I really wanted

some scotch or a can of soda but I didn't want to push my luck.

He stood up and headed for the kitchen.

"Drei aspirins mit wasser," he said as he entered the kitchen.

And there it was again; the German thing thrown right at me. Suddenly I remembered the ink on Dana's arm. *"nur Offiziere."* Officers only.

Witt was nobody else's idea of an officer but I could see him thinking of himself that way. General Witt. Field Marshall Witt.

There was nothing in the decorations of the room that suggested he had any interest in World War Two or the Nazis. The average person probably wouldn't even know the way that some girls were tagged for brothels, or that some were reserved for officers. But I still couldn't get the idea that Witt was somehow connected to the missing girls out of my head. Something in my gut told me he was dirty. So, how was I falling into such easy conversation with this guy? What kind of hold did he have on me?

He brought me a glass of water and a bottle of Bayer aspirin. I shook three of them out into my hand and gave them a good look before washing them down. Criminal genius that he might be I felt pretty confident he wasn't pressing pills in the basement.

"Bayer is a good German product," I said just to break the silence.

"I can't use the other pain relievers. None of them work as well."

"So... You're from Germany? Originally I mean?"

"I was born in Brazil of all places. My parents were from Germany."

"How'd you end up in Wisconsin?"

"My mother wanted to be with people who looked more like her. She had a sister in Milwaukee... they moved north."

"I'm not sure why anyone would want to live in this climate," I said, "but I see her point."

"My father bought this salvage yard and ran it until he died. I've had it since then."

"Yeah, you said."

He pointed to the bag of corn behind my neck.

"Is that still cold?"

"It's okay. I probably need to get going soon though."

I handed him the bag as I tried to stand up. My knees were shaky but I managed.

"I can make you a proper ice pack that you can take with you," he said.

"You don't need to do that."

He scoffed. "It's a plastic baggy with ice. It's no trouble."

He walked back into the kitchen and tossed the corn into his freezer and grabbed an ice tray. He carried it out of view.

I took a few uneasy steps around the living room to shake the wobblies from my legs. It wasn't a big room but there seemed to be too much furniture in it. The big couch and two end tables. A magazine rack next to the wall. There was no television.

I meandered to the magazines and pulled one out. It was not a deliberate move, just something to do.

The magazine sent a cold chill down my back.

When I was a kid one of my buddies and I discovered his dad's stash of magazines. We grabbed one called High Society because it featured a gallery of nude pictures of Britt Ekland who we'd just seen in a James Bond movie. She didn't go buff in the movie so this magazine showed us everything we'd been missing. She'd made quite an impression on my twelve-year-old mind so I took the issue and kept it under a box in my closet. My mom found it and threw it away when I was in high school and I figured I'd never see it again.

But now I was holding it in my hands. Obviously not the same copy, but the same issue with the same pictorial. Britt was still young and sexy, and naked as the day she was born. It was from the late seventies, long after she was married to Peter Sellers, long after she'd been in the Bond movie and

The Wicker Man and probably ten or eleven years after she'd given birth to her children Victoria and Nic. I didn't know that stuff when I was a kid but this magazine had started obsessions with me, and not just with cool, blonde, Swedish actresses. This magazine got me started on the skin mags in a big way.

How was it possible that this guy had this same issue? And it was in good condition, like he's catalogued it and boxed it the way people do comic books and... other magazines.

What kind of trap had I landed in here?

I was still looking at the cover when Witt returned with the ice pack—a Ziplock Bag with ice cubes in it. He had a cheap towel in his other hand.

He saw me holding the magazine and stopped. We stared at each other for a moment; I was waiting for him to say something and I assumed he was waiting for me.

Awkward.

Just at the moment I half expected him to deny or defend his interest in dirty pictures he said, "Do you remember Britt?"

Do I remember her? Was that stupid question or what?

I tried not to let my embarrassment show as I said, "Yeah, I remember her. She was in "The Man With The Golden Gun."

"She was a very sexy woman."

"Haven't seen her lately. Maybe she still is."

"The Swedish have a gift, don't they?"

I shrugged.

"I don't know anything about that. I was just sayin'."

He gestured towards the magazine in a "May I?" kind of way. I handed it to him, pulling my hand away like it gave me some kind of electric shock. It felt strange to give it up.

Witt took the magazine and opened it to the photo spread. He smiled when he saw the pictures.

"Ah, Britt. So nice to see you..."

He spoke quietly but appreciatively, as if she was an old

friend.

It occurred to me that I had a similar feeling towards her. Maybe it was because I hadn't seen her in so long...

I was thinking about pictures in a magazine as if it was a real person. Why was I letting this get under my skin?

Witt held up the magazine to a particularly memorable page. I couldn't deny that she had a beautiful body. It was the kind of physical beauty that a guy looked for in a woman and rarely found. I couldn't say if she had anything going on in the brain department but she sure was easy on the eyes. Her acting skills never put her on the path to an Academy Award but she managed to make a career of looking good. And these pictures, taken at least thirty-five years ago, portrayed a glamorous figure, sexually powerful and alluring.

I knew from cases that I'd worked that there was nothing powerful or alluring about the porn industry. Even in a city like Milwaukee, where scumbags who made dirty movies were only a notch above amateur status, coercion, drugs and a lot of violence played a huge part. There was nothing liberating about it at all, sexually or otherwise. Many of these girls were trapped in a lifestyle they didn't want or enjoy.

But Britt? She probably got paid a lot of cash during a career slump to do this spread. The big-name magazines with money were always trolling for an actress with an even bigger name to go buff for the camera.

"She has a lovely body, our Britt. Yes?"

Yes, she did, but I didn't feel like saying it to this mouth breather. And I didn't like the way he called her "our" Britt, as if she somehow belonged to us.

I wished the aspirin would kick in.

He turned the page and a short moan escaped from his mouth.

"She had nursed two babies with these breasts at this point," he said. "Yet they are still perfectly formed. And her belly is as flat as a teenager's."

Paging through girly magazines was never a team sport to me and his commentary was really getting on my nerves.

"Look at her," he said. It was a request, not a demand, but there was something manipulative about the way he said it, as if he'd found a chink in my armor and was going to shoot an arrow through it. "You can't *not* want to look at her."

"No, I've seen it. You're right. She's very pretty."

"There is no one greater when you are talking about pure sex appeal. Not Marlene Dietrich, not Romy Schneider, not Raquel Welch."

On any other day I may have argued that last one with him but I had no desire to get into a dispute on the subject. I just wanted to go.

"Thanks for the ice pack," I said picking it up from the couch where he'd set it down. "I gotta get going."

"Did you want to borrow the magazine?"

My mouth would have said yes; fortunately, my brain kept me from talking. I nodded a goodbye and headed for the door.

"Why do I suspect you will be renting one of Britt's movies on the way home?"

I shook my head and endured the pain that came with it.

"Nah," I said. "On days that I get my head stomped on I tend to spend some time at the hospital." I opened the door to go. "Have a good evening Mister Witt."

Chapter 27

I didn't go to the hospital. I went to Kryptonite to get the taste out of my mouth with Seagram's Seven and Seven Up and the picture of Britt Ekland's body out of my head with one of the dancers who were working tonight. It didn't matter which one, it didn't even matter whether they were pretty or not. I just needed a different image in my head and if they didn't have perfect breasts and belly, well… all the better.

I ordered the Seagram's but passed on the Seven Up. I didn't want to push it with the sugar and soda was a killer.

Milos set the drink in front of me and leaned over the counter resting his chin on his folded arms. He looked the same way in grade school when he was falling asleep at his desk.

"Slow night," he said.

It was a slow night. There were only a couple other guys in the club and neither looked like the kind that were going to settle in for the long haul. These were guys who were stopping off to blow off steam on their way home to their families.

Kind of like I was doing.

I told myself I was long passed the age of getting off looking at naked girls, whether it was in a magazine or on a stage and to an extent that was true. I wasn't the kind of guy to take a girly magazine into a bathroom, or anywhere else, and pleasure myself looking at the pictures but there was something about naked women that got my attention in a big way. Did that make me a bad guy? I didn't think so. I never had cheated on Carrie, no matter how rich my fantasy life was. I could imagine doing the deed with someone else but it was Carrie who I was happy to come home to.

You can't prosecute someone for thinking about doing a crime, not until they act on it. There were many times I interviewed a suspect who told me they thought about committing a crime but they never did it for one reason or another. The ones telling the truth got to walk for the simple reason that they didn't do anything illegal.

Thinking about something isn't wrong, right?

Looking at these girls at Kryptonite wasn't wrong, was it? Not unless I actually touched one of them. Then I'd have done something Carrie could nail me on.

The truth was that Milos would have stopped me before it came anywhere near that. He might just grab my arm and say, "Are you sure about this?" and I'd come to my senses. He was that kind of friend, not that it had ever come to that.

My head was spinning. Maybe the whiskey was a bad idea too. But I hadn't drunk any yet.

I needed to get home.

I grabbed a five from my wallet and set it on the bar.

"See ya," I said.

"What's this for? You didn't drink nothin'."

"The floor show."

"Don't get me wrong, Kenny. I appreciate the dough but I'm not gonna take yours. Keep it."

He flicked the five towards me with his index finger.

"'Sides," he said. "I'd probably just buy bacon with it anyway."

He smiled and walked away down the bar, making it clear the conversation was over. I grabbed the bill and shoved it in my pocket on the way out.

Carrie was curled up on the couch, her feet tucked underneath her as she watched a TV show—one we didn't watch together.

I dropped onto the couch beside her.

She didn't look from the TV.

"You stink," she said.

"It's been a long day. I'll take a shower."

"You smell like the bar. And sweat."

"I told you, I'm gonna take a shower. You wanna join

111

me?"

"No."

"Come on, Carrie. We haven't showered together for a long time. It'll be nice."

"It'll be cold. And I'm watching this show."

"I can wait."

"Yeah, please don't. You're pretty bad."

"It was a tough day."

"If I kissed you would you taste like booze?"

"What's the problem, Carrie? Are you mad about something?"

"Yeah, you could say I'm at least half mad about something."

I sat up a little on the couch and turned towards her.

"So, do you wanna play a game of twenty questions or are you just waiting for a commercial?"

She pointed the remote at the television and turned it off.

"You're gonna miss—" I managed to say before she cut me off.

"I'm recording it."

"So, what are you half mad about?" I said.

"First tell me what happened to your face."

So she had noticed. My nose was still swollen and I was sure there was a serious bruise developing on my face, but the opposite side from where she was sitting. I did that on purpose when I sat down.

"Some scum bag did a little jig on my face," I said with a shrug as if it happened every day.

"Yeah? What's he look like?"

"Don't know. I never saw him. So, what are you mad about?" I said steering the conversation back to her anger.

"There was a Brewer game tonight," she said. "Tonight would have been a good night to take Toby. We all could'a gone," she said spreading out her arms with her hands up like I'd intentionally ignored her.

"I just got home. It's too late now."

"You don't answer your cell phone so I called the squad.

Wash said you left hours ago."

"I left the squad; that doesn't mean I was done working for the day."

"So, you were working at Kryptonite?"

"I stopped there on the way home. Probably wasn't there for ten minutes. I didn't even have a drink."

"So, why'd you go there?"

"To see if Milos needed me to work next week."

She was quiet for what seemed like a long time, just staring at me. I couldn't tell if she believed me or not but I also couldn't figure out why I was lying to her. I guess I just didn't want to have that conversation at that moment.

"Come on Carrie. What's really going on?"

"There's nothing 'going on', Ken. Your son wants to go to a ball game with you and you keep giving him the runaround on it. "

"So, we'll go to a game!" I could hear my voice rising a bit. Worse, I could feel my blood pressure going up a bit too.

"When? He said he's talked to you about this and you just keep pushing it back." She took on a mocking voice and said, "This weekend... next week... next month..."

"Is that tone designed to embarrass me or something?" I said standing up. "I guess it worked."

From my shirt pocket I removed four tickets to Sunday's Brewer game at Miller Park and dropped them on the couch beside her.

"Except right now I don't feel like going," I said.

I went to the bathroom and took a shower.

I was rinsing the shampoo from my hair when I heard the door open and someone enter. I knew it was Carrie; the kids would never come in while I was showering.

"You change your mind about joining me?" I said it with an angry edge in my voice that I really didn't feel.

"I'm sorry for squeezing your shoes about the game," she said. "I only mention it because..."

I heard her take a breath over the sound of the water.

"You make promises but you don't keep them."

I put my head under the running water and let it run over me. She was right, I had done that a few times in the last few months.

"I'm gonna do better," I said. "I just gotta get out of this slump at work. It's been tough."

"The kids don't hold that against you. Neither do I. Let us help you."

Should I tell her about the diabetes? Or Stephen Witt, who I believed more and more had something to do with Dana Hujet's death? Maybe she'd like to hear how I was still the red-headed stepchild in the squad and my new Lieutenant hadn't taken much of a liking to me yet. Or how seeing an old High Society magazine with Britt Ekland was making me feel all randy.

Nah. I didn't want to talk about any of them.

I pushed the curtain aside so I could see her.

"Are you coming in here or what?"

I don't believe she thought I was serious at first, but after a moment she gave me a slight smile and a look that said, "why not?" and got undressed.

She stepped into the tub and I let her stand under the water until she was completely soaked. She used the water and her hands to push her hair back from her face and turned to me.

I tried to kiss her but she grabbed two handfuls of my hair and held me away from her.

"Don't hurt me again," she said. She looked into my eyes, demanding a response.

"Okay," I said and pressed my mouth into hers.

Chapter 28

The Goateed Man rolled out of the bed, picked his briefs up from the floor and put them on, then left the humid room. He was covered in sweat and there was even a little blood on one of his legs; not his own, that was from 90028.

After tonight he knew he was going to have to get rid of the girls. Two visits from the detective in one week was too much of a coincidence to ignore. It was time to start clearing out, at least for a while.

There was the cottage up north, but even that wasn't big enough for all six of his guests. And he wasn't going to move that far out of the city just to keep them alive.

No, he figured, it was better to just kill them now and dump the bodies where they either wouldn't be found or couldn't be tied to him.

As he dressed, he wondered what the best way to kill them would be. There was a lot to think about: how to do it so the others don't hear? That would only cause further problems. How to kill without making a huge mess that he'd just need to clean up later? Was there a humane way to take a life? He had a gun; was that a good way to do it? Then he'd have the noise and the mess, so that ruled that out. A knife? A baseball bat? Choking them with a rope or belt or something? Could he do that? Those were pretty intimate ways of killing somebody and he doubted he had the strength of character to do any of them.

Then he thought about the time he could spend in prison for his personal concentration camp.

I guess I could do it if I had to, he thought.

The more he thought about it the more he realized he needed to do the killing someplace else. He would take the girls for a ride, let them think he was going to let them go somewhere in the hinterlands and then take care of them.

Take care of them. That sounds good.

He would get them back in the van and take them for a ride, then figure out how he would do it when he got... somewhere.

He wondered who should be first and decided 90028 would get the honor. He'd just spent an hour with her and she surely wasn't expecting him to return right away. No, he was done with her in every way imaginable. And she hadn't shown any interest in him in a couple years, not since he realized she was trying to take control by seducing him. He'd caught on to that and put an end to it right away. The beating he'd given her that time had almost killed her, this time he just needed to finish the job.

Yes, 90028 was the best first choice, he decided.

He unlocked the door to her chamber, walked across the cold floor to the bed, grabbed a handful of hair and dragged her from the room.

Chapter 29

"Hey Wash, there's something I gotta tell you."

"I told you, I'm not gay!" Wash said loud enough for everyone in the squad room to hear.

His comment didn't bother me; he'd made the same joke a hundred times and everybody was used to it. What hacked me was that I wanted to say something on the QT and he was drawing attention from everybody in the room.

"You done?" I said, bring the volume back down.

"What's up?"

I leaned across my desk with the stacks of folders and said, "I'm still liking this guy, Stephen Witt."

"Liking him for what?"

"I think he's involved in this Dana Hujet death. I got a strong feeling about this."

"A strong feeling isn't evidence," Wash said. "A Grand Jury won't indict on a strong feeling. We can't even arrest him on a strong feeling."

"I'm trying to make this work."

"The evidence isn't there, Brady. Besides, wasn't Witt in jail when she got snatched?"

"He went to jail after."

"So, what? How'd she survive the whole time he's in jail?"

"I don't know. Like I said, I'm trying to make it work."

"You think he's got a partner or something?"

"That could be, but I don't know who would be friends with a mook like him. I was thinking he might be part of something bigger. Like some Neo Nazi thing."

"Some whacky Hitler club? That's why they ink them"

"They don't have to be Hitler fans. Maybe they just like tagging the girls. Maybe it gives them some kind of power over them."

"A tattoo?"

"Maybe it keeps them scared. It's not like Witt is a very frightening figure on a good day."

Wash sat back in his seat, considering.

"But the tat is in German," he said. "They wouldn't even know what it says."

"Sure. That makes it even scarier."

He shook his head.

"I still don't see it. I don't know why you have this mad on for him, but…"

"Maybe you should go see him and tell me what you think."

"I got a case to work," he said. He put his glasses on and resumed reading the file on his computer.

I couldn't blame the guy for not wanting to give Witt any freight. He'd never seen him, never spoke with him and never seen the razor wire on the fence. And even if he had, Wash wasn't the kind of cop to give his gut any attention. He was a good detective, maybe even great, but he didn't close cases intuitively. He collected data, conducted interviews and found the holes in people's stories. He was more like Columbo that way.

I always wanted to be Sherlock Holmes, a character I admired from the first time I read a Classic Illustrated comic that adapted a couple of Conan Doyle's short stories. I read through the entire canon several times, along with a whole bunch of books written by other authors, none of which had Sir Arthur's gift for legitimate imagination.

Holmes was based on a doctor named Joseph Bell who, it was said, could diagnose a patient with amazing accuracy the moment they walked in the door simply by observing the details. Apparently, he was a one-man crime scene investigation team without all the high-tech stuff you see on television, most of which is bogus anyway. Doyle took Bell's gifts and gave them to Sherlock Holmes who used them to solve crimes both large and small. It's a tribute to the quality of the writing and the stories that many people believe Sherlock Holmes to be a real person.

But if you try to solve crimes using Holmes' methods, you'll drive yourself nuts. There is just too much forensic information to any one person to have encyclopedic knowledge on the subject. The guy that is an expert on ballistics might not know squat when it comes to poisons. The blood splatter guy probably couldn't tell the difference between a Cutco knife and a K Bar. To know every brand of tobacco by the ashes was a fantasy that today's detective couldn't indulge.

And let's not even think about how the legal system has changed in the last fifty years, let alone the last hundred and fifty...

"I got something for you to see," Lieutenant Gold said. This guy had a talent for sneaking up on me. "A friend of mine in records dug these up for me this morning."

He dropped a couple files on my desk.

"Does it relate?"

"You tell me," he said.

Wash and I each grabbed a file and took a look.

The name in the file I grabbed was Ellen Urmanski. She'd gone missing four years ago from a Polish neighborhood on the south side of Milwaukee. She was thirteen at the time.

The picture is what grabbed my attention.

It was taken at a birthday party not long before she disappeared. She was with her friends or relatives, clearly enjoying herself based on the big smile on her face. She had big, beautiful, brown eyes and jet-black hair.

She could have been Dana Hujet's sister.

I looked up at Wash. He held up the picture from his file the way he would hold up the picture proving the existence of Bigfoot.

Same look. Dark skinned, dark hair.

"What's going on here, Lieu?" I said. "We were looking at these jackets for days to identify that Hujet girl. How did we not see this before?"

"I hope you just hadn't gotten to it yet," Gold said.

"Are these girls related?" Wash said. "I mean, are they

the same family or something?"

"Other than the way they look there's no connection," Gold said. "They're not even from the same nationality originally."

"How'd you know to look for these?"

"I remember the cases. They happened pretty close together. I didn't know about the Hujet girl until you caught the case so I didn't put it together." Gold looked at his shoes. "I'm almost ashamed to say it was my wife who reminded me about them."

"Is your wife on the job?" I said.

"No, she's just on my case."

Great. Now his wife was going to tell us how to do our jobs...

"What are we supposed to do with this now?" I said. "Two more girls... what? Taken by the same guy? That's what I'd assume."

"Run with it," Gold said.

"But there's no connection," Wash said.

"Except they all look pretty similar. You might think they have a notable ethnic look."

"You're saying they all look like Jews."

"Yeah, Brady. I'm saying they all look like Jews."

"So, you think we ought to be looking for a hate crime component?"

"All crime has an element of hate to it," Gold said. "You don't steal from someone you love, and you sure don't kill 'em. Nobody commits a crime against someone because they think it'll do the victim good."

I couldn't think of anything off the top of my head to poke a hole in his theory, but I wasn't gonna say that.

"But you think there's a definite racial component to these abductions?"

"I think whoever is snatching these kids, if they're all the same guy, is a sick twitch. Whether it's racial or not... I can't say. He sure seems to have a certain type of girl he likes."

"And in a city this big there are plenty of gals that fit the same physical description," Wash said.

"This whole thing might just be a game to this guy," Gold said. "I'd hate to steer you in the wrong direction but I wanted to let you know about these girls too. If anything jumps out of the file; if there's someone you think is worth re-interviewing... whatever."

"And maybe we should be paying attention to this Jewish angle."

"If you think that's going to help, sure."

"This guy might just be a big World War Two buff," Wash said. "Might not be any Jewish angle."

I could see Gold's temperature going up. He was getting a little redder in the face and he was drumming a stack of paperwork on my desk with his fingers.

"You got any kids Lieu?" I said.

"I got a boy in high school," he said. "Why?"

"I just didn't want to think that you had a daughter at home that fit this description too and that was the reason you were so fired up about us looking at this angle."

"I'd be wanting you to look this hard regardless," he said without hesitation.

"You sure?"

"What is it with you Brady? Am I the first Jew you've ever worked with? You wanna see if I got horns or something?"

"Nah, Lieu. You aren't the first Jew I've worked with. Not even close."

"So, what's the problem?"

I really didn't want to have this conversation, not in the squad room anyway. I knew how it was going to sound when I said it but Lieutenant Gold gave me the impression he wasn't going to let it go until I answered him.

"My experience, Jews on The Job are trying to prove something."

"You think so, huh?"

"My experience, that's all I'm saying."

Gold looked at me, considering what I'd said. I don't

know if he thought I was being plucky or a racist jerk but he didn't answer right away. I imagined he was sizing me up.

For the first time I wondered about his previous assignments; whether he'd ever run a squad before. It would be just like the bureaucrats to assign him to an elite squad like SCU based on him being a minority. Maybe that was the reason Voight told me I needed to look into this guy. Or maybe he did have something in his deep, dark past that he was trying to distance himself from. God knows, we all got secrets.

But I was being totally honest with him. The bosses I'd had that were Jewish always seemed like they had a chip on their shoulder. Was that every one of them? Probably not, but I still didn't know anything about the new Lieutenant.

"Something to prove, huh?" he said looking as though he was giving it some serious attention. "You're not wrong."

He turned and walked back to his office.

Chapter 30

Gold and I avoided each other for the rest of the morning. I don't know what he was thinking but I didn't feel like getting into it with him again. After a while defending yourself against a claim of racism, no matter how factually eloquent you make it, starts sounding like, "Nuh huh," even if you're a cop.

Especially if you're a cop these days...

At eleven-thirty I went to grab my lunch from the fridge in the break room. I'd packed a brown bag before Carrie woke up so she didn't see what I was doing and start asking questions I didn't want to answer yet. I picked up a couple cans of diet soda on the way to work hoping that I could choke the stuff down. I suspected the taste would grow on me but I still needed to actually get started.

I sat at the table, appreciating the solitude, and pulled out a Tupperware filled with baby carrots and a baggie of sliced cheese. I'd stuffed a smaller plastic dish with peanut butter and started dipping the carrots in it. It turned out to be pretty good, but then how could it not. Peanut butter made everything better, which was a clear sign that it couldn't be good for me. I made a mental note to moderate my intake of the stuff, or at least find a brand that wasn't too bad.

Wash walked in just as I was popping a can of diet cola and stopped. He stared at the meal I had on the table.

"What is your problem?" he said.

"I'm hungry."

"Then don't eat like a rabbit. What is all this stuff in aid of?" He pointed to the diet soda. "Are you dyin' or something?"

"I like carrots. I like peanut butter."

"I see that. I also have seen you eat a triple hamburger for lunch. Does this have something to do with your doctor visit the other day?"

I took a drink from the can and tried to make a contented face. It was a wasted effort. Wash knew me too well and could tell I hated it. Diet soda always left a dull feeling in my mouth that only made me jones for sugar even more. If I was gonna make this diet work I'd need to start drinking water or unsweetened tea.

"Yeah..." I said when I'd choked the vile liquid down. "My doctor says I need to make some changes."

"You? Make a change? That I wanna see."

"I don't have much choice. I have diabetes."

"No kidding," Wash said nonplussed. "You gotta give yourself shots and stuff?"

"Not yet. I need to make an appointment with someone on our health plan to make a... plan."

"You're probably going to need to monitor your blood sugar levels. You'll be poking your fingers every day to draw some blood."

"I can live with that," I said. "Doc said I need to get cracking with diet and exercise. I think I can beat this."

"I don't think you beat diabetes. I think you keep it under control, but I don't think you can get rid of it."

"Yeah? Watch me."

I took another pull from the can and immediately wanted to spit it out.

"Okay," I said. I don't think I can do this..."

After lunch I made some phone calls, trying to set up meetings to interview people involved in the earlier abductions Gold had given us that morning. I was having no luck reaching anyone—apparently people worked during the day or something—and was in an ornery mood when a one of my fellow squad members wandered sheepishly into the room.

Paul Murphy was one of the guys I considered a friend. We'd both joined SCU around the same time; we were about the same age, with the same interests and had been partnered on many cases. Paul had been to my house many times and even taught Toby how to ride a bike during a Fourth of July picnic one year. On 'The Job' I can only describe him as "a cop's cop." He always had your back, ready to stand with you no matter what the situation. I believed he would lie for me and probably take a bullet for me.

Though I hoped we'd never find out.

Seeing his forlorn mug in the squad nearly broke my heart, not only because he was usually so happy, I had a feeling I knew what the look meant. We didn't have a rigid dress code but his sweat pants and hoody weren't workplace attire. He clearly wasn't a cop today.

I hopped up from my seat.

"What's happening, Murph?"

"I, uh…" he sputtered, pointing towards the locker room. "I just came to… get my stuff."

"What's *really* happening?" I said.

Wash walked up behind me but didn't say anything. Claire had turned in her chair to hear what was going on too. The other guys in the squad stayed away but I knew they were all straining to hear what we were saying.

Murphy took a breath and looked around. There was an agitated quality in his manner. He let the breath out and said, "I'm out."

"How long a rip?" Wash said.

"I'm done. I'm out. I had to turn in my gun and shield this morning."

I couldn't have been more shocked if he'd told me he was dying. I expected some departmental disciplinary action but I never thought he'd lose his job over this. He'd popped a few pills to stay awake during a stakeout. It wasn't unheard of. It wasn't common, but it happened. And that stakeout had led to a major score for the narcotics squad he'd been loaned out to. Now Internal Affairs was hanging him out, and for what? Being a good cop and doing what he needed to do to close a case and put a half-dozen world-class humps in prison.

"I'm sorry, Murph."

He waved a hand at me.

"It's my own fault," he said. "I should have known better."

"Come on, man."

"No, I should have known better."

"I think this is a bunch of nonsense, Murph. You don't get rid of a cop for popping a few pills."

He actually rolled his eyes at that.

"That's what you heard? That I popped a few pills?"

"That Padgett from I.A. called you an addict but didn't give it no attention."

"You know how those guys exaggerate everything," Wash said.

"Yeah," Murphy said. "Sometimes they don't."

It was as much of a confession as he was going to give to me, and more than I needed. I wasn't going to bust his chops about the amphetamines and he knew it.

"Ah, Murphy…"

"Yeah…"

"Don't take this lying down, man. You need to talk to your delegate or something."

"The Association will take care of you," Wash said.

"Forget it guys," Murphy said. "I'm done fighting this one. It's over."

He looked at me like he wanted to say "Goodbye" and get out of the building. I didn't want to make it any harder for him than it needed to be but I didn't want him to think I wasn't on his side.

"Let's get together, Murph. Come on over to the house tonight. We'll have a few beers… or something."

He shook his head and said, "I can't do it tonight, Kenny. I got a few things I need to do."

"Okay," I said. "We'll do it tomorrow, or some other day. Just…"

"Yeah," Murphy said. "Yeah, that'd be nice. I'll call you tomorrow. We'll make some plans."

"I'm serious, Murph. Give me a call. Bring Lo and we'll grill out or something."

"I can't promise Lois will join us, but I'll call you."

"You better."

"I will."

As he passed through the squad to the locker room, I knew that he was never going to call me.

Chapter 31

The neighborhood in West Allis was quiet when I got there. It was starting to look like rain and most parents probably pulled their children inside already, if kids even played outside anymore. It was a very different world than the one I grew up in and I wasn't so nuts about the way of it. Kids got fat sitting on the couch playing video games with a diet of potato chips and soda. Not that I believe the government, or the President's wife, had any right to tell us what to eat; I just think parents need to do a better job being parents.

Like I did with Jake and Nicole... Yeah, I'm a hypocrite. And now I was pretending to be Amanda's father.

It was Amanda who opened the door when I arrived, but Johnny D was standing a few feet behind her looking scared but not hiding from me. He was even faking a smile. Amanda wasn't happy to see me at all.

"What do you want, Ken?" she said.

"Can I come in?"

"What do you want?" she repeated.

Johnny twisted his body around nervously as if he didn't want to be there.

"I just wanted to see how you're doing."

"I'm fine. Look," she said holding her hands up and doing a graceful turn. "No bruises. No broken bones."

"Except for that hand you have in a cast," I said.

Johnny D stepped out of the hallway through the nearest door. I wanted to smile but I didn't want to give Amanda the impression I was amused by any of this.

"Yeah, well. That's last week's news."

"And what's next week's news gonna be?"

She rocked back and forth on her feet and said, "There's not gonna be any news next week. Johnny's being good to me."

Now I had to stop myself from laughing.

"Johnny," I called down the hall. "Get out here." I waited a few seconds. "Come on, you gutless punk. Get out here."

"He probably thinks you're gonna beat on him again," Amanda said.

"I might beat him if he doesn't come back."

I don't know if he heard me or not but Johnny stepped back up behind Amanda, careful to keep her between us. He managed to choke out a quiet, "What?"

"She says you're being good to her," I said.

"He is."

"I'm helping her," Johnny said. "I'm doing what you said."

"Are you gonna hit her again? You gonna lay hands on her again?"

"No."

"Why not?"

"I don't want you laying hands on me," he said.

"That's the wrong reason," I said.

"Well what do you want?"

"I want you to leave her alone," I said. "And I want you to do it because beating on girls is wrong and only a piece of crap would do it."

"I'm not going to do that."

"I don't believe you."

"Come on, Ken. You gotta give him a chance. You can't accuse him of something he hasn't done yet."

"Look at your hand, Amanda. He has done it."

"I'm not gonna hurt her again," Johnny said.

"You better not."

"I think you need to get going now, Ken. Leave us alone."

I knew how I wanted to respond, but I knew it wouldn't matter to Amanda. She was going to do what she wanted to do whether it made any sense or not. I couldn't fathom why she'd want to be with a guy that slapped her around the way this guy did but there was nothing for it but to leave her alone.

It broke a piece of my heart; I really wanted to help this

girl. We'd become friends when she became my C.I. and I truly hoped for better things. But now, as I looked into her eyes and saw that she was in earnest about me leaving her alone, I got the strongest feeling that I wasn't going to see her alive again. I didn't want to see her laid out on a table at the morgue like Dana Hujet but that seemed inevitable at this point. And then I'd have to track down Johnny D and...

"All right, I'm going," I said. "But remember what I said. He isn't gonna change."

I didn't stick around to hear if either of them replied.

Chapter 32

I didn't want to give Amanda up as a lost cause but it was looking like that was the case. I couldn't pretend anymore that she was going to listen to logic or reason. Girls stuck with guys who kicked the crap out of them; it happened all the time and there was no explanation for it. Her saying she loved the guy through swollen lips and a jaw wired shut sounded too stupid for words, but there it was. *It is what it is.* Probably the most meaningless phrase in the universe...

She wasn't going to accept my help, or even my advice, so why should I stick around and wait for Johnny D to take one swing too many?

It made me feel useless.

I drove back to the lakefront and had dinner at The Smoke Shack, easily the best BBQ joint in Milwaukee. I skipped the thirty-two-ounce soda and filled myself up with brisket and four-cheese mac and cheese instead. The carbs would turn to sugar eventually but I didn't care. I needed comfort food and I got it.

Sitting alone in the darkened restaurant, ignoring the music that was too loud and too modern for my tastes gave me time to think as well. I thought about my case that was going nowhere and it didn't take my mind long to circle around to Stephen Witt and his High Society magazine.

Extra sensory perception doesn't solve crimes, and it sure doesn't get convictions. That takes evidence—mountains of irrefutable evidence. I was still trying to find a connection between Witt and any of the girls that had been abducted.

Could I even say for sure that they'd been abducted? That was the most likely scenario but it was possible that they'd up-and-gone all on their own. None of their families would have found that theory credible but we were still looking for proof that they'd been snatched.

So, why couldn't I get this Witt character out of my noggin? He'd even been in jail when some of the abductions occurred. That took him off the chart right there, didn't it?

I pushed my plate aside and thought about smacking my head on the heavily lacquered tabletop. Then I remembered the boot I'd taken to my head-bone and figured some headaches weren't worth it.

Who had attacked me? And why? I still hadn't figured it out. I hadn't even told Lieutenant Gold or the other guys in the squad what had happened. I wasn't keen on them finding out that I'd taken the ride out to Witt's junkyard anyway. They knew I suspected Witt was dirty but they also knew I had no solid evidence to warrant a visit.

So what? I thought. I needed to know what it was about Witt that made me want to bust him so badly. Why did I keep seeing his ugly mug when I thought about this case?

I paid my bill and walked back to my car. It didn't take more than two or three nanoseconds to decide I was going to pay this guy another visit. I grabbed the Kansas, Audio Visions CD from the passenger side visor case, popped it in the player and started north.

I left my windbreaker in the car, which I parked half a mile up the road from Witt's. The walk would do me good and if someone chased me it wasn't too far to run.

Too far to run? What was I thinking? I was still carrying my handgun in a leather waistband holster. My steel, collapsible baton was on the other side of my hips, right next to my pepper spray. I wasn't planning on running from anybody.

I turned my cell phone off and removed the battery, just in case somebody tried to use the GPS to find me. It felt a little paranoid but then again, I was about to do something illegal.

I found a section of fence away from the road, hidden

from view of the apartments and houses in the area by thick bushes and, using a pair of bull cutters I'd brought along, cut the chain in eight places, making it easy for me to pull back and crawl through.

There was the smell again. Who'd have thought that corroded metal could stink so bad?

I walked slowly toward the house, listening for any sign that someone was there or that the dogs were wandering loose in the yard. I was also trying to remember the last time I'd had a tetanus booster shot; there was a lot of rusty crap lying around and the soles of my shoes weren't going to stop any of it from going into my foot if I put my full weight onto it.

One more bit of incentive to lose a few pounds.

I reached the spot where I'd gotten my head stomped on and crouched down next to a Dodge Grand Caravan that someone had taken for a roll on the highway. The sun was setting, casting long shadows. I tucked in as close as I could to the minivan and took a look around.

There was a wrecker truck that wasn't too much nicer than many of the cars I'd passed walking through the yard. It was canary yellow and had a Witt's Salvage sticker on the door.

Apparently, Witt was home. So much for just walking in the front door.

Over the years as a cop I'd learned a lot of tricks about opening doors and windows. It was a requirement of the job to know how punks did what they did. Occasionally we'd see something new but once we sussed it out we became experts on that too.

Witt's house wouldn't be any problem for me to get into; I just needed to figure out when I was going to do it. I didn't know anything about Witt's schedule or sleeping habits. I hadn't even considered that before arriving and I really wasn't prepared to sit there for hours until this goober, not to mention my legs, fell asleep.

I considered putting the battery back in my phone and making a call to the phone number on the door of his truck, telling him I was broken down on the highway and needed a wrecker. As ideas went it wasn't my worst but I had to consider the potential problems with it. What if he recognized my voice? What if he went on the call and found no broken down vehicle? Would it tip him off that someone was watching him? Or that somebody may be in his house at that very moment?

I gave it up as a bad plan.

I was considering heading back to the hole in the fence and my car when I heard the unmistakable sound of a front door opening and the screen door getting sucked shut as the air gets pulled into the house. Before the flimsier door opened, I'd shuffled as far back as I could, assuming the lowest profile possible.

I peered between the damaged vehicles to make sure it was Stephen that was on his way out the door. I didn't have the best view but his size and mincing way of walking was unmistakable, it was Witt and he was getting into the wrecker. Apparently, someone else really did break down on the highway…

I waited for over a minute after the truck sped away before I walked over to the house. I was still listening to make sure that nobody was around but everything seemed clear. When the dogs got a whiff of me and started barking loud enough to wake the dead and nobody's face appeared in any of the windows, I knew I was okay. Fortunately for the mutts they were on the other side of their pen; I wouldn't hesitate to shoot any of them that came after me.

The front door was mid-century and fairly flimsy. He hadn't stopped to use the deadlock so I only had to crack the lock on the knob.

Too easy for an old dog like me.

I pulled the stainless-steel lock pick from my back pocket, squatted down and looked at the lock. I figured it would take me less than a minute to get inside using the tool.

Instead I stood up, pulled a credit card from my wallet and slid it between the door and the frame, pushing the mechanism out of the strike plate.

The door opened and I stepped inside.

Chapter 33

The living room looked the same as when I'd been there the day before. It's possible that it was a little cleaner but that may have been my imagination. I couldn't see Witt going around with a dust rag cleaning the joint up. Then again, it didn't look like a college kid's apartment either so maybe he did do the occasional once-over.

There was one change to the room: the High Society with Brit's beautiful breasts wasn't in the magazine stand, it was sitting out on the coffee table open to the photo spread that had captured my attention so completely.

My first thought was that he left it there for me. My second thought was that if he'd gone to that much trouble, I should just take it.

It took a monumental effort to walk past it into the kitchen.

There was nothing special about that room either; it wasn't spotless but then it wasn't a mess either. There were a few dishes in the sink awaiting a wash and half a cup of coffee on the table that was still warm.

The cup made me think that he might be back soon so I didn't want to waste any time. If he came back while I was still there, I could get in a major jackpot. I had no right to be wandering around his house and I certainly didn't have a warrant. And I couldn't think of a story that would be believable explaining my presence there three times in one week.

Even if I found something in his house there was no way I could use it as evidence. All I wanted was to know I was headed in the right direction with this guy. I rationalized that I was there to clear Stephen Witt as much to confirm his guilt.

My quick search of the kitchen revealed nothing except

that he hadn't bought new utensils since Clinton was President. His heavy-duty pizza wheel had oxidized in a few places and the plates had chips. No laws against that.

The stairs leading to the second floor were behind the kitchen, near the back door. I couldn't find steps to a basement, which seemed odd in a house this far north, built in the mid-twentieth century.

I walked up to the second floor, stepping on each step and listening for revealing squeaks or creaking. If I needed to get out on the Q.T. it would help to know which stairs might give me away. It helped that they were carpeted; they hardly made any noise at all.

The hardwood hallway was a different matter. Every step seemed like a symphony of noises. It was fifteen feet long with four doors, one of which was a bathroom.

The first one was a musty smelling bedroom that was cluttered with dirty clothes and model cars. There was a poster on the wall for a movie called "Damaged" with a young woman holding a butcher knife in one hand and a younger girl in the other. They were sitting backed up against a wall and the one holding the knife was clearly protecting them from something. I'd never heard of the flick but I made a mental note to find out what it was all about. It must have meant something to Witt.

I closed the door and walked to the next room.

The sun was setting on the opposite side of the house and I had to stop myself from flipping the lights on to see. The window faced the junkyard but I still didn't want to announce that I was here.

This bedroom was bigger than the first and clearly where Witt bunked down. There was a queen-sized bed covered with an eiderdown quilt that must have been sizzling in the summer. Like the kitchen nothing in the room looked new. The furniture was probably handed down from his parents and the carpeting was stained with food and motor oil. The wallpaper had been painted dingy green years ago and was beginning to peel at the seams. There was dust on a ceiling fan that clearly hadn't been run in a very long time. Beyond the dilapidated condition there was nothing weird in this room either.

The third door was at the end of the hallway and closed, but there was a gap at the bottom unlike the others in the hallway. It was also the only door that had been closed—I would need to remember that when I left.

I pushed the door open to find it as dark as the room facing the junkyard. There was a window on each side but they each had blackout blinds and heavy curtains covering them. I still wasn't going to chance turning on the light but I figured I could use my Mini Maglight. I pulled it from my pocket and twisted the top to turn it on.

As I looked around my body seemed to drop ten degrees and I felt a strange pressure on my bladder. I suddenly felt like I needed to find a toilet.

The room was filled with Nazi memorabilia. And not just the kind of antique store crap that any run of the mill white supremacist would have laying around the rec room. Oh, there were pictures and even a red, white and black Swastika flag pressed under glass, but that barely scratched the surface. There were letters from the desk of Heinrich Himmler to Rainhard Witt matted and framed. Another letter that looked like a commendation signed by Field Marshall Jost prominently displayed next to a photograph of what I presumed was the soldier and Witt's... father? Grandfather? A shadow box held three Iron Cross medals and the skull and crossbones insignia from an SS officer's hat.

nur Offiziere.

It would never hold up in court. It wasn't proof of anything but a tasteless collector.

There was an antique silver table in the corner with a glass lid. The piece was a hundred years old and probably very valuable, especially in the well-maintained condition it was in. What was inside was worth quite a bit more.

There were medals and ribbons, the kind a soldier would affix to his dress uniform. Any text on them was in German and words I didn't recognize. It became clear to me that the collection was from more than one person, most likely several soldiers. It was possible that many were purchased from other collectors or on the internet but the way there was no dust on any of them made me think that at least some of them had sentimental value to Witt.

The prize piece of the collection was a Luger resting on silk bedding in the middle of the silver table display. It was a beautiful 9MM pistol that despite being meticulously cleaned and oiled had seen better days. The end of the barrel showed signs of rust, as did the ejection port on the upper body. My guess was that it spent some time under water and I doubted that the gun could fire safely anymore. It was a valuable paperweight but not much more—not that most people would know that when it was pointed at their face.

I turned the flashlight on a nearby bookshelf not unlike one I'd made in high school shop class my sophomore year.

Every book was about Hitler or The Nazi Party. There were copies of Hitler's and Rommel's books, both of which looked like collector's pieces and could pull a pretty penny if Witt ever wanted to sell them. There were two different series of Time/Life books loaded with pictures and enough text to keep a reader busy for months. Half the books were in German.

The Third Reich was not a passive or passing interest for Stephen Witt. He was the real deal, this guy. He'd devoted time and a lot of money to learn what he could about the Aryan dream.

nur Offiziere.

If I'd looked through these books would I find a picture of that tattooed on a young woman? Or read about it?

Witt was my guy; I was sure of it. Meeting up with him had been an accident; a coincidence, if you believe in them, but my intuition told me that he was the guy I was looking for. My gut told me there was something wicked about him and now I'd verified it, to my satisfaction at least.

Chapter 34

I turned the beam of my flashlight to the corner of the room to the left of the door, away from the museum of Nazi artifacts, and found several boxes stacked up.

Not several boxes, there were at least twenty of them, the kind a comic book collector would have, except bigger. And they were all labeled on the front end with black marker; "Oui," "Penthouse," "Hustler," "High Society," "Playboy." There was one marked "Miscellaneous." The dates on the boxes went back to the late 1970s and ran up to the present.

Witt really did collect skin magazines. He really did catalogue and protect these things.

I took the cover off a box and pulled an issue of "Hustler" from it. The paper was still glossy but it showed signs of wear. It had clearly been thumbed through many times over a period of more than twenty years. In some places the pages stuck together, a result of static and not anything more nauseating.

I put the issue back where I had taken it from, careful to return it to the exact spot.

I rolled the beam of light over the collection, amazed at the effort that had gone into not only collecting them, but maintaining them as well. I'd never seen such a comprehensive collection of adult entertainment magazines and I had to admit, I was impressed. The dedication of time and money to this library was staggering. And these twenty boxes couldn't hold every issue of these magazines from the last thirty-five years. There must be a garage full of containers like these somewhere.

I put the flashlight in my mouth and pulled the cover off another box. It was full of Playboys, but not the American publications; these were all German.

The guy collected in two languages.

For a moment I gave Witt credit that he actually bought the magazines to read them but quickly changed my mind. That could be possible with Playboy but nobody collected issues of "Hustler" and "Oui" because they contained great journalism. I don't think I ever noticed words except for the title on the cover.

I checked a miscellaneous and found it full of bondage magazines, the kind you don't find at the Open Pantry convenience stores. These were serious, hardcore and very violent images using every sort of sexual toy you could imagine and a few I'd never believed were real.

Was this Stephen Witt's thing? Was he into this bondage thing? If he was, where was the evidence of it? There were no hooks or gimp outfits in his bedroom. I didn't see any whips, chains or leather straps even. If this was his bag he must have a dungeon someplace.

And how does someone make the jump from looking at pictures of naked women to hurting them?

"Don't hurt me again."

Carrie's words echoed in my ears, only this time they were accusing me.

We enjoyed a hearty physical relationship; you might even say vigorous. We took pleasure in our lovemaking and I liked to think I give as good as I get. We didn't dress up like something from a Mad Max movie or try to asphyxiate each other but I think we were plenty adventurous. I certainly never tried to hurt my wife but apparently I got carried away on a few occasions.

Maybe it wasn't as long a jump as I thought.

I shoved the magazines back in the box with considerably less care than the others I'd found. Something made them far more distasteful than the other nudie books and I couldn't quite put my finger on it. I never indulged in hardcore porn, as some called it, but I never had any real prejudice against it. I'd investigated deaths that bled into that subculture and while violent death always troubled me my attitude was always live and let live with the bondo crowd. There was an intrinsic violence to the S&M lifestyle, just like there was with homosexuals, that didn't appeal to me but I couldn't make a case that it made them bad people. For all I knew the girl who cut my hair or my dentist might be into this. So, why now, at this moment, was I offended by it? Was it because I thought the guy who owned it was a pedophile murderer?

Seemed like a good reason to me.

I shut the light off and was turning to the door, anxious to get out of that room when I heard the unmistakable sound of a vehicle pulling to a stop outside.

Chapter 35

I pulled the shade away from the window, the one that faced the junkyard, only to find it had been covered by a thick layer of black paint.

As quietly as I could I walked back to the bedroom and looked out that window. That glass had not been painted over but it was covered with a film of dust that made the visibility lousy.

I could see the full yard from this point, including the vehicle that had driven in. It was a full-sized white van—maybe a Ford—and it had driven past the house to the pen where the dogs were going crazy. The driver stepped out and the dogs settled down.

I squinted through the dirty pane but couldn't get a clear look at the guy. The sun was setting on the opposite side of the house, which didn't help me any either. I thought about wiping a section of the window but I didn't want to make any noise that might tip this guy off and give away my position; I surely didn't want to leave any proof that I'd been in Witt's room. The driver opened a lock on the gate and drove the van to an outbuilding that wasn't visible from the ground. Careful to not run over one of his mutts he backed up to the only door on the building.

Whoever it was knew the layout. More importantly, the dogs knew him. It could have been Witt; I couldn't get a clear view of his face. Maybe Witt had switched the wrecker for the van so he could transport something easier and without the whole world seeing it. The other truck really wouldn't have room to hide anything effectively.

I stepped away from the window and pulled the phone from my pocket. I'd forgotten that I'd turned it off and scrambled to power it up again. I hadn't turned the volume down so when it powered up it played a four-note jingle that made jump a little and drop the phone. It bounced on the hardwood floor and I scrambled after it.

To me it sounded like a gunshot in the quiet of the house but when I'd managed to get my hands on the crazy device and looked out the window the driver had opened the back doors of the van and was moving into the building.

The van was pointed in the direction of the house, not exactly towards the window where I was but not too far away. If he'd taken a moment to look towards my particular spot he would probably see something moving in the shadows of the bedroom.

I slid my finger across the screen to get to my menu and punched the icon for my video recorder. Being the cheap, piece of junk phone that it was it took about fifteen seconds for the camera to turn on. Making sure to stay below the windowsill I held the camera with my forefinger and thumb so that it was pointing at the van, hoping I'd be able to scrub a good image or two from this section of digital video.

It didn't take long for my arm to get tired and my hand to start shaking; no doubt the sugar in the barbecue sauce playing a part. I gripped my right wrist with my left hand and tried to balance on the sill. I could see what I was filming so the arrangement worked out pretty good.

Fortunately, I didn't have to wait long. Whoever it was came out of the building looking like he was carrying something to the back of the truck. The open door blocked my view so I couldn't tell if it was a person or a bag of concrete mix. For just a moment I thought I heard a whimper over the van's engine but nothing I saw supported it. The driver, who I still couldn't quite make out, didn't slow down as he hopped in the driver's seat and drove away.

I stopped the phone's recording and shoved it back in my pocket. Drawing my pistol, I ran out of the room and headed for the stairs.

By the time I'd burst out of the front door the van was

turned onto Grandville Road, it's taillights fading from view. The motorized, chain link fence/door was sliding back into place. There was no way I could have made it to my car and followed; he was way too far ahead of me.

I looked back at the house and wondered if I should keep looking inside. Was there more to find beyond the Nazi shrine and a ginormous collection of nudie magazines? I didn't imagine there was so I holstered my weapon, walked up the stoop and shut the front door making sure I locked it.

As I made my way back towards the hole I'd made in the fence, I realized the dogs were barking at me again. But it wasn't the dogs that captured my attention. The building where the van had been parked suddenly had my interest.

What would I find behind those walls? Is that where Witt kept his larger stash? Or maybe it was a private dirty movie theater. Maybe he was sick of the quarter peep shows and had built himself a place to watch his, no doubt extensive, movie collection.

Or maybe that was his dungeon.

There was no way I was going to find out that night, not with those dogs pushing each other out of the way to jump over the fence and rip my throat apart. I figured I was safe on my side of the fence but any part of my body that crossed over would end up in the stomach of one of these crazy bitches. I thought about shooting them but I didn't need that kind of attention either. It was probably best that I left before Witt, or whoever it was came back.

My guts were still churning as I crawled through the hole in the fence and walked back to my car.

Chapter 36

It was just after ten o'clock when I got home. I needed a shower, as much to clean myself from the discoveries I'd made in Witt's house as to wash the sweat and dirt from my skin.

I had seen enough to convince myself that Witt was the guy who was responsible for Dana Hujet's abduction and death. There was still a major problem with that theory: what happened to her while he was in jail? I didn't have the answer to that question, but that didn't mean there wasn't an answer. I didn't want to think that there was some kind of group, or club or whatever that also indulged in the abduction of young women. In this day and age was it possible for that to exist without somebody saying something? Guys like Jeffrey Dahmer were able to continue what they did for so long because it was a one-man show. He didn't bring anyone into his inner circle while he murdered and defiled his victims by the most gruesome methods.

I hadn't been involved with the Dahmer case, but I knew a few guys that were. They'd seen some pretty wicked stuff and even though they were experienced detectives it still had a profound effect on them.

In my time on The Job I'd seen some gnarly things as well. I'd investigated the deaths of people from infancy to autumn years. Every method of killing you could think of I'd seen, plus some stuff you'd never imagine in your darkest dreams.

So, why was this Stephen Witt, with his Nazi memorabilia and porn collection make my skin crawl the way it did?

I was standing under the shower head, the hot water rinsing the shampoo from my hair for the second time. I reached for the bar of soap to start scrubbing the rest of my body down when I noticed a small, plastic brush that Diane used to clean herself with.

It was shaped like a fish. A clownfish even, like that Nemo cartoon. But a fish.

For some reason I couldn't figure out the idea of fish bothered me. I hadn't eaten any in a long time and we didn't own a fish tank. The image was making me uncomfortable.

There was a washcloth that I wasn't using hanging on the shower faucet. I grabbed the cloth, wrung it out and dropped it on top of Diane's brush so I wouldn't have to look at it. The image was still in my mind but at least now I didn't have to stare at it.

What was it all about anyway?

I grabbed the soap this time and raised it to my chest, which was the exact moment it slid from my grasp and landed in the collected water with a splash.

I muttered an expletive and reached into the water to grasp the soap again. I squeezed too hard and the soap flew from my grip again, this time ricocheting off the wall and the cast iron of the tub before landing in the water with another splash.

I squatted down to pick it up this time, imagining I looked pretty silly and glad nobody was there to witness my impromptu comedy routine. It reminded me of the time I was in Lake Geneva and I'd caught a walleye but couldn't get it into my bucket. The thing just flopped around on the dock and...

Another fish story. Another fish.

What in the world...

There was something I wasn't connecting, or something I wasn't remembering. Clearly it had something to do with a fish, but... that's as far as I got.

I carefully picked up the soap, careful not to squeeze it too tightly, and lathered up my torso.

The shower was invigorating and had even helped get my mind off Stephen Witt, but my confusion regarding aquatic vertebrates had completely derailed me. If I was ever going to fall asleep again I'd need to erase the whole concept of anything to do with water life.

Carrie was in bed, but I could hear music coming from Toby's room. It wasn't loud enough that he needed me to say something about it. In fact he probably just had it on in the background while he played a video game or did whatever it is teenage kids do these days. Diane's cell phone was sitting on the kitchen table. I knew she wouldn't leave the house without it so I could safely assume she was in her room as well.

I could safely do what I needed to do.

I turned on my computer and plugged the phone into a USB port. It took about fifteen minutes for me to transfer the video I'd shot from Witt's window from the telephone to my computer.

I opened the video player on my desktop and dragged the corner to make it as large as I could. It turned out to be too large so I made it smaller. When I found the sweet size it was only about three by four inches in size.

Someday I'd need Diane to show me how to set the resolution higher.

The image was shakier than I thought it would be and I probably shouldn't have zoomed in so far. Most of the time the driver of the van wasn't even in frame and when he was the image was unrecognizable. The picture was so bad I couldn't tell if it was Brad Pitt or Barack Obama.

I grabbed and exported a couple frames, one of the driver and one of the front end of the van. My idea was that I might be able to do something with them in Photoshop to scrub them a little cleaner, but they were still too dark and out of focus.

I needed one of those machines that they had in that movie Blade Runner, the kind that creates a virtual, three-dimensional world from a two-dimensional photograph. Yeah, that's what I needed—a machine that didn't exist. I could set it right next to the proof of Witt's guilt that didn't exist.

I was spinning my wheels.

I scratched my head, which was still wet from the shower. I rubbed my leg, drying my hand on the pair of shorts I'd thrown on and, using the mouse, moved the cursor to the Explorer icon and merged onto the information super highway.

The high-speed connection put me on the Internet in seconds and it wasn't long before I'd checked my email and moved on to a well-known site.

There was a page that catalogued scenes from movies where actresses were nude. It didn't matter if the actress was young or old, famous or mostly unknown; this web page had them. They were catalogued by first and last name as well as the title of the movie or television show that displayed their body. I'd discovered that it wasn't exhaustive but that was probably due to copyright issues or lawsuits from actresses who hadn't imagined a site like this existed when they went over the nudity clause in their movie contract.

I entered the site as a tourist and immediately clicked onto the "What's New" section. A list of actresses' names appeared, a couple I had even heard of. Nowadays the big thing in porn was to find a willing actress who looked like an A-list star and shoot a movie in a garage, wealthy person's home or a tool shed in an afternoon. Filming high definition video allowed for instantaneous upload onto a computer for editing and immediate posting on an Internet host. The whole process could be done in a day and subscribers could be watching what happened in the morning by dinnertime. Lunchtime if they were really quick about it.

I never liked the celebrity lookalikes. It defeated the purpose, knowing that the person in the movie wasn't the real actress. Watching an actress who vaguely resembled Julia Roberts wasn't going to show me what Julia Roberts looked like in the buff. It just wasn't the same.

"One fisherman always sees another fisherman from

afar."

It popped into my head without my even thinking about it. One fisherman always sees another fisherman from afar was a Russian saying that I'd read someplace years ago. The idea is that if you see someone who is like you, has the same job as you, the same background as you or the same hobbies or interests as you—you're going to see those qualities right away. You know your own kind.

Over twenty years on The Job had made me recognize fellow cops even when I was in other states. Cops know cops. Dirt bags know dirt bags.

Porn addicts know porn addicts...

Until that moment I'd never considered myself an addict. Yeah, I'd been looking at it for decades but I always thought I could leave it alone anytime I wanted. In fact, I had. Many times.

I thought about the full context of that and began to understand that I really did have a problem. I'd tried to stop looking at the magazines and web sites but something continued to draw me back, some lack of impulse control that didn't even register with me. Photos of naked women? Stag films? So what? Didn't it just make me appreciate women even more? Didn't it make me thankful for Carrie?

I guess I couldn't answer those questions. Or maybe the answer was buried somewhere in the lengths I went to keep my fascination with naked women and sexually explicit material a secret from her and everyone else. If I were a smoker, you'd smell it on me. If I were a boozer you'd catch a whiff of it on my breath and see my job performance hit the toilet. And drugs? It would show up in my blood tests. Those were things I couldn't hide for long, but I had kept my secret for decades. It didn't leave the same kind of signs that other addictions left.

So, what was the problem? I wasn't hurting anyone, was I? It wasn't that kind of an addiction, was it?

"Don't hurt me this time."

150

Did hurting Carrie have anything to do with me looking at porn? Again, I didn't know the answer to that. I guess I'd lost control during our lovemaking and gone a bit too far. I know I tried a few things that she was uncomfortable with and I'd had to work hard to regain her trust on a couple occasions. But had I crossed a line? And did that make me a bad person?

What effect did that mountain of pornography have on Stephen Witt?

I had just committed a felony trying to make the connection between Witt and Dana Hujet and the two things I found were lots of Nazi stuff and copious amounts of naked women. Evidence showed that Hujet had been sexually abused over a long period of time. Witt had clearly been building his collection for decades. Was it possible that the magazines and movies had flipped some switch in him that turned him from passive magazine thumber to sexual predator?

I remembered seeing a video interview with Ted Bundy, one of the more notorious serial killers in America during the 1970s, filmed on the day he was executed where he'd talked openly about his fascination with pornography and how it compelled him to kill at least thirty women. At the time I'd dismissed it as a last-minute manipulation and an attempt to shift the blame off himself.

I wondered what affect the magazines had on Witt. Was it possible that Bundy was telling the truth about the effect that material had on him and was Witt an unknowing disciple of Bundy's theory? Had the nude women got so far under his skin that Witt was compelled to rape and murder to satisfy his urges?

And what affect did it have on me?

I didn't think I was a violent person, a couple incidents with Carrie notwithstanding. I was less than gentle with Johnny D's hand but it's not like I dragged him outside and tuned him up. I didn't slap my kids around or anything like that. There had been a few times in the last twenty years that I'd had to fire my weapon but those had been in response to someone attacking me, not just throwing random shots at someone because I was hacked off.

The more I thought about it the more I kept coming around to how it affected my relationship with my wife. Or how it shaped all three of my marriages.

There had been a change in me while my first wife Terri and I were together. That was a time I was really indulging in videos and strip clubs and I could tell, looking back that it all had an effect on how I treated her. I wanted her to be as energetic and wanton as the girls I was seeing in the videos, even after she'd given birth to two kids and was tired from the time she woke up. Me coming home with half a drunk on and shaking her awake to satisfy me was too much. I never hit her but it wasn't any kind of stretch to call what I did mental abuse, which she did in the divorce.

My short marriage to Randi was about sex and nothing more. I was a cop during the day, she was a dancer at night. We slept when the other one was at work and when we were together we were wild and naked. Some of the guys thought it sounded like the perfect marriage but it wasn't and it self-destructed in a very short period of time.

Was my marriage to Carrie perfect? No, but no marriage was perfect. It was just a matter of how many things weren't ideal about your partner and how far you were willing to compromise. For Carrie and the kids, I was willing to take a bullet. In my way of thinking that meant I loved them. As imperfect as I was, I still loved them.

What was Witt's story? Did he ever have a wife? Did she leave him because of his sexual tastes? Did that cause him to abduct girls and abuse them? The more I thought about it the more I realized I knew squat about this guy. And much of what I thought I knew about him was speculation.

Was he a murderer? I thought so. Did having a pile of dirty magazines play into him being a murderer? I honestly couldn't say, but I couldn't honestly say it didn't. All I could say with any certainty is that my own fascination with sex, fueled by magazines, movies and girly websites had an effect on me.

I slammed my palms down on the desktop, careful to avoid the keyboard and mouse.

What was I afraid of? That looking at that stuff would turn me into a pervert or that it already had? Wasn't I disciplined enough to keep that from happening?

What would my wives have to say about that?

Being sexually promiscuous alone wasn't a criminal act. Even the S&M stuff from Witt's magazines wouldn't get you arrested, not if you didn't take it too far. Was it credible to think that every person who ever got into nudie pictures was going to abuse women? I didn't think that was the case.

So, why was I so worried about myself?

Was it because I wanted to give Johnny D the beating of his life? Was it because I spent too much time in an interview room talking to pus buckets who I would just as soon have shot in the head and dumped in Lake Michigan? Was it because I saw death every day on The Job and I'd heard a thousand people say, "I never would have guessed he'd snap like that?"

Was I better than the scumbags I hunted? I had a badge but that didn't make me perfect. I was more intelligent than the majority of them but smarts weren't going to help me when I had a serious mad-on and couldn't stop myself.

I knew what I was capable of, and it didn't make me comfortable.

I moved my cursor as quickly as I could to close the page, but my hand on the mouse was shaking, either from blood sugar issues or irritation from what I just now recognized as a personal weakness and it took three attempts. Instead of shutting the computer off I flipped the switch on the surge protector, killing the power to the computer and a desk lamp and plunging my world into darkness.

Chapter 37

In a lifetime marked by bad nights' sleep, that was one of the worst. I'd crawled into bed and Carrie had even moved her body against mine, probably to get warm and not to initiate intimacy. Her body was naked and cool to the touch and even in my frightened state I couldn't help being aroused by her. I slid my arm around her so her head was resting on my shoulder and held her protectively. After a minute or so she had lifted her head to look at me, maybe letting me know she was still awake, but she didn't speak. I figured she knew something was bothering me so she put her head down and went to sleep.

It took me a couple hours.

I'd hardly set foot in the squad room when Lieutenant Gold brushed past me and said, "My office."

My first thought was that he'd discovered how I'd spent the previous evening and was going to bust me out, but when he called for Washington to join us, I relaxed and followed.

"I got a call from Waukesha County," Gold said when we were in his office. "Another body turned up this morning. Dump job at a quarry right off the highway. They didn't even make much effort to hide her."

"Let me guess," Wash said. "Dark skin? Dark hair? Tattoo number on her?"

Gold nodded and said, "It's the same guy."

I couldn't speak. Part of me wanted to tell them what I saw but I would be admitting I committed a felony. I wasn't ready to do that yet, even though I was sure that Witt was connected to all this.

Had Witt left in the wrecker to switch vehicles so he could dump the body of the girl? It was certainly possible, but it still seemed a little strange. Why wouldn't he keep his van at the salvage yard?

"Was this girl all cut up too?"

"Strangled. Based on the ligature marks they assume it was with an extension cord."

I hated to admit that the strangulation fit my theory: that Dana Hujet was escaping and climbed through the razor wire on that fence.

So, why had he killed this girl now? Had something I'd done or said given Witt the impression that I guessed he was involved and now he needed to get rid of however many women he had left?

Did I help kill this girl?

"Were they able to…" I cleared my throat, which had suddenly become very dry. "Did they identify the body?"

"Yeah," Gold said. "Her name was Margaret Lockley. Her paperwork in on your desk."

"How do you know that?"

"Because I gave it to you a couple days ago."

I read Margaret Lockley's file from cover to cover, which didn't take very long. There wasn't a whole lot in it aside from her picture and family information. There were really only a few details about her abduction and one fact jumped right off the page.

She'd been abducted three years ago, while Witt was incarcerated.

Somehow this whole thing was bigger than Witt. It had to be. The guy was dirty, and he was involved with these murders, I was sure of it. My gut told me, and my experience agreed. And, unfortunately, I knew this guy better than I wanted to admit. We had too much in common, and that was bothering me too.

I had to stop thinking like that…

Clearly there was somebody else involved, at least in the kidnapping aspect of these crimes. If Witt didn't grab the girls then who did? And who whacked me in the melon the other day? He'd mentioned a nephew but there was no indication of anybody else living in his house. Did he have someone helping him out at the salvage yard?

For a second and a half I entertained the idea that Witt was completely innocent and all the concerns I had about myself were for naught. Unfortunately the idea didn't take root in my brain; I knew he was a bad guy and no matter how I tried to redirect his guilt it just didn't wash. I needed to get this dirt bag off the streets.

How was I going to do it? I couldn't arrest him; I had no idea what part he played in all this because I had no evidence.

I needed help if I was going to figure any of this out.

I checked my watch, looked up at Wash and said, "Let's grab some lunch."

"It's only ten o'clock," he said.

"It's ten twenty-two. If you don't want to eat you don't have to. Just come with me."

We walked over to the George Webb on Wisconsin Avenue and ordered coffee. I thought about getting a hamburger too but decided my body was screwed up enough and passed on it.

"What's goin' on with you? Is your blood sugar thing making you weirder than normal?"

"No. Maybe. I don't know. I just didn't want to talk to you about this in the squad."

"I'm listening."

I definitely heard some concern in Wash's voice, which wasn't his natural tendency. Both of us gravitated to sarcasm, especially when speaking to each other. I knew he was taking me seriously.

"This case…"

He waited for me to say more. After a few seconds he nodded to let me know I could continue.

"I still like this guy, Stephen Witt."

Wash rolled his eyes and sat back in his seat.

"Come on, man. You got jack on this guy. He's a white

whale."

"No, it ain't like that. That first girl—Dana Hujet—I bet she got cut up climbing through the razor wire on his fence."

"You said that before."

"And now he's getting rid of the other girls because he knows we're onto him."

"But we're not onto him."

"Okay, I'm onto him. He knows I like him for these kidnappings at least."

"You think he gets that from you talking to him that one time? If he's that smart we ain't never gonna catch him."

A waitress delivered our coffee and asked us if we needed anything else. I told her not right now and she went back to the counter and helped an older, overweight couple in matching windbreakers.

"What are you not telling me?" Wash said. "There's something else about this guy, isn't there?"

I hesitated and Wash picked up on it right away.

"What did you do?"

"I went out to talk to him."

"When?"

"The other night. That's where I got my face kicked."

"Witt did that to you?" He looked and sounded incredulous.

"I don't know who did it," I said. "It wasn't Witt though. He had stepped inside to answer the phone."

"Why did you think it was a good idea to go talk to him?"

I shrugged and said, "I wanted to get a look inside his junk yard. I made up some story about looking for a part for a car."

"You don't know nothing about cars," Wash said. "He probably saw through that right away."

"I think I did a pretty good job until someone blind-sided me."

"What did Witt do?"

"Brought me inside and made me an ice pack."

"Nice. So, I suppose you two are like blood brothers now

157

or something? Home boys."

I didn't want to tell Wash how much we had in common, but if I wanted his help, I was going to need to confide in him. He was my partner and I needed to trust him.

I said, "There's more," and told him about the night before and all I'd seen. He just sat and listened, letting his coffee get cold. I didn't leave anything out, including how all the dirty magazines made me feel. Wash knew I occasionally surfed the adult web sites but I could tell he was surprised that I was making such a strong connection with Witt based on a mutual fascination with sexual media.

When I was done, he was silent long enough for me to finish my cup of coffee.

"You're serious about this?" he finally said.

I was serious and I told him so.

"I don't see what you're talking about," he said. "So, what if you and him both looked at nudie pictures? I looked at nudie pictures too." The way he said "nudie pictures" made me feel dumb, like they were baseball cards or something.

"It's not something I can explain, man. It's something I feel in my gut."

"Your gut is a mess, Kenny. Ever since you started eating the diabetic food."

I didn't bother to tell him that there was no such thing as diabetic food. Or that it had nothing to do with liking Witt for the abductions.

"I know he's involved."

Wash held up his hands to put the brakes on me.

"Okay," he said. "Let's say, for the sake of this discussion, that you didn't commit a crime finding all this stuff about Witt out."

"Okay."

"And let's pretend it actually did prove that he was guilty of… anything."

I shrugged and said, "Sure."

"What are you gonna do about it?" He counted his points

off on his fingers. "You can't arrest him, you can't get a warrant, you can't use any of what you saw in court, you would probably find yourself prosecuted… you'd lose your shield at the very least." He held out his thumb. "I can't remember my fifth point. I had one but I forget."

"This is why I'm coming to you," I said. "I don't know what to do."

"I hope you don't think I got an answer."

"I was sort of hoping you would."

"Well, you're out of luck. The only alternative is to put him down. Get all Dirty Harry, Charlie Bronson on him. But I don't believe you got the stones for that."

Could I kill the guy? It would be as simple as pointing a gun at him and squeezing the trigger. Mechanically, yeah I could do it but I didn't want to—and it wasn't because I didn't have the stones.

I didn't want to think that death was the only way out for people like Witt. Something made me want to believe that he could be saved, maybe even rehabilitated. He didn't need to live until his natural death as a monster.

"I don't want to kill him," I said. "Let's take that play off the board right now."

"Then I don't know what to say. I don't know what it is you want me to say because you got nothing."

His phone chirped and he dug into his pocket to get it.

"Just think about it," I said. "Help me find a way to nail this guy, 'cause he'll snatch another girl sometime. And one or two of those other girls might still be alive—we don't know."

"I'll do what I can, but I ain't breaking into houses or setting up surveillance on some guy without a warrant. I don't have any *gut feelings* about this guy."

He slid a finger across the screen of his smart phone and read the text message he received.

"It's from Claire," he said. "She said we gotta get back to the squad."

Chapter 38

Police Department squad rooms aren't known for being quiet, so I knew something was up while we were still coming up the stairs. The usual keyboard clicking and telephone chatter wasn't happening the way it should and even the fluorescent tube that hummed so much you thought you were in a bee hive was quiet.

Claire was standing on the opposite side of her desk, close to the catching bench and the doorway when Wash and I stepped into the room. She didn't say a word, just nervously turned her head towards Lieutenant Gold's office.

Lance Padgett, the Internal Affairs rat, was by the Lieutenant's desk, pacing with his hands shoved deep into his trouser pockets. He looked aggravated which, I had to admit, made me happy. He was talking to Gold but in a quiet, controlled tone, not his usual bluster. Something told me he'd stepped on his own shoelaces.

Gold was seated at his desk listening. I could see him interject every once in a while, but most of the time he just leaned forward and rubbed his eyebrows.

"Schmidt," I said. The detective turned around, first taking a look at the Lieutenants office. "What's happening?"

"Something to do with Murph," he said. Then he turned back to his desk and whatever newspaper he was reading.

"What's going on here?" Washington muttered.

I just shrugged.

There were a couple other detectives in the room but nobody knew what was happening in Lieutenant Gold's office. I don't know how Schmidt knew it had something to do with Paul Murphy. He was gone. Why would Padgett be here regarding him anymore?

"All right everybody, listen up."

160

I hadn't even heard Gold's door open but there he was, standing in the front of the room, his own hands in his pockets, holding his coat open. Padgett was standing behind him, leaning against the wall making as small a profile as he could.

The other guys got up and walked over. Claire stepped closer, holding several files tightly to her bosom.

"What's going on, Lieu?" Wash said.

Gold planted a foot but scanned the room just below our faces like he didn't want to catch anyone's eye. It wasn't shame he was feeling, he looked like a parent that was about to give the kids bad news.

"I just found out…" He cleared his throat. "I just heard that Detective Paul Murphy… killed himself last night. I don't know much more about the details; those'll probably be coming out in the next few days."

My chin dropped to my chest and I felt sick to my stomach. I couldn't catch my breath for a few seconds.

Murphy was my friend—not just me but the whole squad. We'd worked alongside him and even spent time at his house. He was one of the few guys I could count on to have my back, and he knew I had his back.

I don't know everything about those stages of grieving but I went from disbelief to rage in world record time. I took a couple steps closer to Padgett, pointing at him as if I were driving my finger through his chest. If he weren't ten feet away, I would have.

"This is on you, you cheese eating piece of crap!"

I felt Wash's hand on my arm and Gold stepped between me and Padgett.

"Take it easy, Brady," Gold said.

Padgett looked at me impassively. I wanted to hit him; the jerk didn't care that he had driven a good cop to killing himself.

"Are you happy? You do this to a good cop and go on your merry way? You're scum; you piece of…" I trailed off without repeating myself.

Padgett's lip curled and he said, "He was a doper."

"No, he wasn't a doper! He popped a few pills to stay awake so he could get an even bigger piece of crap than you off the streets. He did it so your kids—god forbid you ever have any—so your kids can walk the streets of the city or play at the park without getting shot at!"

"You need to calm down, Detective."

I knew I needed to calm down, but I wasn't going to. I couldn't.

"You're garbage," I said. "You do more harm than good."

"Keep talking," Padgett said.

Gold put a hand on my chest. I pushed it away.

"You rats... all you do is divide good squads and good cops. Make us look at everybody sideways so we can't trust each other."

"You keep telling yourself that there are no dirty cops on the job," Padgett said.

I wasn't going to bite on what he was fishing for with that comment.

"Then go after them!" I said. "Let the good cops do their job."

"That's what I'm doing, Brady. I don't drop my finger on a name in the Policeman's Benevolent Handbook and decide to investigate them. By the time I get to where you see me there's already an investigation with plenty of evidence. Quit acting like what I do is any different from what you do."

"You don't have any idea what I do."

"I know plenty of what you do."

That caught me short for a second. Was he saying I was under investigation for something? Was that possible?

Padgett saw the look on my face and said, "You think we don't have a file on you?"

"You got nothing on me," I said.

"We got a file on everybody, Brady."

"You got nothing, you bum. You're a lot of gas; that's all

162

you got."

"You keep telling yourself that."

I stepped forward but Gold hooked his arm around me. For a smaller guy he had a solid grip.

"If you got something on me, use it. You're nothing but a rat. You're a rat that probably can't satisfy his wife so you gotta take down good cops."

He hesitated for a second, looking for words. Then he said, "Anything else? This is all good material."

"Yeah, take that material, roll it into a cone and jam it."

Gold pushed me towards my desk.

"So, that's what's going on," he said. "Get back to what you were doing." He turned towards Padgett. "You got anything else before you leave?"

The Internal Affairs man shook his head and said, "Nope."

"Then you know the way out." Gold turned to me and said, "Come on." He gestured to his office.

I closed the door behind me and turned to the Lieutenant.

"What is the matter with you?" he said, not hiding his irritation.

"What's wrong with me? A friend of mine—one of my partners just killed himself after that fink took his job away."

"Murphy did what he did. You don't have to go to bat for him against every P.P.D. joker in the department."

"That guys a jerk," I said gesturing to the empty section of floor where Padgett had been standing.

"Of course he's a jerk, but you let him get to you and you become the jerk."

"That's crap Lieu. He didn't need to come down here to our squad. He could have called and told you about Murphy over the phone. He was spoiling."

"And you gave him the fight he wanted. You feel better now?"

I didn't feel better. I felt lousy but I wasn't going to tell Gold that. I kept my mouth shut.

"Where are you at with that Lockley girl's body?"

"Nowhere yet," I said. We were going through the sheet when all this nonsense started."

My cell phone started ringing in my pocket. I pulled it out and looked at the number.

"I gotta get this," I said.

Gold nodded, then he said, "Sorry about Murphy."

Chapter 39

The phone call was from Todd Griffin, a uniform cop I'd worked with on a couple of cases. We weren't buddies or anything so I guessed he was calling on business. I stepped into the squad room and answered.

"Brady, it's Griffin. You got time to talk."

I didn't think I did but I lied anyway.

"I'm calling because I know you use a C.I. named Amanda, right?"

"Yeah, she's out of the picture right now, but yeah."

"Apparently, she's staying at 201 Chandler, over in West Allis. Did you know about that?"

"She told me. In fact I was over there the other day checking up on her."

"You might wanna get over here, Kenny," he said. "We got a D.O.A."

So that punk finally did it. Johnny D finally took one too many swings at Amanda and now she was dead.

I didn't even wait for Griffith to give me the details. I hung up, mumbled a few words to Claire and rushed out the door to my car.

What a day this was shaping up to be. Murphy kills himself and now Amanda gets herself killed. I wanted to help both of them—I'd offered to help both of them...

I pounded on the steering wheel as I wove through the I-94 traffic. If I wasn't so hacked off, I probably would have cried. Right now, I couldn't work up the tears because I was too busy thinking about what I was going to do to Johnny D when I found him.

And I would.

Johnny D didn't have the brains to get out of town, find some place to lay low for a while. I'd probably find him parked at the same stool at the same bar where he was the night he put Amanda in the hospital. He was a creature of habit and I was going to use that to bring him down. The best thing that could happen to him is to be picked up by a radio car.

I wasn't thinking straight. For all I knew the uniform cops already had him. I felt a migraine coming on…

There were three radio cars blocking the street near 201 Chandler. A crowd of civilians had gathered on the sidewalk as well, being held back by a single uniform cop. They hadn't put any tape up because the body was inside; there was nothing to see. I left the Impala crooked in the street, held my shield in my hand and made my way through the crowd.

I wasn't anxious to see Amanda's corpse; in fact, I didn't want to see it at all. I had an idealized image of her, born out of a photograph she'd shown me several months ago. In the picture she was a scrappy teenager with long hair and a big smile. It was before she'd started walking streets and shooting junk. There was beauty, and promise, and maybe even a bit of hope. It gave me a baseline for where I wanted her to end up again: in a house of her own, with a husband and a couple kids that she could take care of. Happy. Fulfilled.

A shameful memory popped into my head as well. I remembered a time when I sat across from her in that hell hole she called an apartment, wondering what she would look like if she cleaned up, inside and out. I wondered what that body of hers looked like with nothing on.

Years of abuse had ravaged her body and I had wondered what she looked like naked.

Now it was all out the window. The nice house, husband, and kid scenario as well as the sweet naked body. She was gone and there was nothing I could do to help, or hurt her anymore.

I leapt up the stairs onto the porch and pushed my way

into the house, holding up my shield so the uniforms wouldn't try to stop me. I passed one in the hallway and said, "Griffin?" The Officer pointed towards the back of the house.

I walked further down the hall, passing the kitchen, to a landing where the stairs went up. Another cop was coming down the stairs and I asked if Griffin was upstairs. He said yeah and brushed past me.

As my foot hit the first step my stomach started to turn. I felt the coffee I had at George Webb rolling back up on me and I had to force myself not to puke. I bit my lip to stop it from quivering.

By the time I reached the top stair I was sweating, and not from the heat. It surprised me how tweaked up I was getting about Amanda being dead. I never thought I had given her that much of a place, but now I was turning into a mope.

Come on, Kenny. Get it together.

Griffin leaned out of a doorway, saw me and gave a half-hearted gesture.

"That was quick," he said.

"What happened?"

"Near as I can tell the vic was taking a shower when someone went all Norman Bates. The weapon is between the wall and the toilet."

"Nobody touched nothin'?" I said.

"We know better than that."

"You got the guy that did this?"

Griffin gave me a look of confusion and shook his head.

"What are you talkin' about?"

"The guy that killed her," I said. "I'm pretty sure it was a guy called Johnny D on the street. Real name is John Delacroix."

Griffin's confused look didn't go away as he said, "You need to see this Brady."

He beckoned me to follow him into the bathroom.

The room was small but I was able to squeeze past Griffin

and get a look into the bathtub where the body was laying in a haphazard mound. The first cop on the scene had turned the shower off but the white basin was stained pink from blood. A puddle was collecting under the victim's right kidney where it had been punctured.

The violence of the murder wasn't what surprised me the most. What I was looking at made no sense to me at all.

"There was a wallet in the pants pocket on the floor," Griffin said. "Driver's license was still inside it."

He handed the wallet to me.

"This is John Delacroix."

It was Johnny D looking up at me, his eyes frozen in the most horrifying stare I had ever seen.

Chapter 40

"Any idea where she is right now?" Wash said.

I had called him to tell him what was going on and see if he had any suggestions. With everything on my mind my brain was fried and I could use his help.

"Amanda's in the wind right now," I said. I was walking through the house, looking for any clues about what happened here today. "I don't want to jump to any conclusions. This might not have been her doing."

"You believe that?"

"I want to believe it. There're no signs that she packed in a hurry or anything."

"It's not her house. Did she even have anything there?"

"I don't know," I said. "Quit harshing my mellow..."

"You don't have the facts yet, man. Let the forensics team get in there and see what prints they lift. I'd bet money she did it, but if you wanna hold out hope, that's cool with me. I don't know the ho, y'know?"

I didn't appreciate Wash talking about her like that but he was right, he didn't know her. I wanted to believe she was innocent and that Johnny D had made some other enemy. That didn't sound so farfetched to me. But somewhere inside me I knew that Amanda had done this.

I heard someone down the hall say, "What's SCU doing here?" When I looked, I saw two detectives out of the 6th District house on 27th Street. Their suits gave them away.

"Yeah, well..." I said to Wash.

"I'll see you when you get back here," Wash said and rang off.

Griffin stepped up to the detectives and said, "He knew the victim. We're pretty sure he knows who got him dead."

One of the detectives approached me and said, "You

169

probably don't remember me. My name is Markham."

He was right, I didn't remember him. Apparently, we'd crossed paths before, but I'd be dipped if I could remember.

"Yeah, sure," I said. "You guys caught this one?"

Markham jabbed a thumb in Griffin's direction.

"This guy says you know who did this maybe?" he said. "Maybe we can all go home early."

"Yeah and no," I said. "The vic's girlfriend is a C.I. She'd been staying here since she got out of the hospital."

"Who put her there?" Markham asked though he sounded like he knew.

"The vic—Johnny D they call him. He beat her up on a pretty regular schedule. I'd been trying to convince her to get away from him but she wasn't listening. The prevailing wisdom is that she snapped and went all ginsu on him."

"You wouldn't happen to know where she is now by any chance, would you?"

I shook my head.

"You would tell me if you knew, right?" He added quickly, "I'm just asking you to ask. I'm not saying anything."

"I really don't know, and yeah, I'd tell you if I knew."

I didn't enjoy lying to other cops but then I didn't enjoy giving up a friend either. I was troubled by what was happening and I just wanted to understand it.

There was too much I wasn't understanding right now: The whole thing with Witt, Murphy killing himself, and now this. All this stuff was gnawing at me and I really didn't know how much more of it I could take.

I felt my phone vibrate in my pocket just before it started ringing. I pulled it out and looked at the number but I didn't recognize it. I separated myself from Markham with a gesture and steeped out the back door.

"Hello," I said.

"Kenny?"

My blood froze when I heard Amanda's voice. For a moment I couldn't speak, couldn't move, couldn't do anything. Then I looked around as if I might find her watching me from one of the other houses that surrounded me.

"Where are you?" I said.

"You were right," she said. "You were right."

I could hear the pain in her voice. She was holding the phone so close to her mouth that every breath was like a windstorm.

"Tell me where you are," I said. "I'll come get you."

"No, I'm not gonna... I can't do that. I just wanted to tell you that you were right."

"Right? What was I right about?"

She sobbed and said, "He was never gonna change. Like you said. He was never..."

So that's what happened. He'd beaten her again. He smacked her around and she'd had enough so she killed him.

"Tell me what happened, Amanda. I can help you if you tell me what he did."

She exhaled a ragged breath and said, "We were talking... then we were fighting. He was screaming at me. Then he stopped." She took another breath. "Then he said he was gonna take a shower because he needed to cool off."

"So, what happened then?"

"He took a shower."

"Did he touch you? Did he hit you or anything?"

"He was in the shower, and I snuck in the bathroom. I snuck in and I stabbed him with a knife from the kitchen."

"Did he hit you?" I said again.

"He never got the chance," she said. "He was pretty surprised to see me with the knife."

Oh, man. What was she saying? What in hell did she do?

"You killed him? He wasn't beating you up or nothin'? You just killed him?"

"He didn't hit me this time," she said. "But you were right. He wasn't gonna change."

Chapter 41

The squad room was empty when I returned, not a surprise since it was after five and SCU didn't have a night shift. The lights were off and the only illumination came from the windows. I walked through the darkness to my desk and booted up my computer.

I wished I could restart this entire day as simply as I restarted the desktop PC. It had been a disaster since I'd first stepped through the threshold this morning. My entire day had been awash in death. Margaret Lockley, Paul Murphy, Johnny D. And lurking above it was the specter of Stephen Witt. The day had gone to crap so quick I hadn't even had time to think about him.

It felt like there was a hurricane passing through my head. I needed to calm down. I connected to the internet and typed in the address of an oft visited web site.

In a few moments I was in familiar territory, taking in bodies that were both hard and supple, skin that was smooth and clear and facial looks that projected wanton sexuality. They were Photoshopped to perfection, which was just what I needed. I didn't want to think about my day; I just wanted to lose myself in beauty where I wouldn't have to think about my blood sugar level, or Amanda or… Witt.

Why did I keep coming back to Witt? This guy had almost as much a hold on me as the women. If I didn't get something on this guy soon—

"What are you doing here, Brady?"

It was Doug Haggerty, one of the detectives in the squad. I hadn't heard him coming up the stairs and now he was walking towards his own desk, further back in the room than mine.

I considered scrambling with the mouse to get rid of the

page I was looking at but I knew how that would look. Haggerty didn't seem like the kind of guy that would squeeze my shoes about it anyway. He was fairly new to the squad, maybe six months, and was still trying to make a good impression. He was a good detective too.

"Hey Haggerty," I said. "I'm just... doing some research on this Hujet case."

"What a pain that one is, huh? You can't seem to catch a break on it. Wash was telling me about it before."

He walked past my desk and looked at the computer screen. If he was surprised by the images of nudity and animated gifs of hardcore sex, he didn't show it. In fact, he was amused.

"That's the kind of research I can dig my teeth into," he said. Pointing to a picture he added, "I think I went to school with her." His laugh made it clear he was joking.

"There's a guy I'm looking at for these abductions," I said. "He's into this kind of stuff."

"Lots of folks are. It's not like I never indulged."

I recalled that he was engaged to be married for the first time at age thirty-seven.

"Does your fiancé give you her blessing?"

"We don't sit down and surf the sites together if that's what you're asking. I only do it if she's not around."

He went to his desk and opened a drawer. From it he withdrew a small, gift-wrapped box with a ribbon and bow on it.

"And I didn't get you anything," I said.

"It's Glenda's birthday. I forgot her present. That'd be perfect, huh? Show up to dinner empty handed. That'd make for one long, lonely night, huh?"

"You'd probably end up sitting here next to me, looking at this stuff."

"Yeah, I don't know," he said. "It's not something I really want to do. I mean, when I look at that stuff all the time it's not Glenda I end up thinking about."

"What do you mean?" I said turning around in my chair

to face him.

He leaned against the next desk over and said, "If I walk into the apartment and she's standing there with nothing on we will go to town. It don't matter whether I've eaten dinner or not." He emphasized "go to town," making sure I knew what he meant. "If I'm looking at web sites or watching dirty movies, I can start wondering about pretty much anybody. I come in here in the morning and see Claire and I start wondering what kind of underwear she has on and if she waxes, if you know what I mean."

I knew exactly what he meant, and I said so.

"Not that Claire's not a pretty girl or anything," he said. "It just doesn't help my relationship with Glenda any." He stood up and said, "Plus, I read someplace that porn is addictive as heroin."

He stood there as I thought about what he said. Addictive as heroin? How was that possible? It's not like I was shooting something into my blood that was giving me a physical, chemical change. I was looking at photographs. Where's the harm?

"Don't hurt me again."

And again, I was reminded of Witt and his collection.

"You better get to your girl's birthday," I said.

Haggerty jumped up from the desk with a lighthearted spring. He tossed the gift box in the air and caught it.

"See you tomorrow, Brady."

I muttered a "See you later" as he walked out the door of the squad room.

I stared at the women on the screen and wondered what effect they were having on my marriage. I thought about the effect they'd had on my first two marriages. If I were being honest with myself, I could see that it was an enormous elephant in the room.

And it was an elephant that had settled in. My house had been built around it and it was threatening to knock the whole place down.

I hated thinking in metaphors like that, but it was true. Dirty pictures had probably claimed Stephen Witt's humanity and I wasn't ready for them to claim mine. I knew what I had to do if I was going to be able to live with myself.

And I had to do it now.

Chapter 42

Everyone has secrets. I don't care who you are; you have secrets. Every relationship has secrets. Parents keep secrets from their kids; kids keep plenty of secrets from their folks; even best friends keep secrets from each other. Husbands and wives have secrets.

And if being a cop for over twenty years taught me anything it's that secrets don't stay secret. Sometimes you out the secret and sometimes it outs you.

I met Carrie at Jason Voight's retirement racket. She was there with another cop that she'd been seeing for a couple of weeks, a relationship that didn't last the next couple of weeks, mostly because of me. She was mid-thirties—a little younger than me, with short, blonde hair and killer legs. We played eye games across the bar before I bought her a drink and moved ourselves to a quieter corner of the room. It seemed like we told each other everything that night; I told her about my two busted marriages, she told me about hers and the two kids. She even told me that she was a closet Cubs fan. It seemed like we were trying to scare the other away before everything got too crazy.

If that was the plan it didn't work. She got her hooks into me and, if she is to be believed, I got my cuffs on her, at least figuratively. Even her kids liked and respected me.

The courtship was brief and the wedding was simple: her, her kids and me. My kids didn't show.

We prided ourselves on being able to talk about anything; except for the stuff I couldn't tell her about regarding The Job. I even told her about that sometimes. She knew if I was in one of my sullen moods to just leave me alone, give me some space and eventually it would pass. She understood that sometimes I just needed to be by myself.

I don't think she ever considered I was keeping anything from her. Of course, there are things we kept to ourselves; like grabbing drive-thru on the way home because you're too hungry and can't wait for dinner. That kind of stuff doesn't matter and Carrie wouldn't think less of me if she knew I'd eaten a Chili-Cheese Burrito while driving.

But there were other things about me—about who I am that would make a difference, and I'd waited way too long to tell her.

I'm no believer in mental telepathy or E.S.P. I do believe that we have senses that don't fall under the normal five we are aware of. Whether it's a gut feeling or instinct or whatever, it's saved my hide on many occasions. It's also warned me that something was wrong when Carrie was in one of her moods.

But tonight it was Carrie who could tell something was up.

I'd been sitting in my office, staring at the computer for half an hour when I saw her standing in the doorway. She was wearing one of my old Packer t-shirts that hung down to about mid-thigh. She still had killer legs.

"Ken," she said gently. "Are you all right? I don't remember you coming in to kiss me."

She was right; I hadn't kissed her. I couldn't kiss her. I could hardly even look at her at that moment. I felt lousy about that too, but there was something I needed to get off my chest.

"My dad..." I started, "never really taught me anything about women... sex... any of that stuff."

"Ken?"

"I didn't have that kind of example that other kids had. My old man mostly yelled at mom. I don't know if he slapped her around or not. I saw him shove her down one time so I guess you could say he was physically abusive."

Carrie sat in the chair on the other side of my desk. She pulled her feet up under her.

"What happened Ken?" she said. "What's going on?"

177

"I swore I'd never be like the old man. I didn't hate him but I didn't love him neither. He died when I was sixteen—I didn't cry or nothing. I mean, it's not like having him around made us feel safe. Even my sister didn't seem too broken up about it."

"Does this have something to do with the case you're working on?"

I wanted to tell her it did, and that wouldn't have been a lie. If it hadn't been for Stephen Witt I wouldn't have felt the need to have this conversation at all.

"I'm sorry," I said. I wanted to tell you that."

"Sorry for what?" Carrie said. "You're not like your dad. You've never hurt any of us."

"I've never laid hands on you that way but... "I couldn't believe how dry my throat got in that moment. "But I know I've made you do things... things you didn't want to do."

She stared at me for a long moment and I could see her go from total confusion to thinking she knew for certain what I meant. I'd never seen her look so mortified.

"Are you talking about...?"

"In bed," I said. I couldn't even look her in the eye. "I'm talking about—"

She cut me off with an uncomfortable grunt and a wave of her hand.

"I'm really sorry."

I looked up at her, hoping for a look of forgiveness or some sign that she accepted my apology. Her face was still a mask of confusion.

"You gotta tell me what's going on in your head, Kenny."

"I was nine years old the first time I saw a dirty magazine," I said looking away at the citations I had framed on the wall. "One day after school I went to my buddy Gene's house to play... I don't know, cards or something. We were playing in the basement and we found his old man's stash of Playboys, Hustlers, High Society. We must've sat there for hours looking at them until his parents got home. I'd never seen a naked woman before that."

Carrie stared at me and waited for me to continue.

"I couldn't tell you how many times we cracked open that collection and looked at the pictures. Some of those women are still... burned into my brain."

I tried to shake the memories from my head, but they were still there. I knew they'd always be there. I didn't have a mental broom big enough to brush them away.

"When we got older his parents subscribed to one of those early movie channels that ran skin flicks after ten o'clock. I Am Curious... Yellow was the first one I saw. The old Emmanuel movies... saw 'em all. That and, like, a hundred others. Sometimes we'd even watch them with his dad."

I could tell she was uncomfortable with what I was saying, but I needed to continue.

"That was all such a long time ago. You don't have to..."

"In high school I started watching more x rated stuff. There was a video store nearby that had a curtained off section and every time my parents were gone for the weekend or something, I'd have a 'Behind the Curtain Party.'"

"What does that mean?" I noticed her voice was becoming colder now.

"The video store had a section they curtained off with all the x-rated stuff. I guess I looked eighteen to whoever was working. That or they didn't care that they were renting dirty movies to a kid."

I took a breath and soldiered on. "By then I'd started buying my own magazines. And I'd go to the bookstores to read the books by 'Anonymous' —just stand there in the fiction section reading. There were other series of books, a series of westerns with some trashy looking covers. They had sex in them too. I'd skim them until I found some hot scene and read that. You know, it didn't even matter that my dad never taught me anything about sex before he died. I learned it all from movies and reading those books."

"Okay stop," Carrie said. "I'm not sure why you think I'd want you to tell me all this. I mean, we're talking about thirty years ago."

"And I should have told you about it a long time ago."

"Why? Did you think I imagined you grew up in a monastery or something? Or that in this day and age you'd never seen a dirty movie?"

I leaned forward on his desk, holding my head in my hands.

"It's not that easy, Carrie," I said. "I let a genie out of a bottle and it doesn't go back in very easily." I shook my head and said, "It's an addiction."

Carrie was quiet. I imagined her just staring at me, and then she said, "Are you kidding me?"

"I've tried to quit, believe me," I said looking up at her. The look on her face was one-part denial, three parts furious.

"I was at the academy when I got a call from Gene's mom. He'd been getting into asphyxiating and accidentally hung himself. His wife came home and found him in the garage. That night I burned every magazine I had. I got rid of all the video tapes... everything. I thought I had it kicked. I really did. When Terri and I got married I hadn't looked at a dirty magazine or movie in years.

"Then one day, not long after I got my shield, I'm working a homicide on the south side. Some dancer at a... 'gentlemen's club' gets beaten to death by one of her admirers. I'm standing in this club, interviewing these girls, and they're all standing there with nothing on and I gotta look at them to keep my mind off the stink of this place, and the stink off the body that's lying between the dumpsters out back. I'm fighting with myself to not look at them like a piece of product, but they're standing there with nothing on, not even trying to cover up. I'm trying to pay attention to anything else about them; their eye color, their moles, the track marks on their arms, and finally I just say to myself, 'Forget it. She's an attractive girl. There's nothing wrong with admitting that.' And the minute I give an inch the dam breaks and all that crap I'd pushed back—the movies, the magazines, the books—it's all right back in my mind. All the stuff I tried to forget..."

180

I hit myself in the forehead with the palm of my hand trying to chase away decades' worth of images. The memories of women's bodies that I'd only seen in magazines or videos and others I'd seen from a distance, through the smoky haze of a topless bar.

"Is that why Terri left you?"

Carrie and I had agreed years ago that we weren't going to talk about our past marriages, but considering I was the one who'd opened this can of worms I couldn't hold back now.

"Yeah," I said.

"And Randi too?"

I shook my head and said, "Randi was a mistake from the beginning. I left her."

There was more to that story but I didn't think those detail would have made a difference at that moment.

Chapter 43

It seemed like an hour before Carrie spoke again. She looked at me, looked around the room, at the floor and at her hands before she said, "So, how do you expect me to respond to all this?"

In some part of my mind I hoped she'd take me into her arms and tell me that it was going to be okay, that she would hold my hand and walk me through this dark place I'd been living in for so long. The rational part of my brain told me that was optimistic at best. What did I think she'd do? I had no idea and told her so.

I could see her trying to process all this and wanting to ask me a hundred questions. I wanted her to ask them; I imagined they would help her understand what was going on in me. I had already prepared answers for most of them. Leave it to Carrie to ask me one I hadn't even considered.

"Where do you keep your stash?"

"My stash?"

She waved a hand around in an all-encompassing gesture.

"Your magazines and movies," she said. "You're telling me you're an addict but I haven't seen so much as a Playboy. Where do you keep all your smut?"

I didn't even need to say any words to answer her. I turned the computer screen towards her, typed a few keystrokes and in a matter of seconds the screen was full of sexual images.

"Oh no…" she moaned. "Is this what you…?"

Even with everything I had been telling her Carrie was still shocked to see the web page I had up. You couldn't even call it smut—it was far worse than that. There were pictures of women, most of them looking like they were only minutes past their eighteenth birthday—if that. They were in positions or doing things that I wouldn't consider trying to get

Carrie to do, and she could get adventurous. On the side of the page were animated gifs of things she probably wouldn't discuss with her closest girlfriends.

She pushed the thin computer screen with both hands, sending it crashing to the desktop face down where it scattered a pile of notes. She collapsed to the floor and sobbed into her elbow, waiting for me to say something.

"It's that easy," I said. I spoke gently but I needed to be firm. "Today you can get this stuff on your cell phone."

"Oh my god. Oh my god..." she moaned. "What are you doing, Ken? What are you doing to us?"

"I'm telling you something I should have told you eleven years ago."

"This is great," she said lifting herself up to her chair. "My husband tells me he's a pornography addict..."

Pornography. The word was like a punch in the gut. It wasn't a word I used very often, even in police reports. I'd certainly never heard Carrie use it.

I nodded and said, "I guess, if you want to call it that."

"That's what it is."

I didn't feel like getting hung up on terminology so I pushed ahead. "Okay, fine. It's porn."

"So, what do you expect me to say?" she said. "That everything is okay? That I'm okay with it?" She gasped for a second as her next words got caught in her throat. "Aren't I enough for you?"

This was an avenue I really didn't want to go down. There was no good way to answer her question.

"It's not like that Carrie," I said. "I don't look at this stuff because I get off on it. The truth is I don't even find it arousing anymore."

"But you can't stop? Is that what you're saying?"

"I'm saying this isn't about you. This is a problem I've had since... long before we even met."

She pulled herself up on the chair and stood behind it.

"Of course, this is about me," she said. "I knew when I turned forty things were going to change, but for crying out loud…"

"Carrie, you're not listening." I needed to keep her from thinking she had something to do with this. I definitely needed to keep her from thinking I wasn't satisfied with our physical relationship. "This is a problem I created when I was a kid. I have no idea how I'm gonna beat this but I gotta do something. Right now, I'm admitting I have a problem."

"You've been hiding this for thirty years? Who else knows?"

"Terri figured it out," I said. Randi might have known, I don't know. I don't think she would have cared either way."

"Well," she said. "Now all of your wives are up to speed. Thanks for feeling the need to drop this bomb on me too."

"I swear I didn't tell you this to hurt you."

"Then why did you tell me?" she said. There was still strength in her voice, but also a good measure of pain. "Seriously Ken, was everything going so well in our marriage that you thought you needed to screw it up? You could have kept this to yourself and I never would have guessed."

"I think I wanted some accountability," I said. "And I wasn't being honest or fair to you."

She scoffed and shook her head.

"So…" she said. "Strip clubs?"

What could I do? Should I keep lying to her? That's what was kicking my guts already. I bit the bullet and told her the truth.

"Sometimes."

"Other women?" She threw it out there so unemotionally that it felt like she slapped me in the face.

"No," I said. "No. Never. I swear, I have never cheated on you."

For a second I thought she was gonna slap me for real. She leaned forward, holding herself tightly to keep from shaking. When she spoke, her face was masked with fury.

"That's rich," she said. "You never cheated on me? That's good…"

"I didn't!"

"You did! Every time you set foot in a *gentlemen's club*. Every time you looked at some woman doing her routine on a pole. You betrayed me every time you said you were checking your email or surfing the net and then came in here to watch that slop." She looked away and shook her head. "In my house. With my children in the next room."

It sounded pretty bad when she said it like that. I couldn't believe I'd never considered what effect my addiction had on Toby and Diane.

"I'd never hurt them," I offered weakly. It sounded lame even to me.

"Why? Why are you doing this?" she said. I could tell by her voice that the anger was moving towards pain.

"I... I guess I'm scared," I said.

"You're scared?"

She said it as if I had no right to be afraid; as if the damage was happening to her alone. My first response was anger, but I held it back. I had to make her understand but I couldn't push her even further away as I did it. I blurted out, "Yeah, I'm scared. I'm scared now 'cause I see I'm addicted to this crap—just like this guy I'm almost positive is kidnapping girls and molesting them and killing them and..."

"What are you talking about?" she said. "What has that got to do with anything?"

"The guy that's snatching these girls," I said. "I'm pretty sure I know who it is. I was in his house and I saw... his collection."

"Collection of what?" Then she figured it out. "His collection of pornography?"

I nodded my head, unable to talk. It seems weird that, as hardened to all the junk I'd seen on the job I was having such a hard time articulating to my wife.

She picked up on it too.

"You're not making any sense," she said. "Are you trying to say that you're like this guy somehow?"

"I'm not doing the stuff he's doing—"

"I hope not!" she said. That man is a monster!"

"Listen to me," I said.

She turned away from me and took a step towards the door.

"You're not saying anything," she said. A tone of denial was back in her voice.

"Just listen," I said slapping the desktop. I was keeping my voice low to not wake Toby or Diane so it came out like a growl. It was dumb anyway; for all I knew they were already awake.

I held up my hands in a gesture of apology, then motioned for her to sit in the chair again.

I could see her considering whether or not she should do what I asked. I wouldn't have blamed her for bolting. Usually when I had a chat with someone around a desk like this they didn't have the option of leaving. Tonight, I was the one spilling my guts and no matter how many times I tried to convince someone confession would make them feel better… Tonight I wasn't buying it.

But Carrie didn't run. She slowly moved towards the front of the chair and sat down.

"I go to work thinking I'm gonna do somebody some good. It's the whole reason you do this job. It's the whole reason you're willing to lose your first two wives… because you think you're going to save someone else. Or a bunch of someones. Then, before your morning coffee is cold, you're up to your belt in something hideous you couldn't have imagined when you went to bed the night before. Kids beating their grandmother with a table leg because they think she has some money hidden away some place. A strung-out mother lets her boyfriend of the week have sex on her seven-year-old daughter so he won't kick her out on the street. Teenage girls kidnapped and held in…" The words caught in my throat and I had to clear it before continuing. "Held in a basement for years, treated like an animal. Violated. Starved."

"Half the guys I work with have some kind of substance abuse issue. Some of them are oilers, some of them pop pills just to get to sleep, others just to stay awake. Nobody talks

186

about it. Nobody jams anybody up over it. You just figure it's part of what you gotta do to keep from eating a bullet on this job."

"So, I'm lucky, I guess," Carrie said, the sarcasm dripping from her words. "I get the husband who's hooked on internet porn. And now you tell me... what? That you've bonded with a serial killer?"

"I didn't say..."

"You're telling me that my daughter, who we've been raising together, might be in danger... from you?"

"No," I said.

She leaned forward in her chair, looking me in the eye.

"No? How am I supposed to believe you? You don't sound like you know what's going on in your own head."

"No, I don't know everything," I said. "And since my blood/sugar has gone all kittywumpus I am having problems thinking clearly. But one thing I'm sure of: I gotta do something about this. In A.A. they say the first step is admitting you have a problem. This is me telling you I have a problem."

"So, tell me," she said, "is porn the problem or a symptom of another problem?"

"I don't know," I said. I hated to admit it but I really didn't know. I looked down and started sputtering. "I... god, this is... My ideas about sex didn't come from the great example my parents—my dad set up for me. And I probably never treated you right that way. I'm sure if I went to the Psych Services guy, he'd say my condition was unhealthy."

"Ya think?" She didn't say it in a playful tone.

"And what I'm afraid of... what scares the living... heck out of me... if I don't do something now, if I don't change... ten years from now I'll find myself like this guy I'm hunting now."

I looked up and saw her staring at me with her mouth hanging open.

"Are you serious?"

I looked back down at the desk.

There was a long moment where neither of us moved. It didn't seem like we were even breathing. I could feel my heart pounding and the pulse beating behind my ears.

"You want to change?" Carrie said. "I'll make it easy for you."

She got up from the chair and walked to the door. She stopped herself from leaving with a hand on the frame. She stood there for a moment and when she turned back to me she had tears in her eyes.

"I'm going to bed," she said. "I want you gone when I get up."

"Carrie…"

"You know," she said wiping a tear from the corner of her eye. "I may have been an idiot not to see. Maybe I did know something wasn't right. Maybe… I don't know. Maybe I loved you too much to notice."

She closed the door and was gone.

Chapter 44

I could either take Highway 45 or 76th Street to go up north to Witt's place. I decided to take the highway because I could burn some gas and hopefully some of the rage I was feeling. I was ready to kill that greasy worm if I had to, and part of me was almost angry that I didn't do it when I was there a few hours earlier. Of course, my life hadn't taken its unexpected turn at that point.

I didn't know what the worst-case scenario of telling Carrie about my addiction would be, but I guess I hadn't considered that she would tell me to leave. A week of sleeping on the couch? Maybe. Get out? That was a surprise.

I didn't bother getting any clothes before I left; they were all in the bedroom anyway, and the last thing I wanted to do was bother her anymore. If I had to, I could always buy some skivvies and a shirt to hold me over until I could get back to the house and collect some duds. I'd have to go sometime when I knew Carrie wasn't there.

This line didn't occupy more than a few seconds of my thoughts. All I was thinking about were the many ways I would beat Stephen Witt until he told me where the rest of the girls were. I wanted him to feel like I felt—like the world had deserted him and all he had to look forward to would be a lifetime of pain.

At least for him it could be mercifully short; his type didn't always last long in prison. It's weird to think that there is some kind of code among hardened criminals but people that abused kids are pretty low on the totem pole and often find themselves the victims of fatal accidents. Even guys like Jeffrey Dahmer, who the average person on the street thought was as evil as a human being could be—and probably was, didn't last real long once he hit the penal system.

Stephen Witt would get eaten alive.

The problem was what I had in mind wouldn't put him through the system. The best I was hoping for would be rescuing a couple more girls that I suspected he still had imprisoned. I didn't have a warrant and intuition was no replacement for probable cause. There was a good chance I was done being a cop after tonight. Frankly, that was okay with me at that moment. My personal life was on the trash heap, why not my professional life too?

I drove the Impala off the highway at the Good Hope exit, passing a minivan on the ramp. It was after midnight and there wasn't a whole lot of traffic, even on this major road. I didn't even need to slow down when I ran the red light at 107th Street.

I took my Smith and Wesson out of its holster and set it on the seat next to me. Whatever other surprises I might find when I got to Witt's salvage yard, I knew I could count on meeting up with his two dogs, and I had no intention of letting them slow me down for a second. I also didn't want whoever bashed my grape before to take another shot at me.

I was angry and I was alert.

But as I turned onto Granville, I could see a glow over the trees ahead of me. There was nothing around that should be putting out that kind of light at this time of night—no malls, parking lots or office buildings. I was probably within a mile of Witt's place when I noticed the smoke, illuminated in the orange flickering glow of fire.

I started beating the steering wheel of my car and screaming a torrent of profanity that would have got my mouth washed out with soap when I was younger.

It was Witt's house that was burning; I knew it before I got close enough to see the fire trucks and the half dozen MPD cars keeping traffic away from the blaze. I hit the lights on my own car and pulled up to the first checkpoint.

"What happened?"

The Uniform looked at my shield and said, "Someone lit

the place up," in a way that sounded more like, "What do you think happened, dope?"

I drove on and parked on the side of the road a hundred feet away from the rescue and fire trucks. Holstering my S&W I climbed out of the car and headed towards the confusion.

I didn't think I could get any hotter that night but that walk changed my mind in a hurry.

It was already a hot night but the heat that emanated from the burning house was more intense than anything I'd ever felt before. I'd been in breweries, factories and steel mills but this was way beyond any of that. Whatever started this fire had some help, and lots of it. By the smell I'd say someone had spilled kerosene on the floor and probably the walls and furniture as well. The Fire Marshall would have the final word but if this wasn't a clear case of arson, I'd eat my underwear.

It looked like there was already an investigating team on site along with a couple MPD detectives by the looks of the cars cluttering the street.

My blood pressure was already high and I'm sure my blood/sugar would have been messed up if I'd checked it. Despite the heat I still went cold when I saw Ray Schmidt step back from the crowd and look at me approaching. He said something to the man next to him who turned to look as well.

It was Lieutenant Gold.

The two of them broke off from the group and came towards me. They didn't run but I felt like I was about to be on the receiving end of the Malachi Crunch and I really was in no mood to let these guys push me around.

Gold was looking as angry as I'd ever seen him and it didn't take a genius to figure out he was hacked off at me. I couldn't wait to find out why.

"What are you doing here, Brady?" he said when he arrived in my face. I could smell the Wrigley's Doublemint

Gum he was chewing. The whole act was designed to put me on the defensive, to put me in my proper place but there was no way I was gonna play that game. I had questions of my own that I needed answered.

"I was out for a drive, Lieutenant. What are you doing here?"

Schmidt, who was standing a couple feet behind Gold, decided it would be a good time to chime in.

"We're here because of you, Brady."

"What is that supposed to mean?"

Gold wasn't going to answer my questions directly; I knew that. I wasn't surprised when he answered my question with one of his own.

"Were you here earlier tonight?"

The question surprised me, not because I had been there but because he suspected I had been. Was he having me watched? Had he set his dogs on me for some reason? Why would he do that?

"Why would you think that?" I said.

"Because we have a witness that says they saw you getting into your car and tearing out of here."

"They described your clothes, they described your car, they even gave your license plate," Schmidt said with a certain amount of glee in his voice. I suspected that he was having a good time stabbing me in the back. Problem was these things always came back to bite you. One of these days I'd be holding the knife and this tubby idiot was going to wearing the target.

"Well I was at home," I said. "Did anybody bother to check? I was there until about twenty minutes ago and based on what I know this fire has been burning longer than that."

"Were you here earlier tonight?" Gold asked again.

I decided I wasn't going to get anywhere avoiding the question. He knew, or he would find out anyway. I needed to control this conversation and so far it wasn't happening.

"You know I was. So what?"

"I gave you your assignment," Gold said. "I told you to forget this Witt guy. What were you doing out here again?"

"I still like the guy for these murders. You know I do. I was on my own time."

"You broke into his house—for what? What did you get?"

I didn't try to tell him that I hadn't broken into his house that night. Would it have mattered if it were today or a few days ago? Probably not. He seemed to know what I was doing anyway so why split hairs.

"I know he's the guy."

"You don't know squat!" Gold yelled jabbing his finger into my chest. "Your gut isn't going to get a search warrant much less a conviction."

"Now Witt has disappeared," Schmidt said. "And any evidence that he had anything to do with kidnapping or murder is up in smoke."

"There's a building near the back of the yard. It's half underground. I think that's where he was keeping the girls."

"It's gone, Detective," Gold said. "The hose jocks say that it was where the first explosion came from."

As far as Gold was concerned, that was it. I knew that Witt and/or Peter wouldn't have left the girls in the house or that outer building when they lit the place up. They weren't the brightest bulbs in the bunch but they would know that fire couldn't be expected to destroy all the physical remains. There were always partial pieces of bone that survived being burned and that would be enough to satisfy any jury. This case was still alive, but not because Witt and his nephew were innocent like the Lieutenant thought. It was still alive because they were guilty as hell.

"So, all the evidence is gone?" I said.

"If there was any? Yeah, it's probably gone."

"So, that ought to tell you that I had nothing to do with starting the fire. Why would I destroy everything I was looking for?"

"I don't understand anything you've done lately Brady,"

Gold said. "I'm giving you the benefit of the doubt that you can keep working with your blood/sugar imbalance."

He knew about that too? Great...

Even worse, I was beginning to feel light headed. It could have been any number of things causing it. The heat probably had something to do with it, my fight with Carrie was playing a huge part too, but I realized I hadn't eaten anything since I'd taken the call from Amanda and that was at least seven hours ago.

Maybe I wasn't as alert as I thought.

"You can't seriously think I'd torch Witt's place." I hoped it was an accurate statement but I didn't know Gold well enough to guess what he thought about anything. Unfortunately for me it wasn't Gold who replied.

"Can't we?"

I took a step around Gold to grab Schmidt's shirt but the Lieutenant did a smooth little side step and held me back with one arm. For someone so small he had a lot of strength. It made me think his position wasn't just an Affirmative Action fulfillment.

"Tell me something Dumb," I said looking past Gold. "Where's that witness you mentioned? Who's the good citizen says they saw me here before?"

"We haven't found him yet," Schmidt said. "But that don't mean nothin'. You admitted to us you were here before."

"But I didn't start this fire. I didn't even get past the gate tonight. Whoever did this was covering up what went on here. My guess is we aren't ever gonna see Witt again."

"I don't care about Witt!" Gold said. "You got nothing on that guy! You broke into his house and still couldn't find anything on him."

"You don't know that."

"If you had anything you would have told me."

"You don't think that presupposes that I can trust you?"

Gold looked almost amused by that. It was a pretty dumb

194

thing for me to say; he'd never given me reason to distrust him. I'm sure it was my wonky blood/sugar talking, and the fact that I was monumentally hacked off about the way things had been falling that day. Gold offered me an out but I was too screwed up to take it.

"I don't care if you trust me or not," he said. "From now on Washington is taking the lead on this one. You can work it from your desk."

"I'm not driving a desk on this one, Lieu. This is my case."

"Not anymore." He turned to Schmidt and said, "You're going to help Wash. Anything you dig up I want you to get to Brady."

"No way," I said. "I'm not taking a back seat to this tub of goo."

"If you want to stay on this case at all you will."

"This is crap."

"Yeah? Well, when you're the boss and I'm in your command you can assign me anywhere you want. Until then I'd appreciate it if you'd shut up and let me be in charge."

"You're doing a bang-up job so far…"

"I got a better idea," Gold said stepping up to my face again. "Why don't you take some time off? Go grow a beard or do something. Anything but is anywhere I am."

"You bouncing me from SCU?" I couldn't believe what I was hearing. I'd been on this team for years and now he was gonna give me the boot for… what? What was he kicking me out for? Insubordination? Yeah, that'd hold up with my union delegate.

"I'm telling you to take a vacation," Gold said. "I don't need some rag-ass who can't figure out which side of the legal street he's playing in my command. Come back when you can get your head in the game. Until then, I don't even want to see you in the squad."

"You can't do that," I said knowing full well how untrue it was and how lame it sounded.

"Yes I can," he said, "You're off. And be glad I don't push it further."

He turned and headed back to the Fire Investigators. His lapdog followed him.

"This is crap Lieu, and you know it!"

He didn't even turn his head to me when he shouted, "You're off!"

As I watched them walk away, I couldn't decide who I would like to shoot the most: Gold, Schmidt or myself. The person I really wanted to shoot was Stephen Witt, but that didn't seem likely to happen anytime soon. And even if I could shoot the chuckle-head—would it do me any good? I still hadn't proved he was the guy who kidnapped, assaulted and killed those girls. I knew he did it but Gold was right, my intuition wouldn't get us a conviction.

But it didn't matter. I was off the case. I was on vacation. Only it wasn't the vacation Carrie and I had been talking about for months. About the only thing that was the same was that I'd be sleeping in a hotel.

I checked my watch to make sure it was still early enough to get to a bar. I needed a drink.

Chapter 45

Peter Bohn stood with his hand on the chain-link fence, watching the children swim. He hadn't known about this park before today; he just noticed it as he drove west on Hampton Avenue. Madison Park and Golf Course, with a good size public pool as well.

It was a warm day and the pool was busy. Families sputtered around in the shallow end of the pool while the older kids took their turns jumping or diving off the three diving boards. In between people tried to swim laps but were invariably stopped by the paddlers who crossed into their lanes, not paying attention to anyone else.

Swimmers laid out their towels on the concrete deck, occasionally taking a break from the water and laying out to dry off and work on their tans.

These were the people that Peter was focused on. With his sunglasses on nobody could tell exactly where he was looking and he was careful to move his head so nobody would think he was staring.

And there was plenty to stare at.

It wasn't just the tween and teenage girls that he found himself gawking at, with their lithe and supple bodies in swimsuits that left very little to his imagination. He found himself engrossed by a group of women who he guessed were in their early thirties and displaying bodies that he didn't think were worth putting on display.

He found one of the women particularly sickening, with her two-piece suit so small that she looked like a muffin from Starbucks. Her thighs looked like a white garbage bag filled with cottage cheese and he wondered how any man could find that attractive. He knew there were guys who were into that, he'd seen the magazines, but there was no way he was ever going to be interested in someone like that. Not when there were still girls like Marta around.

Marta. She was still a sensitive subject with Peter. She had taught him so much and her death had a profound effect on him. There was no question about it; she was his first love. His own mother had been about as sensitive as a toilet seat but not quite that warm so when he made a connection with this beautiful, brown eyed girl it was extra special.

Even now, years after she passed, he held her up as the ideal: dark hair, olive skin, full lips and hardly an ounce of fat on her. Not like the fatties that shamelessly flaunted their obesity with immodest swimsuits at the public pools he liked to visit.

Fortunately, there were the younger, more attractive girls for him to fixate on.

There was a girl in a red, one-piece suit that was exactly what he was interested in. Her skin was chestnut brown and her hair was shiny black, though that may have been because it was wet. She was thin, with long legs and her chest was underdeveloped. She couldn't have been more than sixteen.

Peter watched her as she splashed around in the water, laughing and joking with her friend, a blonde girl that he had no interest in. Every once in a while, she would go to the diving board and do a graceful leap into the clear water, the lie down on the deck, stretching out her lean body on a towel.

He could feel himself getting aroused as he watched her and knew he had to be more careful. The last thing he needed was to look like a creep while he was figuring out how to abduct this girl. Drawing attention to himself was only going to get him caught. Besides, he was getting hungry anyway. Peter kept food in the van and there was a soda machine over by the building. He could keep an eye on the gate in case the object of his affection finished her afternoon recreation and left for home.

He would need to follow her anyway, try and establish a

pattern of movements. He knew from experience that teen-age girls were unpredictable and grabbing her was going to be difficult, maybe even dangerous, but he didn't care. Things had changed and everything he'd collected was gone. He wasn't missing the house and even all the Nazi crap was getting old. That was his old man and his uncle; he was never much committed to anything political. No, Peter was miss-ing the girls and he was anxious to get something going with a girl again.

Things had been slow for a while anyway, ever since the one girl had climbed over the fence and got away. He still didn't know how she'd made it out of the hut much less climbed through the razor wire at the top of the barrier but she did, and in the process received the lacerations that killed her not much later. She'd died in his arms, the way he hoped to die someday, being held by someone who loved him. And Peter genuinely believed he loved her. She was his favorite of the girls who had been left. She had the same beautiful hair and eyes that Marta had.

Peter wished he could remember her name.

It was almost three o'clock when the girl walked through the gate, said goodbye to her friends and climbed on her bi-cycle.

Peter sat up in the driver's seat of the van and congratu-lated himself on his good luck. She could have left with her friend, or in a car. Her leaving alone was a gift he couldn't ignore. He was ready to grab her if the opportunity arose or-ganically but he wasn't going to force it. Today was about reconnaissance, not abduction so he expected to leave empty handed but he wasn't going to question fate.

He put the van into drive and followed her out of the park-ing lot into the neighborhood.

Her bike wasn't a ten-speed or a racing bike and she didn't ride like she was in any hurry. Peter watched as she weaved from side to side in a carefree manner. She seemed like a pleasant person, loving life and the fresh air of summer. He couldn't wait to get to know her better, find out what she liked, what music she listened to and what television shows she watched.

Maybe she would be different from the other girls he'd brought home. Maybe she wouldn't want to get away from him; he hoped she wouldn't. True, his living arrangements were up in the air for the moment but that would be sorted out soon enough. He'd have a home where they could be together and enjoy each other. There was that "getting to know you" period that they had to get past, when he would need to give her time to learn that he wasn't a bad guy. That was when she would fall in love with him and, as sad as it was, he would have to keep her locked up until she did.

Maybe this one wouldn't take as long as the others.

Peter followed her at a safe distance even turning onto a parallel block from her and tracking her between houses for a while. His only concern was that she would turn into a driveway and he wouldn't know which one. Each time he saw her at the cross street he smiled.

She turned south on 105th Street, actually riding right past him while he sat at the stop sign pretending to look at a street map. Their eyes even met for a moment and a spark of excitement ran up his spine.

But how to get her into the van and make sure that some Dudley Do Right staring out the window wouldn't see him?

He was astonished when the solution presented itself, and it was completely of the young girl's doing.

While Peter watched she rode her bike into the back entrance of Pine Lawn Memorial Park.

A cemetery.

Chapter 46

It was a huge stroke of luck and it was perfect for what Peter wanted to do. Pine Lawn had plenty of trees and bushes that blocked the view from the streets and homes surrounding it. He couldn't see anyone wandering around or working either. The place was as good as a ghost town and the irony of the thought didn't escape him.

He waited on 105th Street for her to get a few hundred feet into the cemetery before slowly moving in her direction.

The further he drove into the graveyard the more he liked his chances. Peter was convinced that nobody would see him—that nobody could see him. The roads went in circles, each one with blind spots and dark areas, even at this time of day. The aged trees cast long shadows over the whole area. It could be perfect but he would have to do it right. It would require an Academy Award performance.

He turned the Econoline down the road that she was riding on and drove past her, holding up the map as though he were looking at it. At the next turnoff he rounded the corner, stopped, backed up and turned around. He figured he looked like an old lady looking for a specific headstone.

Peter stopped in the middle of the intersection, put the van in park and placed the map against the steering wheel. Keeping his hands below the level of the window he opened a plastic bottle and shook the contents onto a rag careful not to spill any. The chloroform was colorless but it had a sweet odor that might tip the girl off that something was weird.

She was about twenty feet away when Peter waved a hand at her.

"Can you help me out?"

She looked over her shoulder, realized he was talking to her and stopped a few feet from the window.

"I'm supposed to make a delivery on… Auer. My directions say it's back there." He pointed a thumb in the direction they'd come from.

The girl pointed in the opposite direction and said, "I think it's that way, on the other side of the parkway."

"I don't know," Peter said. "I don't see it on the map."

"Just go out of the cemetery over that way. Go south on highway a hundred about… I don't know. Half a mile."

"I'm not seeing it?" He turned the map towards her. "Can you show me on here?"

She rolled a bit closer. "Let me see."

He turned the map towards her and said, "I think we're here someplace."

"We're in here," she said pointing to a green patch of the map. Her finger moved to another part of the map. "You need to be looking here."

Peter placed his finger on a nearby portion of the map not far from hers. He got a thrill from being so close to her. He was looking forward to being with her all the time.

"Does Auer turn off this highway?"

She leaned closer to find the road he was talking about.

You won't get a chance like this again.

Peter let go of the map and used his left hand to grab the back of the girl's head. He moved so fast she didn't have a chance to react, clamping his right hand and the cloth over her nose and mouth.

He held her tight as she fought against him, pulling her body against the van. The cloth kept her from crying out loud enough to do any good. She kicked against the door and slapped at Peter with her arms but he didn't let go.

It didn't take long for the chloroform to do its job.

Chapter 47

I found a bar not far away from where Witt's place was burning and ordered a beer then I ordered another beer followed by a whisky or two maybe three but I was only half oiled when I fell asleep in the back of my car and when I woke up in the morning my head was killing me and the seat was wet from sweat and puke but my pants were dry so I didn't have no accident.

I bought some aspirin at a gas station pounded them down with a bottle of warm water I found under the seat and drove to Carries house even though I knew she wasn't there because I knew she wasn't there so I grabbed some clothes and headed for a hotel where I could rent a room for a week and had a kitchen when I realized I hadn't eaten nothing for almost a full day so I drove through Burger King or Wendy's or something I don't remember but they messed up my order by putting mayo on the sandwich and I spit the first bite back out the window before going to the front desk and asked for a room on the first floor so I wouldn't have to hump up and down the stairs every time I came home even though it wasn't my home and I was hungry.

I used my credit card at another gas station that sold scotch at a ridiculous markup but I didn't care and bought the six bottles they had carrying them back in a big, brown grocery bag where they clanked together the whole way and I had to stop and make sure they weren't broke and spilling all over the dozen candy bars I bought as well so I would have something to eat but when I ate them it just made me more light-headed so that when I drank the scotch I got my load on fast and usually fell asleep watching baseball or HBO only to wake up in the middle of the night and run to the john and puke up everything I'd eaten and drank which wouldn't take long since it was just the scotch and chocolate.

This went on for a few days I think because I didn't go to work and it didn't matter what day of the week it was not that it mattered the hotel had my credit card number so I could stay as long as I wanted and the cleaning ladies that didn't speak much English learned really quick to just skip this room while they did their rounds because I didn't want them to be coming around here all the time especially because they weren't much to look at anyway not that I had any interest in women not even the women on the HBO original series who took their clothes off all the time because it was HBO and not network television and you couldn't show naked women on network even though I only wanted to see Carrie but I felt like that was all over as much as I hoped it wasn't.

Carrie. I missed Carrie.

I found myself thinking about Randi my second wife and our whirlwind romance that started in the back of a gentleman's club where she worked and lasted a little over two years and was filled with adventurous and experimental sex, ending when she took too much interest in a fellow dancer that she invited into our bed and while I didn't complain about the experience I couldn't stand the idea of my woman hooking up with another woman no matter how willing she was to let me do pretty much anything I wanted just because I'd never done it before even though it was illegal in several states and I was still a cop.

I wondered where Carrie was right then maybe taking the kids to the mall or a park or doing some work around the house cleaning out my clothes from the closet and dresser or burning my stuff in the fire pit in the back yard except I never got around to building it so she was probably using a fifty gallon drum that I kept in the garage for wood shavings and stuff but now thought I should ride over Niagara Falls in.

I was out of chocolate and I was out of scotch so I decided to go back to the gas station but I couldn't find my keys or my pants and I didn't want to go outside without pants and I couldn't go outside without keys so I went back to sleep and dreamed of Stephen Witt and the girls he'd kidnapped, molested and killed and I dreamed that each one of them was standing in my hotel room with me and they were asking me why I couldn't arrest him or shoot him or choke him or something as they walked past my bed in a single file line as if I were a corpse on display for them to view instead of the other way around and then I figured that maybe I was dead and they were all coming to tell me I wasn't worth bringing into heaven because I wasn't good enough and I guessed they were right about which time I noticed Witt laying on the bed next to me patting me on the leg like I'm his buddy which is when I lifted my gun up for him to see before I realize he's the one holding the gun and placing it in his mouth and suddenly I don't want him dead mostly because I don't want to end up that way myself and I feel like I'm in some lover's pact with this loser so I scream to stop him but the scream turns into a gunshot and then everything goes red.

I woke up in a hospital room with an IV in my hand and Wash sitting on a chair watching me.

Chapter 48

"I never imagined I'd be waking up to your face," I said.

"Not exactly my dream scenario either, Kenny." He stood up and walked to the bed. "How do you feel?"

I hadn't thought about it until he asked and when I did I wished I hadn't. I felt awful and told him so.

"No surprise there. You drank enough to drown Dean Martin."

"What are you doing here, Wash?"

"I'd been trying to find you for a couple days," he said. I noticed his tone was more concerned than angry. He wasn't jacking me around; I think my partner actually cared about me.

"Yeah?" was all I managed to say.

"I called Carrie," he said. "She told me what happened."

"Carrie didn't know what happened."

"She told me she gave you the boot. She told me why."

Great. So, by now the whole squad knew I was some kind of pervert with a pornography addiction. That's all I needed. And as far as practical jokes go: cops are the worst. I could probably expect to find piles of skin mags on my desk when—if I got back to the unit.

Apparently, he saw something on my face because he continued almost sounding apologetic.

"I don't even care about that, man. You got your deal; I got mine. I'm not gonna hold it against you, you like to look at dirty pictures."

"It's not just that, Wash," I said. I wanted to tell him how I was afraid it would take me over completely the way it did Witt. I wanted to tell him I saw something in Witt that I recognized in myself and that it made me uncomfortable. No, uncomfortable wasn't even the right word. It scared the hell out of me.

"You don't have to explain anything to me," Wash said holding up his hand like he was blocking what I was going to say. "That ain't why I'm here anyway."

"How did I get here?"

"I found you yesterday afternoon over at the hotel."

I pinched the bridge of my nose, trying to chase away a burning feeling in my sinuses. I suspected they had me on some oxygen for a while. Had I really been that messed up?

"I don't even remember what hotel I was at."

"Safari, over on Appleton," he said. "I didn't figure you would stay at the Plaza or a Double Tree."

"I didn't think I drank that much…"

"The doctor said your glucose level was pretty high."

"That'll happen when you don't eat real food I guess." I held up my hand with the IV attached to it. "This ought to get me regular, huh?"

"I hope so," Wash said. "Because I need you to come with me."

It wasn't a gesture. It wasn't him reaching out to me to lift me up off the floor. It was a statement of fact, nothing more. He needed me to come with him. Either I did something pretty bad while I was pool eyed or SCU needed my help. I wasn't about to lay odds on which was more likely.

"Where we going?"

"The House on Silver Spring," he said. I was worried until he added, "Another girl got grabbed yesterday."

That really wasn't what I wanted to hear. Obviously, right? Part of me hoped that Witt died in the fire, even though I knew it wasn't probable. Nah, he was still out there and up to his same tricks. Now there was another girl missing and we had nothing to go on.

Or did we? I had nothing in mind, but that didn't mean the other guys at SCU hadn't shown up for work. What did Wash need to take me to Silver Spring for? I weighed the benefits of being coy or asking him outright and decided to plow forward.

"Did you get something?"

Wash's head tilted sideways and he looked at me with an offended expression.

"Get something?" he said. "Did I get something? I got the kidnapping son of a whatnot."

"What do you mean, you got him?"

"What do you mean, what do you mean? I got him. I pulled him over less than half a mile from where he grabbed the girl." He looked at me for a long moment before dazzling me with a smug, toothy grin.

I was impressed. How could I not be? I'd been lead on this one for a week and come up with squat. Now Wash goes out and catches the bag of meat in the act of abduction.

What a messed up, stupid world…

"How'd that go down?" I asked. I think I was able to hide my frustration but my head was still pounding and I couldn't be sure.

"I was set up on him for a couple days, watching him—"

"Hold up," I said interrupting him. "You were set up on him? How'd you clear that with Gold?"

"I didn't ask him. Aren't you the one that says it's easier to ask forgiveness than permission?"

I guess I had been known to say it. I just hoped my kids never turned it around on me.

"So, you saw him grab the girl?"

"He used a map and asked directions. Then he slapped a cloth over her face with some kind of anesthetic—probably chloroform. He threw her bike in the back of his van and tossed her in beside it."

I couldn't believe it; it was just like I thought. Just like I imagined while I was piecing together all those old abductions.

"Was it a white van?"

"Yup. An Econoline with a bogus pizza place painted on the side. Pretty gutsy. I wonder if anyone ever called the number."

I lay my head back on the pillow and sighed. They caught him. Wash caught him in the act. There was no way that he could get out of this one. I couldn't wait to get to the House and see if he still had that smug look on his face.

"How soon are we leaving?" I said.

"Soon as we get you unhooked," Wash said.

I used my left to peel the tape back and, ignoring Wash's protests, pulled the needle from my hand.

"Where are my pants at?"

"Hang on a second, Kenny. There's one more thing I gotta tell you before we leave. Something I think you should know."

"Save it," I said figuring he wanted to give me some kind of encouragement or lame pep talk. "I want to see Witt's face when I step into that interview room."

"Sorry I gotta tell you this, man. It isn't Witt,"

I fell back on the bed.

Chapter 49

The station house on Silver Spring was getting some cosmetic work done; paint on the walls, new ceilings, lights and such. There was scaffolding and guys walking around in white overalls spotted with a variety of colors. For some reason it reminded me of Twin Peaks even though the building was bigger and there were less donuts in sight.

I have to believe that Wash would have kept me from eating donuts anyway but I was glad to step into the interview room.

The first thing I noticed were the acoustic tiles on the wall and ceilings, many of which were stained with brown spots of… something. Coffee? Puke? Blood? Something worse? I'd hate to see the tune up that happened to fling scat on the walls.

I thought about taking that approach with Peter BOHN but I didn't feel like I could carry it off. I was still feeling like a stiff but even beyond that I didn't believe it would work on this guy. He didn't seem like the kind of cupcake that would respond to the rubber hose much as I'd love to beat the dog-snot out of him. This was going to take something else and, no joke, I had no idea what that was.

Peter was sitting up at the table, his feet bouncing beneath his chair. I noticed his shoes: gray Starters with two Velcro straps, the kind that kicked my face in a little while back.

I expect he recognized me too.

I dropped a stack of files the size of a Milwaukee phone book on the table across from him and sat down. The whole time I'm looking him in the eyes.

He was looking back at me too, trying not to be obvious about recognizing me and failing miserably. I'd love to play poker with this chump; I'd beat him dirty just watching his eyebrows. It was his "tell," raising one of those bushy monsters like he found out he'd just eaten a bad clam. Maybe I could use that in the interview.

"You look like you know me," I said. "Where'd you know me from?"

Peter leaned forward like he was taking a closer look and said, "I don't know you." There was no accent or anything but his directness was definitely Teutonic. The loud swallow was a sign that he was feeling at least a little frightened.

"Okay," I said opening the top file. "Sometimes people know me from somewhere and I have no idea who they are. One time a guy was into me and I had no clue. Turned out we went to grade school together. Can you believe that? Almost thirty years later this guy still knows me."

"I didn't go to school with you."

"No, I'm not saying that. You weren't even born when I was in grade school. I'm just saying is all."

I wanted this twitch feeling comfortable, but not too comfortable. I'm sure he thought I was gonna throw him a beating and I wanted to use that to my advantage even though the game we were playing was going to be entirely psychological. He was no different from Billy Trava—well, actually he was a lot smarter and even more evil, but as far as getting him to tell me what I needed to know there was not a lot of difference. It was a chess game and I had to take away his best pieces.

I took a photo from the file and held it up to look at it. There was a light behind me that made it transparent so Peter could tell what was on the glossy page as well.

It was Dana Hujet, dead in the overgrown parking lot of the old drive in, taken by the CSI team. He shifted in his seat.

I looked at the picture for a long while, then threw it back in the folder and closed it.

"So," I said. "Attempted kidnapping, huh? What's up with that?"

He didn't say a word, didn't move, didn't take his eyes

off the tabletop.

"Come on Peter," I said. "Or do you prefer Pay-ter?"

He didn't speak or even look up but he shook his head slightly indicating he did not like the German pronunciation.

"Come on, buddy. You're in some deep doo-doo here. This is a real hinder-binder and you're not going to be getting out of it. We have a cop who saw the whole thing and a witness who videotaped it on her phone. You're in a six-foot hole with a five-foot shovel. There's always a chance that some clever lawyer could get you off but I don't see you as that lucky."

He looked up at me.

"I was not kidnapping the girl," he said. "I was giving her a ride home."

I shifted the folders around and grabbed one from the middle. Opening it up I read from another sheet.

"I have the report with her statement right here," I said. "She says you grabbed her and put something over her face."

"Not true."

"And Detective Washington, who I've known for twenty years, says he saw you throw her and the bike into the back of the van"

"Also not true."

"Okay Peter," I said closing the folder and leaning back in my chair. "Let me give you a word of advice: you gotta stop saying everything I'm telling you is not true. First of all, I'm gonna smack you a bit. Second, when we get that video off the ladies phone, we'll have all the proof we need and it won't mean jack—whatever you say. The only thing's going to keep you from twenty-five years in jail is to give me a statement."

"You can't get me to give a statement for something I didn't do."

I rolled forward on my chair and leaned my head against my fist. It was a weak gesture and I knew it; I did it on purpose trying to get Peter to relax a bit. I didn't know what he was trying to do—he had to know we had him dead to rights. Or did he think that I was lying to him? Part of me wondered if he was trying to set up some insanity plea. I needed to get this chuckle-head on my side as quick as I could.

"Come on, man. That ain't gonna fly. If this gets to a jury they are going to hear from a fifteen-year-old girl that you drugged, a twenty-four year veteran of the Milwaukee Police Department and they're going to see video of you tossing her in the back of your van. They are gonna castrate you—do you understand that?"

I could see from the way he squirmed that he was hearing what I was telling him.

"And I hate to be the one to say it but when they find about these other girls…" I patted the stack in front of me. "You need to start thinking about yourself here, Peter."

"What other girls?"

This guy was no actor, no kind of performer. He wanted to sound ignorant but I could tell he knew exactly what I was saying and it was getting to him in a way that shouting at him or slapping him around never would.

"Well," I said. "I got eight missing girls here, four of which have turned up dead—two in the last three weeks. The crazy thing is, they all bear a striking resemblance to the girl you tried to snatch in the cemetery. Now I know that sounds circumstantial but I can almost promise you that if we go looking, we're going to find something solid to tie you to them."

"I didn't kill anybody."

"Okay, I wanted to ask you about that. This girl we found out by Dretska—she was all cut up but we know it happened climbing over or through the fence at your uncle's place."

"Is that how it happened?"

"You tell me."

"I don't know."

"Yeah, we're pretty sure that's what happened. The guys that know that kind of thing tell me that's how it happened."

"So, you know I didn't kill her."

"You didn't carve her up or nothing." I waited a second or two before saying, "Did you move her body after she was dead?"

"What?" he said sounding surprised. "Why would I move her body?"

"I don't know. Maybe you didn't want her to be laying dead in the train yard. Maybe you cared about her. How should I know?"

"Yeah... I don't know about it either."

"It was right by your uncle's place too. Were you living there then?"

"I don't know. Maybe."

I smiled and said, "You and me; we don't know much, do we?"

"I guess."

"Did your uncle grab these girls?"

Peter stared at me like I'd just tried to give him a knee in the crotch, which is what I'd done figuratively. I said it like it came out of nowhere but it was all meant to keep him off balance. I was getting tired of this guy and I wanted to get him talking. Giving him an out was giving him an ounce of hope. Giving him hope was going to get him talking, I could feel it. It doesn't always work that way but I didn't get the impression that Peter and his uncle were that tight.

"My uncle Stephen?"

"Sure, your uncle Stephen. I mean if these were all you... you'd have to have started pretty young." I grabbed another file from the bottom of the stack and baited the hook. "You couldn't have been more than sixteen when this girl got snatched up."

He looked like he wasn't sure I was on the level but I knew he desperately hoped I was. If I'd looked under the table his feet would probably be bouncing like a Whitney piston. He didn't know what to do with his hands so he folded and unfolded them before placing them palms down on the table. If it weren't so serious, I would have laughed.

"And tagging these girls with the tattoos? That doesn't seem like something you'd do. Your uncle?" I shrugged. "I saw all the Nazi stuff in his house. He might do something like that, you think?"

He didn't reply to that either. I had to be careful not to let him think he wasn't in a jackpot of his own, otherwise he wouldn't tell me what I needed to know.

"Listen Peter," I said with a sigh. "I'm not going to lie to you, I know you're the guy that hit me in the head in the salvage yard. That's assaulting a police officer. The gas cans we found in your van are going to tie you to torching the place."

"It's not my van," he said springing forward. He stopped short of rising from the chair; pretty smart on his part.

"Then I'm listening."

He sat there with his mouth hanging open and I truly think he was still wondering if he should tell me anything. That wasn't so smart.

"What do you want to tell me, Peter? It's not your van? We know that. It's registered to your uncle's salvage yard— but you were the one driving it. You were the one that tried to grab that girl. And you're the one that's going to take the fall for a half dozen kidnappings and homicides unless you give me the guy that did them."

"How am I supposed to do that?" he said. "How am I supposed to narc out my own family?"

"He ain't here to help you out in your hour of need, Peter. He's hiding out some place letting you take the blame for this whole twisted mess."

"How can I...?"

"Easy. You just do it." I watched him shiver in this stifling room on a hot day and knew he was going to unload soon. As long as I didn't mess this up. "I'm telling you, Peter, he isn't rushing to your aide right now. He's not lifting a finger to help you. He would leave you to rot in De Pere or

Waupon for the next twenty-five years to save his own neck. Think about that, Peter."

He thought about it for a minute before he started talking.

"I just want you to know, I'm not like my uncle," he said.

"What do you mean?"

"I'm not like him. He's got—he had a whole bunch of dirty magazines and movies. Stuff like that. I think it was the only way he could get off. I'm not like that."

"You don't need the pictures?"

"No, I don't. I had a girlfriend. I can get girls. I don't think he ever could. He was never good at talking to women."

"Not like you?"

"I had girlfriends in high school. Nothing too serious but I never sat home on a Friday night if I didn't need to."

"Okay, fair enough. You're not like your uncle. To be honest with you, I never thought you were."

"That's important."

"Absolutely."

"I'm not like him."

"No, I hear you. See, I even wrote it down."

I showed him my yellow legal pad with the words, "Not like his uncle," written down and underlined.

"But you gotta tell me what went on at that salvage yard if you want the D.A. to go easy on you, Peter. Show some remorse and tell us what happened. 'Best thing you could do."

Peter told me a horror story.

Chapter 50

Gold was just arriving when I walked out of the interview room. He looked confused and angry, especially when he saw me. He marched down the hallway towards me and Wash and, without saying a word gestured for us to follow him to an empty section of the hallway.

Wash and I exchanged a sheepish look and followed him.

Gold turned and put one hand on his hip, pushing back his jacket. I don't know if it's a power pose they teach at Lieutenant school but the psychological effect is pretty good. It revealed both his shield and his handgun which, had I been a skel, would have scared me more. As a veteran detective it just reminded me of the chain of command, which wasn't an issue anyway.

It still made me a little uncomfortable.

"I wanna know why," he said not bothering to hide his anger, "I need to hear that detectives in my squad made an arrest on this case from a desk sergeant in another house."

"We called when we brought him in," Wash said. "Didn't Claire give you the message?"

"No, she didn't." He turned to me. "And with you not showing up for the last four days I thought you were on vacation."

I was about to respond when Wash said, "He was. I asked him for some help with this guy."

"He can talk for himself."

"What he said," I told him. "He came and got me to talk to this Peter Bohn kid."

"That's Stephen Witt's nephew?" as if he didn't know who it was.

"Yeah."

"One of you better gonna run this for me before I lock the

both of you up downstairs. I'm not nuts about the way this is shaking out, especially since I told you to lay off Witt."

I wanted to protest, tell him I hadn't been involved at all, but that wouldn't do any good. Besides, I didn't want to get Wash into a jam, especially when we were so close to closing this case.

"Is there an office we can use?" Wash said. Neither of us wanted to run the case for the Lieu in the hallway.

Gold pointed with his head to an empty interview room and we followed him inside. He sat at the table and I leaned against a wall, waiting for my partner to bring me into the conversation.

"I was at the park—" Wash started but Gold interrupted him.

"What park?"

"Madison. It's over off Hampton, right by Timmerman Airport. Anyway, I saw this guy watching the swimmers and he kind of fits the description I had for Peter Bohn."

"What description? We never had one and Brady never saw him."

Wash and I had anticipated this and were ready for it.

"Witt had a couple pictures in his house," I said. "I gave the description off them."

I could tell by his face that Gold didn't buy it for a moment. He shook his head and gestured for Wash to continue.

"Anyway, this guy was just kind of a creeper, standing at the fence with his hand shoved down in his pocket. He was wrong, Even if it hadn't been Bohn I probably would have taken a long look at him."

"So, you waited for him to go and followed him?"

"I watched him for a while," Wash said. "It became clear to me that he was waiting for someone specifically."

"Did it occur to you that he might have been waiting for a friend or his child?"

"By then I knew it was Bohn, and the way he was acting was suspicious to say the least."

"Go on."

"I watched him as he followed a girl on a bike out of the parking lot. She fit the age and description for the girls that've been turning up lately; teenage, dark hair, darker skin and so forth."

"So, you followed him?"

"I followed them both through the neighborhood and into a cemetery nearby. That's where he tried to grab her."

"Tried to?"

"He did grab her," Wash corrected himself. "He got her to come up to the window and look at a map. Then he slapped something over her face that knocked her out. He tossed her and her bike in the back of his van."

"So, what did you do?"

"I called for backup, followed him and we made the arrest on Highway 45."

"Sounds like you wrapped it all up pretty neatly, huh?" There was a hint of sarcasm in Gold's voice.

"It was a clean bust."

"You don't think a D.A. would be able to poke holes in your story? Or at least find some technicality to get him off?"

"Come on, Lieu," I said, stepping away from the wall. "This guy is a known scumbag who attacked an officer of the law."

"You're sure this is the guy that brained you?"

"I was sure before he admitted to it. Now I have it confirmed."

"Okay, so you brought him to this house rather than downtown. What happened next?" I sensed Gold wanted to get to the good stuff.

"I talked to Bohn for a while, trying to get him to tell me his connection to the other girls and what part he played in the whole thing. I got squat; he wouldn't even hardly talk to me."

"So, you decided to bring in Brady, even though you knew that I'd taken him off the case. Even though you knew

I'd pretty much suspended him."

"I thought I was on vacation," I said.

"Would you rather not get paid while you shack up at the Safari and drink yourself stupid?"

How did he know that? It took Wash half a day to find out where I was; how did Gold know? And how long had he known?

I guess my face gave away my confusion.

"You're a detective in my squad," he said. "You think I wasn't making sure you were okay? Or at least making sure you weren't doing anything too stupid?"

"Thanks for caring, Lieutenant," I said with an appropriate amount of derision. "Nice to know that if I step on the wrong crack or take a leak in the wrong alley that you have my back."

"You have not inspired the kind of confidence and reliability that would allow me to let you wander too far from my view. The last time I saw you I half expected to next see you over Witt's body with a smoking gun."

"It could still happen."

"And I don't see that as a satisfactory close to this case," Gold said. "There are holes in this that I could fly a jet through. Now did you get any answers from Bohn?"

Chapter 51

I told Gold my setup; how I'd got him talking to save himself some jail time, Gold asked if I'd promised him anything I couldn't delivered but I assured him I made no promises at all, just that I'd see what I could do.

"He told me about growing up on the south side, the German part of town. Apparently, his parents moved there from South America in the sixties—he didn't know why."

"South America? Let me guess: his old man was a Nazi?"

"The time frame is all wrong," I said. "He wouldn't have been old enough, not like Witt's parents."

"So, what is the actual relationship?"

"Peter's mom is Witt's sister. So, Peter's grandfather was the goose-stepper in the family as far as I can tell."

"Does he show any sympathy to that stuff? Peter, I mean."

"Not really. I got the impression they jammed it down his throat for a while and he just got sick of it. He's lived here his whole life and in school they taught him that the Nazis were the bad guys."

"It's good to know they still teach some things correctly."

Gold's opinion didn't surprise me.

"He seems to know a lot about it but just as a matter of history. He's not the kind of kid who collects the memorabilia like his uncle. That was never his thing."

"So, what's his involvement in all this?" Gold said. "He couldn't have been involved in all these kidnappings and murders. He'd have been, like, twelve when they started."

"It's Witt, like I been saying."

"You been saying. Have you got any proof now?"

"The kid ratted him, Lieu. He gave me everything but actual dates."

"Did he give you anything we can actually move on? Anything more than hearsay?"

"He told me the whole history," I said. "How his uncle tricked these girls into coming up to the van just like he did with this girl today."

"Gina Douglas?

"That was Witt's."

"Kathy Lloyd?"

"Yup."

"Okun?

I nodded. Apparently, Gold had been paying attention to the details. I guess I should have been giving him more credit.

"What about Margaret Lockley?" Gold said. "Witt was inside when she got nabbed. Was that Bohn?"

"Yeah. He told me he did it. Her and that Lori Kelner girl."

"And Dana Huget?"

"That was one of Witt's as well," I said. "But it was Bohn that dumped her body."

"Did he kill her?"

Gold's voice had taken on a less aggravated tone. He sat back in his chair with one hand resting on the table. In his suit he sort of looked like one of those Italian gangsters from back in the Balistrieri days. Maybe not as slick but he did have a presence.

"No, he didn't kill her. She cut herself on the razor wire wrapped on the top of the fence." Like I'd been saying... I didn't say. "He found her near the dump; said she was still alive but she bled out while he held her."

"What's he doing holding her?"

I took a breath to buy a moment while I tried to figure out how to explain this. I couldn't say I completely understood it myself. I looked at Wash but he just shrugged and rolled his eyes.

"He... uh... He said he loved her."

Gold sat nonplussed, waiting for me to speak again.

"Yeah, he said he loved her and he didn't want her to die in a field by herself."

"So, he dumped her body in the old drive in theater?"

"It doesn't make any sense but he didn't want to have her body found so close to the salvage yard. He was pretty earnest though. I think he actually did feel something for these girls."

Gold sat up and folded his hands in front of him.

"So, what was the deal?" he said. "What were they doing with these girls? Why were they tattooing them?"

"Witt started that before Bohn came to live with him. He'd grabbed four of the girls and... I don't know. It was like he was creating his own concentration camp. He kept them in that underground shack thing I told you about, gave them just enough food to keep them alive, brought them into a special room every once in a while and sexually assaulted them."

"He kept them for sex?" Gold asked. "So, it wasn't about race?"

"It may have started that way but after a while it probably got old. Either that or they just liked taking sex off them. Bottom line is they're a couple of nutburgers."

I did think they were nutburgers. But then, where did that leave me? There was plenty about these guys I understood and way too many similarities with Witt.

Oh, come on. Who was I fooling? I liked naked women. I liked watching videos and looking at pictures of naked women, and not the artistic stuff. The same stuff that Witt had stashed away in his house—in some cases the very same magazines.

That High Society magazine with Britt Eckland cast a long shadow. A thirty-year-old shadow.

"Something wrong?" Gold said, shaking from my introspection. Apparently, I'd left the room while I was standing there.

I dropped into the seat opposite him and rubbed my forehead with the palm of my hand.

"My blood-sugar is probably messed up."

"Are you going to be okay?"

I shrugged and said, "I don't know."

Gold leaned to the side and pulled his wallet from his back pocket. He pulled a twenty from it and held it out to Wash.

"You mind grabbing us something to eat," he said. "Some vegetables; carrots, celery, peppers. That kind of stuff."

Wash looked at him like he'd asked him to shoot the mayor. Apparently, he wasn't excited about being asked to make a grocery run for the Lieu.

"Say what?"

"I'll never ask again," Gold said. "Promise."

Wash grabbed the money and headed for the door.

"This is a one-time thing," he said. "Gonna grab me some chicken nuggets too."

"Take it out of what I gave you," Gold called after him. "And get some peanut butter too."

I don't know what the peanut butter was for; I don't think I could eat it. Probably for him but I didn't see any bread anywhere. Maybe he kept a loaf in his car.

"The veggies will help you," he said. "When's the last time you ate real food?"

I shrugged.

"I'm hungry now so it hasn't been recently."

"How long have you been diabetic?"

"I found out a couple weeks ago," I said. "Same morning they found that Hujet girl."

"How are you treating it?"

"I stopped eating donuts." What was this guy, my mother?

"You're going to need to do more than that," Gold said. "Did your doctor put you on any prescription?"

Did I want to talk to Gold about my diabetes—or any

other problem for that matter? Not really. Then again, he hadn't busted me too badly about doing the interview with Peter Bohn, especially considering I was supposed to be on vacation. And he wasn't asking like he wanted to hold it against me somehow; he was asking like a boss who was concerned about a detective in his squad, which was as good as I could expect, I guess. I suppose I could un-ass myself for a couple minutes and give him some straight answers.

"We talked a little bit about it," I said. "I told him I was going to see what I could do with diet and exercise first."

"Yeah, well good luck with that. It's not gonna happen if you keep drinking enough to smell like a gin mill."

"I've had a tough week." It sounded stupid as it was coming out of my mouth but I couldn't stop myself in time.

"Get in line," Gold said. "You don't get a load on because you had a bad week. You were feeling sorry for yourself. There's a difference."

Okay, maybe I did want to be a smart-mouth with this guy again. The problem was I knew he was right.

But that doesn't mean I liked him talking to me this way.

"All due respect Lieu, you don't know what's going on."

"Sure, and I'm not a detective either. What is it you think I don't know? That your wife told you to get out? That you spent two days stiff in a hotel?"

I steeped closer and said, "What do you know about my wife?"

"I know she's married to a cop," he said. "And cops' wives talk to each other. And it doesn't take long for news like that to get around. The Captain called me and told me about—Carrie, is it?"

I didn't answer other than a quick nod with my chin.

"Apparently, it came down the line," Gold said. "Hard to believe cops wives are so indiscreet, huh?"

I'm sure cops' wives were no more chatty than anyone else, but I took his point. And I sure didn't appreciate my marital problems being broadcast throughout the squad this way. If it got to Gold's wife, I'm sure Wash and Schmidt knew about it too. Wash hadn't said anything but if he was like everyone else on The Job, he was keeping it for a hole card; something to bring up when he could use it to his advantage.

Or maybe he was just being cool.

"So, does this have anything to do with this thing with Witt?"

Did it? How was I supposed to answer that? I mean I'd had my… problem long before I ever saw Witt or his collection. I'd used three wives to satisfy my own sex drive. My head was full of all sorts of sexual thoughts, most of which I'd never have come up with on my own. I could describe in detail the bodies of any number of actresses from memory; legit artists like Madeleine Stowe and Julianne Moore as well as performers in the adult film industry.

Was any of this Witt's doing? No, I suppose it wasn't, but he wasn't helping matters. I felt a blissful ignorance before stumbling on Stephen Witt and I truly believed I wasn't hurting anyone, not even myself. But how big a leap was it from being a guy who was into porn to being a guy who devalued women so much that he would abduct and molest them?

I knew that not everyone who read Hustler and Playboy was going to go out and assault women. Still, what was the difference between someone like me and a killer like Witt?

In my life as a cop there had been times I'd had to fire my weapon at other human being and I'd done it without any hesitation. Twice I'd taken life in the line of duty and hardly given it much thought. Could I ever feel justified, even in my own mind, to do harm to someone to get sex? I know I'd made Carrie do things that caused her physical and mental pain. I don't remember any great feelings of remorse afterwards. I was only beginning to realize now what a selfish lover I had been.

That didn't make me a killer.

But if I were going to be honest with myself, I would have

to admit that there were dark thoughts that lurked fairly close to the surface, masochistic thoughts that included some form of physical violence often including the threat of death. Spending evenings at Kryptonite watching the young, nubile girls who worked there allowed my mind to wander into areas that I told myself I could never go in reality. I couldn't fool myself that I wasn't aroused by what the dancers were doing—I wouldn't be human if I wasn't. I loved watching them and imagining what I would do if they gave me half a chance even though I knew that I would be destroying the trust they placed in me to protect them.

Yeah, Carrie was right: I had betrayed her. Without even touching another woman I'd betrayed her.

It wasn't Witt's fault. In fact, maybe he'd done me a favor by bringing all this crap to the surface and forcing me to deal with it.

I figured it was time to level with Gold.

"Nah," I said. "This is on me. Witt just brought it all to a head."

"So, what is this mad-on you have for this guy?"

"Well..." I took a breath while I figured out how I was going to say it. "There's an old Russian saying: One fisherman knows another fisherman from a distance."

I left it there for him to chew. He didn't take a bite. In fact, he didn't even raise an eyebrow.

"Let's just say that when I first started talking to Witt I knew he was the guy because..." Man, this was killing me. "I saw something in him that I recognized."

"Recognized in yourself?"

It took me two tries and a throat clearing to say, "Yeah."

"Are you telling me you knock off little girls too?"

"Nah, it ain't like that Lieu. I've never murdered or molested anyone. That's not what I'm saying."

He shrugged with his hand and said, "So?"

"It was just weird," I said. "Going in this guy's house was like reliving a part of my youth. He had magazines and books, DVDs, all kinds of dirty pictures—most of which I recognized from when I was a kid."

"You were into porn when you were a kid?"

"I was into it until I first got married."

"Did it affect you on The Job?"

"I never thought so," I said. "Who can say what I would have done different?"

"And your marriage?"

"I'm on my third wife. You tell me."

He just stared at me for a few seconds. It felt like half an hour.

"So, you think you might turn into something like Stephen Witt because you had the same dirty magazines and movies?"

"Well, we both had German parents too."

"You referring to me as a kike not-withstanding, you have any Nazi tendencies?"

Wow. I'd forgotten about that. I guess he did hear me.

"I apologize for that," I said. "That was pretty lousy."

"I've been called worse," he said. "But don't think I'm going to allow it again."

"The answer to your question is no, I don't hate Jews, gypsies… whatever."

"So, what makes you think you might end up like Witt?"

I shrugged. "I guess I've been taking a look at what's in my heart lately. I don't usually think about this stuff but something's been gnawing at me. I can't explain it, I just… I don't know."

"I don't understand this soul-searching stuff," Gold said. "What's in my heart can be pretty bad too but I choose not to act on it."

I was about to say I didn't think it would be that easy for me when Wash returned with the groceries. He set the plastic bag on the table.

"Any change?" Gold asked.

"Nope. I drove through McDonald's and spent it all." I

always like the way Wash says Mac Donald's. "I'm lovin' it."

Gold handed me a bag of baby cut carrots and a jar of peanut butter.

"Eat this," he said.

"Together?"

"Try it. I bet you like it."

I did and found out it wasn't so bad. I like carrots anyway and who doesn't like peanut butter? I ate a few and could feel my head clearing up a bit. I liked having solid food in my belly again.

"So, did Kenny run everything for you?" Wash asked.

"Most of it," Gold said. "I just want to know if Bohn gave up where we can find Witt."

"He's pretty sure the old guy is up at a family cottage near Slinger. It's on Cedar Lake."

We ran through a couple more questions; mostly Gold making sure everything went by the book. He seemed to appreciate my technique of writing up the statement and intentionally spelling words wrong so Bohn had to fix them. It was a trick we used to show anyone who might want to use the account against us that Peter had not only read the statement before signing but he'd made corrections in his own hand. It made it tougher for a Defense Attorney to say we'd coerced or beaten a confession out of their client. In the end he was satisfied with how we'd handled the interview.

"So," Gold said. "Let me see if I got this straight. Bohn confessed to be part of the multiple kidnapping, imprisonment and sexual assault of these girls in concert with his uncle, but he says he never killed anybody?"

I nodded.

"Witt is the guy that did the murders?"

I nodded again. "Yup."

"How many girls have there been?"

"Bohn says he knows of eleven," I said.

Gold was as surprised as me when he heard the number.

Eleven girls had gone missing while we were on The Job. Eleven families were missing their daughters and sisters during the time I'd been protecting and serving them.

I knew there was no way the Police Department could catch every criminal; there just wasn't the manpower. It was a sad fact that the skels outnumbered the cops by a pretty sizable majority. That's why catching somebody like Bohn and, hopefully, Stephen Witt was a pretty sizable victory. I wasn't looking for a feather in my cap; I wanted these punks behind bars or dead.

And then a thought floated into my consciousness from I-knew-not-where.

There but for the grace of God go I.

It was not an uncommon phrase, Sherlock Holmes had even used it in one of the old stories, but it wasn't a sentiment I applied to myself before.

I had been dwelling on whatever similarities I believed I had with Witt but I'd never considered what it would take to put a stop to his monstrous behavior. Was it death? Was I—or someone else—going to have to take his life to get him to stop victimizing girls? Prison would certainly change his habits but the fact was: someone like him was likely to become a victim as well if he ended up in the system. It was one of the stranger truisms of the penal system that even the most hardened criminal had zero tolerance for child molesters. A mook like Witt, with no way to defend himself, wasn't going to last long in the land of slamming doors.

Why was I letting this guy get in my head like this? Did I care about what happened to him or what might happen to me?

Chapter 52

Lieutenant Gold drove me back to the hotel where I showered and grabbed my Smith & Wesson. The boss was good enough to wait outside so he didn't get to see the mess I'd made of the small room and all the empty bottles lying around. The last thing I wanted was a lecture on recycling.

I grabbed a fresh pair of jeans, t-shirt and a blue windbreaker, strapped the gun to my belt and climbed into the car.

"You ready to do this?" Gold said.

"Doesn't matter."

The hotel was on Appleton Avenue, not far from Burleigh Street. Gold turned on Lisbon heading west until we reached Capital Drive. Capital took us to Highway 45, which turned into 41, the highway we took up to Slinger.

Neither of us said a word until we were going 55 past the old drive in theater where Dana Hujet's body had been found. I think Gold only spoke then because he could tell I was thinking about what Stephen Witt had done to her.

"A few years back," he said, "I was getting ready to take a leadership course exam. The whole thing was killing me— I was so stressed about it I couldn't sleep, hardly ate anything. I was still living with my mother, who was sick at the time but you'd never know it the way she squeezed my shoes. She had a hard enough time that I didn't graduate at the head of my class in high school. The last time she was satisfied with anything I did was my Bar Mitzvah. Now I'd washed out of college and I'd decided to be a cop. She'd wanted a doctor or a lawyer and ended up with a public servant. I probably don't need to tell you she drove me nuts."

I didn't want to tell him I would have appreciated any attention from my parents.

"Anyways, it's the night before the exam and I'm in my

instructor's office. I don't need to tell you everything that was going on but I'm in his office. Then at one point I'm alone in his office and the exam answer key is sitting right on the table. I figured, 'why not?' So, I take a look. I took a long look. I memorized the whole thing quick as you like. Took the exam the next day and scored the top quarter for the first time in my life."

"You're telling me you aren't that smart?" I said.

"Don't get all Freudian on me but I did better on everything after my mother died."

"She busted your chops, huh?"

"She was born in Russia. I don't have any idea what she went through in her life so I'm not gonna judge her."

"So, you cheat on exams?"

"Just on that one part. There were other sections that I couldn't cheat on, essays and oral and so forth."

"Yeah, well—"

He cut me off before I could finish my thought.

"Anyway, I knew what I did was wrong but after I passed the exams and got my promotion, I didn't want to ruin everything. It probably would've killed my mother if I had. After she died..." He made a frustrated gesture at a car with a Michigan plate that was traveling in the passing lane. "After she died a few things changed in my life. I got married, started a family, I even became a Christian."

I couldn't help laughing at him.

"Yeah, it is funny," he said. "My mother could have been Yente in Fiddler on the Roof and here I was digging Jesus."

"How's that kind of thing happen?"

"I don't know you that well," he said. "So, what happened next... I started feeling guilty about it. I don't know why it started; I don't even remember when anymore but I started feeling bad about it."

"Too late to do anything about it," I said mordantly.

"I did do something about it, Brady. I got a hold of my instructor and told him what I did."

"No kidding? What happened?"

"Nothing. He asked who else I told about it. I told him just my wife. So, he tells me not to tell anyone else yet; he'll take care of it."

"So, he gives you a pass? Why'd he do that?"

"No idea," Gold said. "Maybe The Job needed another minority in a command role."

"Yeah, I'm sure that's it…" I made sure the sarcasm came through. "So, why are you telling me all this?"

"I don't get you Brady," he said. "What drives you, what moves you—I have no idea. I can't tell if you love the world or want to see it burn. But right now, I know something about you that you probably don't want the world to know about—and I don't want you thinking I'm going to use that against you some day."

I had considered that. He'd caught me at the computer, which was a serious breach of protocol. If he wanted to, he could put me in a jackpot. And that to the bender I'd gone on and I might be looking for a new gig.

But Gold didn't seem interested in busting me.

"I need you to trust me Ken, and you're not going to do that if you're waiting for me to drop a bomb on you. Now you know something about me."

"So, that story was calculated to make me trust you?"

"Are you saying it didn't?" he said looking over at me. There was the slightest hint of a smile on the corner of his mouth.

"You know Lieu," I said. "It's not that I don't trust you; I don't really trust anyone."

"That's not going to help you in the department," Gold said. "We need a certain amount of cohesion and if you don't have confidence that your partner has your back…"

"Come on. You know as well as I do that there are plenty of cops, in pretty much every department I've ever seen who are in it for themselves and will take advantage of any opportunity to get over on everyone else in the squad."

"Of course, I know it. But don't let my laconic nature fool you; I see what goes on in the squad no matter whose name is on the reports."

He was talking about me getting the confession from Billy Trava. Nice to hear he hadn't forgotten.

"I wasn't looking for a transfer to SCU but when they offered me the job, I jumped on it—not because I enjoy seeing how nasty people can be to their fellow humans. I took it because you guys have a good reputation and I wanted to be part of a great squad."

"I'd be happy to close a friggin' case," I said. "I don't like these dry spells."

"Nobody does," Gold said. "But you get the bracelets on Witt and I think you'll feel better. And when you get back on your feet you find that Amanda what's-her-name and collar her."

I'd almost forgotten about Amanda. Yeah, I was gonna have to do something about her too when I had the chance.

Right now, I needed to focus on Witt. Getting that guy out of decent society was the first order of business and I finally felt like I was gonna be able to do that.

I looked at the boss and said, "How do we want to do this?"

Chapter 53

The front of the cottage needed a coat of paint at the very least but I was happy that the porch didn't creak when I stepped on it. I was about to knock on the screen when I figured I should make sure I was ready if things turned sour. I took my pistol from its holster and racked the slide to make sure that a bullet was chambered, then returned it to my hip. If Witt tried anything desperate, I would be ready.

I wrapped on the door, which in turn rattled against the frame. I wouldn't have been surprised if it woke the neighbors, the closest of which was about a hundred feet away.

There were sounds of movement inside the cottage but it took almost a minute for the door to open.

It was still warm outside but Witt was wearing blue jeans and a plaid flannel shirt buttoned to the top, looking for all the world like a serial killer. He gazed at me incredulously.

"I wasn't expecting you so soon."

I had more surprises in store for this dirt bag so I didn't give anything away; just stood and waited for him to invite me in.

"How did you find me?"

I shrugged a little and laughed.

"I'm a cop," I said. "We find people."

Witt leaned forward and pushed the door open a few inches. He looked around the yard. He seemed surprised that I didn't come with a S.W.A.T. team or something.

"You are far from your jurisdiction, detective."

I shook my head and said, "Not that far. Besides, maybe I didn't come out here to arrest you. Maybe I just drove out here to beat you bloody."

Witt's eyes went wide for a second, and then he held the door open.

"Then I suppose you should come inside."

I nodded and walked past him into the house.

The front room was paneled with cedar planks and decorated with heavy, wooden furniture. The chairs looked like they each took a whole tree to construct. It was that extra cheesy stuff you'd see at resorts that wanted you to think you were in some Canadian lodge. It looked as cheap and out of place here as it did in Wisconsin Dells.

Witt gestured to one of them, expecting me to sit. There was no way I was going to give him any type of mental advantage so I stood in the middle of the room.

"Something tells me you're not here to physically abuse me," Witt said taking a seat and putting a foot up on the coffee table, another monument to knotty pine cottage furniture.

"Not this time." I took a couple steps towards him and fixed him with my best tough-guy stare. "But I'll be honest with you: I'd love to duct tape you to that chair and beat you with a bowling pin."

Witt smiled and said, "You forgot your pin."

"Like I said, some other time."

"So, what are you doing here?"

I couldn't tell if he really wanted to know or if he was trying to put me off. But since he asked, I was going to press him as hard as I could. Without taking my eyes off him I sat in the chair opposite, leaning forward and leaning close enough for him to smell my minty-fresh breath.

"I thought we could have a little chat."

"Personal or professional?"

I opened my hands and shrugged in a carefree gesture.

Witt shook his head slightly and said, "You want to know about the salvage business?"

This conversation was going to be about me verbally tearing this monster down. Everything I said needed to be a blow to his pride or his sense of security—or both. I needed to pummel him; to beat him into submission without laying a finger on him.

I didn't hesitate to take my first shot.

"No. I need to know what makes a person like you."

Witt laughed. He sounded a bit surprised.

"Good genetics," he said.

"I haven't seen any evidence of that."

Witt pursed his lips and made a "Tch, tch, tch," sound. "That isn't kind, detective."

I wasn't going to shrink from his gaze. I couldn't care less if I was unkind or offensive to this bag of garbage. And that's all he was to me. Instead I leaned closer and spoke in a calm, measured tone.

"You're a kidnapper. And a rapist. Probably a murderer too."

Witt dismissed me with a wave of his hand.

"If you could prove any of that you wouldn't be talking so much."

"So, you have no reason to not talk to me," I said. "Come on Stephen, just talk to me."

"About what?" Something in his voice gave me the impression he was getting annoyed. Good.

"About you."

"What do you need to hear that you don't already know? It's not as though we're all that different, you and I."

"What makes you think I'm like you?"

It was the question I needed to ask; the question I needed the answer to. Tell the truth, it was the question I was afraid to hear the answer to. Even asking it made my stomach turn and, though I'd never let Witt know it, I could feel my bowels turning to water.

"You like the women too."

Okay, that was a deflection I hadn't seen coming. I'd been involved in other cases where killers referred to women he'd murdered as anything but women. "The pretties," or "the beauties," were terms that came up every once in a while. They used other terms to dehumanize the victims.

Witt referring to "the women" was his way of denying the

grip that the sexual material had on him. And he thought I was just like him. I needed to steer this conversation back to him, for my own good.

I don't know why I didn't just do that.

"I have an addiction," I said. "How does that make me like you?"

Witt scoffed and got out of his chair.

"An addiction? You seem to have some strange puritanical notions about women." He walked across the room and brushed an imaginary piece of dust from the mantle over the fireplace. "Appreciating beauty is not an addiction."

"Is that all you were doing when you kidnapped those girls?" I said. "Were you appreciating their beauty while you were molesting them?"

I think my candor took Witt by surprise. His smile was more of a nervous grin.

"My goodness, Officer Brady. You certainly seem to be obsessed with sex."

I could tell that I'd knocked Witt off balance. He was uncomfortable and it seemed like he had lost the advantage. Now was the time to really lay the wood to him. I stood up from his chair and approached the man, crowding him into the corner of the room. It made me uncomfortable treating him this way; like he was a girl I was hustling in a bar but I had no intention of taking it easy on this skel. I wanted him uncomfortable. I wanted him to make a mistake.

"I'm obsessed?" I said. "I'm not the one with forty years' worth of Playboys in my house. Tell me, Stephen, how much did it hurt to set that on fire?"

"Hardly at all," Witt said nervously looking for a place to move to. I had cut off his escape route. "I'm sure you know that there's plenty of... material for a true connoisseur. "

"Oh, sure Stevie. But that was mostly your dad's collection. Were you destroying your last ties to the old man?"

"No!" Witt practically barked in reply. His face transformed into an angry scowl. I wasn't sure if it was the comment about his father or using the undignified version of his name that set him off. Either way I didn't care.

I took another shot at him.

"That's right. You still have all of his Nazi junk, don't you?"

Witt's scowl changed to confusion, then to fear.

"H-h-how did you know about that?"

I leaned forward—close enough for him to feel my breath on his ear when I spoke.

"I do this for a living."

Chapter 54

Witt's face turned red and I watched as he clenched and unclenched his fists. Part of me wanted him to throw a punch. He was cornered and like any cornered animal he was dangerous but part of me wanted to throw him the beating of his life.

And I would have too.

He was getting scared, I could tell. His face had gone from ruddy to bright red and sweat was forming on his brow. He stunk too.

"There's something else you and I have in common, Mister Brady."

The non-sequitur threw me off for a moment, just enough for Witt to try and steal the advantage.

"You have German blood in you as well."

"My mother was born there," I said with a shrug.

"I knew it. When?"

I wasn't sure I wanted to give this dirt bag any personal information, but I wasn't going to learn what he wanted if Witt clammed up. Just keep him talking.

"Just before it got exciting," I said.

Witt placed his hands on my shoulders in a familiar, even familial way. He was trying hard to get the advantage back. His voice teemed with excitement now.

"Your mother grew up in The Reich?" he said.

"Her family was from Potsdam."

"I wonder," Witt said, "do you have any pictures of her in her H.J. uniform?"

I pushed him away and stepped past him to a safe distance. At that moment I wanted nothing more than to drive my fist into his face. This sick puppy wanted pictures of my mother? I could feel tightness at the back of his neck.

"My mother wasn't in the H.J," I said.

"All the children were in the Hitler Youth, my friend. If she said she wasn't she lied to you."

"Then she took the secret handshake to the grave," I said. "She would have been too ashamed to tell us anyway."

Witt walked over to a table in the corner of the room. He picked up a framed photograph and looked at it.

Brady could see it was a portrait of a man.

"My father was proud," Witt said. "He believed in the Aryan ideal."

"Just like you, huh?"

"Ach, no. He was far more committed than I."

"Just not enough to stick around in Germany after the war? He wasn't committed enough to face up to what he did. You were born in... where was it? Argentina?"

Witt put the picture back on the table and returned to his chair.

"What was he supposed to do? The rest of the world would never understand. They still don't understand."

I needed to get this control of this conversation again so I stepped closer and stood over him.

"No, I think they understood plenty," I said. "Once your Fuhrer ate a bullet it was pretty clear that nobody was willing to take a stand for what they did."

Witt made a fricative noise with his lips.

"My god, that's absurd."

"No it isn't."

"Of course it is."

"What's so absurd about it?"

"You don't even know the history," Witt said. "Your mother clearly never told you what was happening."

I sat on the arm of his chair and said, "Okay, tell me."

"Berlin was fallen. What was Hitler supposed to do?"

"Take his lumps like a man."

Witt grunted angrily, throwing his hands up.

"No, seriously," I said. "He spends twelve years building

a thousand-year Reich but he doesn't have the courage to stand up for all the heinous crap he did. Sounds to me like he knew he wasn't gonna be popular with the new landlords."

"He knew what the Russians would do to him if the ever caught him."

I couldn't help but laugh. "Yeah, the same thing he'd been doing to everyone else for years."

Witt spoke through gritted teeth.

"The Russians raped every woman they found. Could you imagine what those perverts would have done to the Fuhrer if they caught him?"

"Are you being rhetorical or are you just an idiot?"

Witt shook his finger with conviction looking a lot like a former President.

"The atrocities the Russians committed… Those are the true crimes against mankind."

"Okay, forget rhetorical," I said, rubbing the stubble on my chin. "You're an idiot."

"Did your mother neglect to tell you what the 'liberators' did?"

"She didn't talk about it too much, but she mentioned how bad it was."

"In the Reich," Witt continued in a contemplative tone, "a woman could walk down the street."

"Unless she was Jewish or a gypsy."

Witt ignored the interruption.

"They were animals," he said. "The things they did… That is why my father left."

"I don't believe this. Your defense of the Nazis is: the Russians were worse? Are you kidding me? Next you're gonna tell me that it doesn't matter that you're the one who started your own private concentration camp in the salvage yard because Peter—Sorry, 'Payter' was more cruel than you. That's about as valid as, 'I was just following orders.'"

He was angry now. I'd insulted his Fuhrer, I'd insulted

his nephew and I pretty much told him I knew what he'd done.

Anger was a strange reaction—not what I'd expected. Fear maybe, but anger? I was glad I'd checked my gun before knocking on the door.

Witt looked away from me and said, "What do you want?"

He wanted me to say it again because he thought I would diminish myself by saying it aloud again. I wasn't going to play it that way. When I spoke to him, I gave him my best hard-cop look and practically growled the words.

"I told you, I want to know what happens to make a piece of garbage like you."

"Why is that so important to you?"

"Because I may have just enough in common to make me think I could end up like you." I lowered my voice and added, "And that scares the hell out of me."

"You talk as though you've never killed anyone."

"Yeah, on the job I've had to kill people, but I've never enjoyed it. I've never imprisoned anybody, or raped and tortured them."

The salvage man looked up at me.

"And you think I have?"

I leaned over and looked Witt in the eye.

"Oh, I know you have."

"You're on a fishing trip, Detective Brady. You're trying to trick me into saying something you can use against me."

"No, I'm not. I don't need your confession. Aren't you wondering how I found this place? Don't you want to know how I knew you'd be here?"

I watched as Witt tried to answer. His mouth hung open but no sound came out. I gave the knife another twist and told him what he'd already suspected.

"Yeah, that's right. Your nephew gave you up."

I had sprung the trap on my prey and frankly, I was enjoying watching the man struggle to form words from a mouth that had suddenly gone dry.

Witt's eyes grew wider and he seemed to have acquired an involuntary tremor in his head. For a second I wondered if he was having some sort of breakdown.

"You're lying…"

"Oh no," I said, the tone of my voice giving away how much I was enjoying the moment. "He's given us names and dates. Lots of details. He told us all about how you would lure young girls to your truck, pretending to be lost. Then how you would tattoo numbers on their arms and keep them in the underground rooms you built, starving them and molesting them whenever you were feeling extra randy. And then you'd have to get yourself all oiled up because you were ashamed of having sex with a Jew."

Witt's lips quivered and he said, "You're lying."

"And how you didn't even care that all but one of the girls weren't even Jewish."

Witt jumped up from his seat and shouted.

"You liar! You're just trying to trick me! Peter would never say those things."

"Okay. Yeah, you're right. I made it all up." I stepped closer to Witt and held out my fist, thumb down. When I opened my fingers a locket fell, dangling from a gold necklace in front of the killer's face. "Look familiar?"

Witt looked from the locket to my face, then back to the locket.

"Peter walked me right to the box where you had this hidden, along with all your other trinkets. Dana Hujet's father identified it as the necklace she was wearing—as if he needed to."

I opened the locket, showing Witt the picture of Dana and her mother. She was young and pure, the way she looked when she'd been abducted.

"You believe what he said?" Witt managed to say.

"I believe the DNA evidence that connects you to Dana. It's more than enough to convict you."

Chapter 55

I watched Witt closely and wondered if he would call my bluff. There was no DNA evidence that would convict him; that stuff took days to get back from the crime lab. But I knew something was wrong with the junk dealer from the moment I'd first seen him. Unfortunately, intuition would never hold up in court.

And neither would Peter's confession. I knew from years of experience that confessions rarely lead to conviction. A good defense attorney would shred the admission like hay through a thresher, or at least make it look like it was coerced.

I had the right guy, but my hand was pretty weak.

If Witt knew how precarious my position was it didn't show. He looked defeated, or at least ready to give up.

"Something to drink?" the older man said.

It probably shouldn't have but the question surprised me, coming from nowhere the way it did. My mouth was dry and a drink was exactly what I wanted. I doubted he was going to offer me scotch. Probably the best I'd get from this nutburger was peach schnapps.

"Got any diet soda?"

Witt stood up and headed for the kitchen.

"I think so."

I took a turn around the living room, looking at the collection of furniture and pictures and wondering why nobody seemed to update the décor of their cottages. I could understand the rustic look of the cedar-planked walls but not the vinyl coated chairs and sailboat prints that were apparently issued to families in 1950 but still hung in the main room of every cottage I'd ever set foot in.

My parents never took any type of vacation that lasted

more than a weekend with one exception. My mother brought me and my sisters to meet the family in Germany. I was nine at the time and remembered virtually none of the trip beyond hating the toilets.

Not long before the divorce my first wife and I drove the kids to Colorado where we stayed in a fairly nice hotel—nothing rustic about it. Carrie and I had flown to Florida and spent a fun-filled week at Walt Disney World but the most countrified thing we did was ride Big Thunder Mountain Railroad.

Cottages were not my thing. This wasn't my world. In school the other kids talked about going up north, but for us that meant touring the Pabst Brewery. My old man never went anywhere he wasn't ordered to go. High living for him was when they started making remotes for TVs.

Witt returned with a plastic cup that matched the mid-twentieth century theme of the house and handed it to me.

"That's not diet," I said after taking a drink. I could almost feel the jolt of sugar hitting my bloodstream. I'm sorry to say it felt good.

"It's all I have," Witt said settling himself back in his chair. "So, what happens next?"

"I place you under arrest and we head back to Milwaukee."

"Are there no jurisdiction issues?"

I smiled. "Did you think we'd need to extradite you? You didn't even leave the state. It took one phone call to set this up with the local boys."

"Does this make you feel good?"

I slid forward to the edge of my chair facing Witt and looked him in the eye.

"You betcha," I said. "It makes me feel great to know that some parents out there aren't going to be wondering why their kids didn't make it home. Knowing that their mothers won't have to identify the body of a daughter they haven't seen in years. Yeah, you better believe that makes me feel good."

"Will putting me in prison help you with your problem?"

Don't let him make it about me again.

"I don't know. Let's find out."

Witt shook his head and made a "tsk" sound.

"It won't. Take a good look at me, detective. I am your future." He leaned forward in his chair. "You wanted to know what made me who I am?"

"You're just talking now."

"You want to know what happened to me. It was the women. You know it was the women. Their bodies. The... feelings they give you when you look at them. Tell me, does it help when you're with your wife?"

I couldn't stop my hand from grabbing his shirt and pulling him towards me.

"Don't... don't mention my wife."

I could feel my blood pressure rising. It was making me light-headed. I pushed him away and took another drink of the soda.

"Doesn't it help with the passion?" Witt continued. "Don't tell me you haven't picked up a few ideas over the years. From the magazines? From the movies?"

"Shut up!"

"Because you know it doesn't stop with the dirty pictures. Eventually your mind goes to wondering what women you see look like without their clothes. The girl packing your groceries or the waitress at McDonalds. Maybe it's the woman in the car next to you—or just someone you see jogging past you in the park."

The most coherent thought I could come up with was, "McDonalds doesn't have waitresses."

"Then before you know it you're fantasizing about your middle-aged neighbor who rolls out the trash bin wearing curlers in her hair and a bathrobe, and it doesn't matter that her hips and thighs are big enough to make her almost grotesque."

"How..." But I couldn't finish the sentence, not out loud anyway. I could feel my heart thumping harder and my head began to throb.

How did Witt know about my neighbor? Had he been watching me? Had he followed me home and watched my family and neighbors? What did this guy know?

Witt slid closer to me but stayed in his own chair.

"I've never been married, Ken. Do the smutty pictures or movies enhance your sex life? And is your wife game for everything you want to try?"

I wanted to say something but I couldn't answer. My mind was becoming a fog and I knew I was losing consciousness. It wasn't a physical reaction to what Witt was saying—he'd drugged me. I'd been careless and Witt had drugged me.

"What did..."

"Has your 'addiction,' as you call it, turned you into a monster? Those women in the night clubs—what will they do for you if you give them enough dollars?"

My head lolled back and my body followed. I landed in one of the log chairs.

Then Witt was right in front of me, his hand on my knee and his mouth next to my ear. For a second I thought he might kiss me.

"There's nothing wrong with me, Ken," he whispered. "You're the one who can't face who you are. You're the one who believes that appreciating a woman's body is a problem."

I could feel the curtain coming down as I said, "You can't get away..."

Witt looked amused as he patted my chin and said, "Neither can you."

Chapter 56

It was a screen door slamming shut that brought me back to my senses. My fingers and toes were tingling but the head was clearing up. I'd only taken the two quick drinks from the cup of soda Witt had given me so I didn't receive the full measure of whatever drug had been mixed into it.

I knew I needed to act—and quickly, if I was going to catch this killer. With all the energy I could muster I pulled myself to my feet.

And collapsed against the arched doorway that led to the kitchen.

The kitchen was a galley-sized space leading to the back door with a narrow stove and ancient refrigerator. Close to the screen door was a sink that held a collection of dirty dishes.

I edged along the counter to the basin, knowing what I needed to do. I found a small bottle of liquid dish soap and squeezed a small portion onto my cupped hand, then turned the water on it.

My stomach was already beginning to turn as I splashed the soapy water into my mouth. It didn't take much effort on my part to gag and then vomit.

When I finished, I rinsed with sulfur-tasting water from the faucet and nearly gagged again. I spat into the sink several times trying to get the taste out of my mouth.

There was an uncomfortable pressure behind my eyes, but my head was clearing. I checked my holster to make sure the pistol was still there and was simultaneously happy and disappointed that it was.

I pushed open the door and went after Witt.

The moon was reflecting off Cedar Lake and I saw the

rowboat moving away from shore almost immediately.

You gotta be kidding me. That's his escape plan...?

I looked along the shoreline and spotted a canoe only a dozen steps away. I'd never been in a canoe before but figured it couldn't be too bad. Besides, what choice did I have. Nobody else was gonna grab this knucklehead.

I pulled the aluminum boat to the water's edge and splashed in up to my knees. The cold water actually helped me to focus. I threw a leg over the side and fell inside, nearly tipping the whole works. There was already an inch of water on the bottom and this didn't help. I hoped there wasn't a leak.

Eventually I found my balance and a paddle, which was all I needed for the moment. Kneeling in the middle of the canoe I paddled after his quarry.

Very quickly I realized I'd need to switch sides often if I wanted to make the boat go relatively straight. I was glad my kids weren't there or I'd be putting money into the swear jar—in big bills. I cursed as I moved across the water's surface in a zig-zag pattern, watching the rowboat get further and further away.

I started gasping but paddled faster and faster, digging the paddle into the water as though it were a shovel and he was burrowing in soft sand. My lungs began to burn as sweat ran down the back of my neck under my shirt collar. I considered throwing my jacket off but didn't want to hesitate for a moment in this pursuit. I also realized that it wasn't the jacket that was slowing me down but the fact that I didn't know what I was doing; throwing away a seventy-nine-dollar jacket wasn't going to get me any closer to Witt.

But something did. I looked up at Witt's boat and was pleased to see was gaining ground. Or water. Or whatever you say on a lake.

But something wasn't quite right. Witt's boat wasn't moving at all anymore. The lake was smooth as a mill pond and the creep's boat was almost directly in the middle.

I couldn't help wondering if something had happened to the old guy or if he was laying some trap. No matter, I wasn't about to stop my pursuit. I paddled towards the drifting boat with renewed energy.

I could see Witt moving in the boat, tying something just below my line of sight with a thick piece of rope.

"Come on Witt," I said when his boat was about thirty feet away. "Do us both a favor, will ya?"

"My father gave me a Playboy when I was twelve," Witt said tying the rope around his waist like a belt. "He thought I was old enough for it. How old were you?"

I stopped paddling and let the canoe float closer to the other boat. It took me a moment to catch my breath.

"My dad never gave me anything."

"Let me guess: you're still waiting for him to teach you about the birds and the bees?"

"The only thing I'm waiting for is you. Come on, let's get back to shore."

"What happens if you arrest me? Will I go to prison?"

I sighed and said, "If there's any justice left in this world."

"Justice?"

"You're responsible for four deaths, Stephen. What did you expect?"

"I don't want to go to prison. I know what they do to child molesters there. I've seen it. I've…"

"I think you should consider yourself lucky that Wisconsin doesn't have capital punishment."

Witt sat up straighter on his seat.

"Look at me Detective Brady. Look at my face."

I looked at him. His face was illuminated by the light of the half moon.

"If you and I are so much alike… it seems there isn't much of a chance for either of us."

"Speak for yourself," I said. "Let's get back on shore and get this done."

"There's only one way out for us."

Witt hiked the rope up his torso until it was around his chest, just under his armpits. Suddenly I understood what he was doing.

"No there isn't!" I shouted. I slapped the paddle into the water, trying to push the boat forward again. It moved forward sluggishly.

Witt reached towards the floor of the boat and lifted a twenty-pound anchor. He held it on his lap and said, "I'm not going back to prison, Ken."

"Put it down!"

Witt smiled.

"I understand now why the Fuhrer did what he did." He stood up in the boat. "Goodbye Detective Brady."

And then, calm as you like, he toppled backward, falling into the calm waters of Cedar Lake.

Chapter 57

Witt had barely broken the surface of the water before I half leapt, half fell from my canoe after him. The water sent needles of icy pain into my body, but it helped me push deeper into the murky lake after him. I had no idea how deep the lake was and I certainly couldn't see anything but it didn't matter; I just kept swimming downward hoping to make contact.

The pressure built in my head and my lungs were burning but pushed on. I knew it would take a miracle to catch Witt but I wasn't ready to give up yet. I desperately wanted to save this guy. I needed to. My biggest fear was that Witt may have been right about him—about them both and I sure didn't want to accept that we were too far gone and the only possible solution to our mutual addiction was death.

I needed to believe there was hope.

Every instinct told me to return to the surface but I pushed further downward, flailing my arms hoping to connect with him, even by accident.

For the second time tonight, I could feel myself losing consciousness. My body screamed in protest and without re-alizing it my mouth followed, releasing the oxygen from my lungs.

The primal shout was somehow invigorating but I knew that I had to surface right away if I wanted to survive. I turned in the direction he assumed was up and kicked my legs.

And something seized my foot.

I knew it was Witt; there was nobody else that it could have been. The older man tried to get a firm grip on my shoe but his quickly hand slipped free.

It wasn't a violent grasp—not an attempt to pull me to the

bottom of the lake. It was the desperate effort of a man trying to survive. I knew immediately that Witt had changed his mind about dying.

Nothing like waiting until the last second. There was nothing I could do. My survival instinct kicked in and I kicked to the surface.

I was still fully dressed and wearing my pistol on my hip but eventually my head broke through the water. I gasped for air, as I tread water.

Witt's boat was nearby. I pulled myself to it and grabbed the gunwale.

Once I'd filled my lungs with oxygen I turned back to the area where I'd just resurfaced, considering another try. But there was no way I could save him anymore. I'd never find him in time.

Stephen Witt was dead. His crime spree was finished.

And clinging to the side of a boat in the middle of Cedar Lake, Detective Second Class Ken Brady wailed like a baby.

Chapter 58

I leaned against my car, wrapped in a blanket and drinking a cup of gas-station coffee that a member of the local constabulary picked up for me. It was awful but I didn't say anything. I appreciated the thoughtfulness. The sun had risen and a team of divers was already in the water looking for Stephen Witt's body. Lieutenant Gold had called them in and he had enough juice to get them there quickly.

It had been the longest night of my life, longer than any night he'd spent on stakeout. What hacked me the most was that there was absolutely nothing he could do but dry off and wait.

Gold had arrived by the time I'd rowed the boat back to the dock outside the cottage. I told him what happened and the Lieu made a few calls while I returned to the cottage to find a towel.

What I found was two girls, one alive though dangerously dehydrated, one mercifully delivered from the nightmare that had been her life for the last several years.

I didn't know for sure but I was fairly certain that the living girl was Leslie Baeten. It would be some time before she would be strong enough to give us any information, if she even remembered her previous life. The abuse she'd suffered at the hands of the two madmen had probably caused trauma from which she would never recover.

I made a pillow of paper bags for her and stayed with her until the ambulance arrived. If my jacket hadn't been sopping wet, I would have covered her with it.

The County Sheriff and the local cops arrived and secured the area. People from nearby cottages wandered out of their summer homes and approached the police cars to find out what was going on only to be sent away. They gathered a dozen yards away and speculated until after the sun had risen over the trees at the far end of the lake.

"You okay?"

I turned and saw Gold heading towards me with another cup of coffee, this one from Starbucks. Apparently, the Lieu hadn't got the message but since I needed the caffeine I didn't say anything.

"I'm alright. Nothing two weeks of sleep wouldn't take care of."

"I might be able to swing the two weeks; the sleep is up to you." He handed me the paper cup of steaming liquid. "This won't help."

I set the first container on the roof of the car and took a drink from the offered cup. The taste didn't do anything for me but the warmth performed a miracle.

"Thanks, Lieu."

"Just a heads up: the captain is probably going to want you to get over to Psych Services. I don't think you have to worry but I wanted you to know what to expect."

"Doesn't matter that I didn't kill this guy?"

"Right now, we have no witnesses or anything. I'm sure when they pull his body it'll bear out your story."

I leaned back against the car.

"I didn't want this idiot to die," I said. "I was trying to keep him alive. Can you believe that?"

Gold watched his detective but didn't respond.

"He said…" It was hard to say, even to this guy who I was starting to trust. At least he was good enough to wait for me to get my act together. I cleared my throat and started again. "He said I was looking at his future. He said I was gonna end up just like him."

"Do you believe that? Do you really think you're going to end up like him? The guy kidnapped and molested children."

"I don't know. Sometimes… He seemed to know something about me. About my thoughts and my… imagination?"

"He knew how your mind wandered when you saw a

256

pretty woman? How you thought about what it would be like to have sex with a woman you know casually—or even work with?"

I looked at the boss and for the first time wondered if he had a similar compulsion or whether I was that transparent.

"Do you think you two are the only men who wondered what a woman looks like naked? You don't need to have a porn habit to slip into that way of thinking."

Gold shifted on his feet so he was standing directly in front of me. The effect was not that of a employee/boss, but a peer.

"I'm going to tell you something that I've never told anybody, not even my wife."

"I'm not a friggin' priest," I said waving him off. "You don't have to confess to me."

"I'm not Catholic either so I don't confess to men," Gold said sharply. "I just want to share something that you may find useful."

Now I had to know, didn't I? I lifted the cup and said, "Share away."

"When I was in college my friends and I used to get together and play Dungeons and Dragons on the weekends. And when I say 'on the weekends' I mean all weekend. We had some pretty extensive campaigns."

"I don't know what that means."

"It's role playing," Gold said. "You create a character and then you play a game as that character; going on adventures, finding treasure, fighting battles. Depending how good your Dungeon Master is you may find yourself in any sort of bizarre situation."

This wasn't what I expected. I wasn't sure what playing a role playing game had to do with molesting children, if anything. I wrapped the blanket tighter around his torso in a gesture of boredom.

"Relax," Gold said. "There's a point coming. Anyway, one of the guys in our game, my buddy Terry, after a while he started having problems keeping track of what was real and what was the game. We weren't sleeping and we were barely eating and he started flipping out. He started acting like his character that was only a couple steps away from being... I don't know... like Conan, I guess."

"A barbarian?"

"Yeah, kind of. We didn't call it that but that's pretty much what it was. At first we thought it was funny and we egged him on. I figured he'd been dropping acid or something; he'd done it before. Then at one point he goes after one of the other guys with a meat cleaver—took a chunk out of the guys shoulder. That's when we realized he had a problem."

"What's this got to do with me?"

"Terry had other problems before he ever picked up a ten-sided dice. He would have had the same kind of problem if he'd been into video games or Monopoly. What I'm saying is, two people can have the same obsessions and it affects them in different ways. Don't get me wrong, you still need to take care of your problem, but I don't think you're going to end up like Stephen Witt."

I wasn't reassured. "How can you say that? I mean, how could you possibly know that?"

"Because you don't have murder in your heart, Ken. You have a problem that nobody can see until you show it to them but you don't have it in your character to kill an innocent person."

I looked across at the Lieu.

"You sure about that?"

Lieutenant Joshua Gold pointed out towards the lake where scuba divers were passing the body of Stephen Witt to two Deputy Sheriffs in a boat. The anchor was still tied to the corpse.

"You didn't kill Witt, and he deserved it. I'm not sure I would have been able to keep from blowing that scumbag away. Yeah, I'm sure."

258

Chapter 59

It was after ten when I arrived home. I parked the Impala in the garage and walked to the post box wondering if the mailman had come yet. It was empty.

I walked in through the garage, entering the house through the kitchen and called out, "Carrie?"

I guess I wasn't surprised that there was no answer; her car wasn't in the driveway or garage. She was probably shopping or bringing the kids somewhere.

I set my holstered pistol on the counter and walked to the bedroom. There were dry clothes in there and my thighs were beginning to chafe from wearing wet pants.

The bedroom door was open, which was not normal for Carrie. She tended to close the door involuntarily, even when she was leaving. It was just a habit she had.

Seeing it open gave me a bad feeling in my gut.

I stepped through the door and at first everything looked normal. The bed was made and everything in the room appeared to be as it should.

But my instinct told him something was wrong, and it was more than just an open door.

I pushed open the closet door and saw my shirts and pants hanging just as they should be, my shoes were on the floor just as I'd left them. But something was wrong. Something just didn't sound right.

I opened the other door to the closet, Carrie's side.

It was empty.

I checked the dresser drawers where she kept her clothes that overflowed from the closet. They were empty as well. Everything—even the plastic tubs she kept under the bed for her extra shoes were gone.

I quick-marched down the hallway to the kid's rooms and

found the same state of affairs. All the big stuff was still there but the clothes were gone. Books and CDs had been picked through but most of them were still where they were kept.

They'd packed up and left in a hurry, probably shortly after me and Carrie had our last conversation.

I had to admit he couldn't blame her for being angry. I'd kept a terrible secret from her for a long time. I may not have outright lied to her but there was an inherent dishonesty in not telling her about my obsession. It had an effect on our intimacy—certainly my sexual conduct and while I hadn't physically betrayed her, I knew I had coerced her to do things she wasn't comfortable with.

Carrie had been good and decent to me from the day we'd met and now I was feeling like a dishonest and depraved liar.

I found her note in my office, written quickly and left on the desk next to his computer monitor. It didn't say much or give any type of hope. It was just a statement that she was leaving.

I folded the note cleanly, placed it in the top drawer and automatically, almost involuntarily, turned the computer on.

The tone of the machine turning on reminded me what I'd done. I sat back in the chair, actually dreading the challenge that this device was placing before me. In a moment it was at my desktop and I stared at a picture I hadn't taken note of in several years.

It was three women: a blonde, a redhead and a brunette, all dressed in skimpy Milwaukee Brewers apparel and holding each other in an intimate, even provocative way.

I hadn't even given the picture a moments consideration in so long—probably since the day I uploaded it from some Internet sports or beer distributor web page. Carrie had probably seen it a hundred times and never said anything. Her children—our children had seen it too but nobody even found it worth mentioning. Were we all so used to provocative pictures like this that we didn't even notice it anymore?

It's gotta end...

I rose from my chair, went to the kitchen and grabbed my firearm from the counter. I grabbed a dishtowel as I walked back to the office and dried the magazine and the receiver. What I needed to do I needed to do in his office. That was where I spent hours staring at porn on the computer. This is where I watched filthy movies on the Internet. And this is where I'd confessed to Carrie that he had a problem. This is where I was going to break the cycle.

I pulled the slide of the Smith and Wesson 9MM back, making sure the action was still riding smoothly after spending some time in the water and the rest of the morning wet. A bullet ejected from the port and smoothly chambered the next projectile.

I raised the gun, noticing that my hands were trembling. Suddenly the metal tool seemed to weigh fifty pounds and I began to wonder if he had the strength to carry through.

I pointed the gun and pulled the trigger.

The bullet tore through the back of the computer monitor with a terrific explosion of metal and plastic, deflected on one of the more solid components and continued on through my padded leather chair, tearing a hole in the material where, had I been sitting in it, my heart would have been.